PRAISE FOR
BAD LOVE MEDICINE
Book 4 in The Bad Love Series

"*Bad Love Medicine* takes these endearing characters to their next level! Without a doubt the best tale in the series yet. This novel intermixes themes of history, sci-fi, and music together to craft a winning story that takes the reader to the edge of their seat. From the depths of the Universe to World War II Germany, it all comes together in this book. Fantastic yet grounded, *Bad Love Medicine* will leave you desperate for more, just as it did me."　　　—Kathryn Raaker, Radio/TV Host and Author, 5 Stars

"Skillful writing (both historical and fantastical), a zesty sense of humor, an appreciation for pop culture, and the ability to create memorably entertaining characters combine to make this an immensely impressive novel—and experience! Very highly recommended."
　　　　　　　　　　—Grady Harp, Amazon Top 100 Reviewer, 5 Stars

"Schewe's artistic ease of combining familiar historical events with cataclysmic fiction is exhilarating. Compelling storytelling transports the reader via time travel, from Hitler and cancer cells, to the Beatles' Abbey Lane without a hiccup."　　　—Marlene Grippa, Retired Librarian, 5 Stars

"A romping sci-fi, historical adventure, the pages of this book are packed with memorable characters, hilarious antics, and, not to mention, a plethora of historical information on the 20th century, WWII, and the Cold War."　　　　　　　—Rachel Song, Editor and Writer, 5 Stars

"If you're looking for the perfect adrenaline-fueled summertime read, look no further, because the Bad Love Gang is back and kicking butt!"
　　　　　　　　　　　　—Jessica Tofino, Educator, 5 Stars

ALSO BY KEVIN L. SCHEWE, MD, FACRO:

BAD LOVE STRIKES
BAD LOVE TIGERS
BAD LOVE BEYOND

BAD LOVE MEDICINE

KEVIN L. SCHEWE, MD, FACRO

Jan-Carol
Publishing, Inc

"every story needs a book"

Bad Love Medicine
Kevin L. Schewe, MD, FACRO

Published July 2021
Broken Crow Ridge
Imprint of Jan-Carol Publishing, Inc.
All rights reserved
Copyright © 2021 Kevin L. Schewe, MD, FACRO

ISBN: 978-1-954978-14-0
Library of Congress Control Number: 2021942553

You may contact the publisher:
Jan-Carol Publishing, Inc.
PO Box 701
Johnson City, TN 37605
publisher@jancarolpublishing.com
jancarolpublishing.com

DEDICATION

I have been a board-certified cancer specialist practicing radiation oncology for 34 years as of July 1, 2021. I am the youngest of three children and have two older sisters, Kathy Williams and Denise Bourg. My first novel, *Bad Love Strikes* was dedicated to Kathy, who remains in remission from her breast cancer. The second novel, *Bad Love Tigers* was dedicated to Denise Bourg, the middle child in our family of three siblings. I am the proud parent of two children, Ashley Daugherty and Christie Schewe. Book three, *Bad Love Beyond,* was dedicated to my oldest daughter, Ashley. This fourth novel, *Bad Love Medicine,* is dedicated to my youngest daughter, Christie.

As she was growing up, I would describe Christie as a student-athlete who naturally made good grades in school and could well play any sport that she embraced. She was a superb cheerleader all the way through college. Christie was an absolute "water-bug" who loved to swim, waterski, jet ski, and go boating while soaking up the sun and listening to music. From her earliest years, it became apparent that she treasured and possessed strong social skills and was anything but shy. She always had a close circle of friends and quickly replenished that sphere whenever we moved to a new location. In one of our fondest memories together, I coached her soccer team when she was ten-years-old. In the middle of close games, we would all huddle together with our hands held in the middle of a circle and scream, "En Fuego!" Our arms would all go up towards the sky as we yelled and then we were "on fire" to be victorious!

Along with her innate social talents, Christie is an instinctive leader, and this has become apparent in her flourishing career in sales and marketing. I love you, Christie and could not be prouder! You have the whole world and the future out ahead of you and I know you will make the most of it!

BAD LOVE
MEDICINE

ACKNOWLEDGMENTS

For 34 years I have worked on the front lines of cancer care as a radiation oncologist in private practice. Receiving a diagnosis of cancer, and then facing the realities of staging, treatment, side effects of treatment, and recovery are challenges that are larger than life. Living with a cancer diagnosis after treatment requires a new view on life and life's priorities. I want to acknowledge the thousands of cancer patients that I have cared for these past 34 years—all of whom have taught me valuable lessons of life and have shown me courage beyond measure, sacrifice, love, humility, victory, real-life miracles, and acceptance. I am eternally thankful to these patients, their families and loved ones—all who have shown me and continue to show me the meaning of life here on earth.

The writing of *Bad Love Medicine* has taken place during the later phases of the COVID-19 lockdown experience and the subsequent lifting of restrictions here in my home state of Colorado. This global pandemic has affected the world in ways that we are only just beginning to understand. As we emerge from these trying times, we have new hope for a brighter future. The *Bad Love Book Series* is rich in actual history uniquely blended with the adventures of time-traveling 1970s teenagers and laced with the unforgettable music of the 1960s and 1970s. These books offer hope, inspiration and refreshing humor to a world filled with new challenges.

AUTHOR'S FOREWORD

RECOMMENDED ACTION FOR ALL YOU TIME AND SPACE TRAVELERS!

In order to get the full sensory effect of traveling through time and space with the Bad Love Gang in *Bad Love Medicine*, I highly recommend that you download the 23-song soundtrack listed on the next page by using your Spotify, Apple iTunes, Pandora or Amazon Prime account. Alternatively, you can use YouTube to play each song as you are reading or simply tell Alexa to play the songs. As each song is boldly introduced throughout the novel, take the time (no pun intended!) to listen to the music and enjoy the full sensory effect of being an honorary member of the Bad Love Gang. Do not be afraid to lip synch, sing and/or break out and dance, play your air guitar or tap your feet as the music moves you!

Back from their mission in *Bad Love Beyond* the Bad Love Gang are knighted in a royal ceremony for the ages at the Queen's Palace on Planet Azur. Bubble Butt and the Bad Love Gang arrange for the music to start during the knighting ceremony and then they play an ensemble of 60s and 70s Earth music during the celebration that follows. Everybody, including Queen Azur and the Azurians are compelled to dance! The music from the 1960s and 1970s paves the way as the Bad Love Gang returns to Earth to deal with the KGB and plan their time-travel trip back to World War II Europe to get the *Bad Love Medicine* breast cancer cure to Hannah Lieb. But before they get the medicine to Hannah, the gang meets with British Prime Minister, Winston Churchill, and they are sent on a mission deep into Nazi Germany to destroy Hitler's darkest secret. Buckle-up for the time and intergalactic space ride of your life laced with the best music the Universe has to offer!

SOUNDTRACK TO *BAD LOVE MEDICINE*

1. "Along Comes Mary," The Association (1966)
2. "Dancing in the Street," Martha and the Vandellas (1964)
3. "These Boots Are Made for Walkin'," Nancy Sinatra (1966)
4. "ABC," The Jackson Five (1970)
5. "Here Comes That Rainy Day Feeling Again," The Fortunes (1971)
6. "SOS," Abba (1975)
7. "A Hard Day's Night," The Beatles (1964)
8. "Reach Out I'll Be There," The Four Tops (1966)
9. "In the Midnight Hour," Wilson Pickett (1965)
10. "Don't Rain on My Parade," *Funny Girl* Soundtrack (1968)
11. "Saturday Night's Alright for Fighting," Elton John (1973)
12. "I Wonder What She's Doing Tonight," Tommy Boyce and Bobby Hart (1967)
13. "Love Child," Diana Ross & the Supremes (1968)
14. "She's a Lady," Tom Jones (1971)
15. "Theme," *633 Squadron*, New Zealand Symphony Orchestra (1964)
16. "Revolution," The Beatles (1968)
17. "Crazy Horses," The Osmonds (1972)
18. "Gypsys, Tramps and Thieves," Cher (1971)
19. "Love Is Like an Itching in My Heart," The Supremes (1966)
20. "Born to Run," Bruce Springsteen (1975)
21. "No Time," The Guess Who (1969)
22. "Penny Lane," The Beatles (1967)
23. "Happy Together," The Turtles (1967)

MAIN CHARACTERS

THE BAD LOVE GANG FROM OAK RIDGE, TENNESSEE

1. **Kevin "Bubble Butt" or "BB" Schafer:** Age 17. Borderline genius, has one foot in reality and one foot in destiny. Great sense of humor. Loves strategy, adventure, and popular music: has a "music brain." A pilot, he discovered the White Hole Project time machine with Bowmar. Plans adventures for the Bad Love Gang. The narrator of the *Bad Love* book series.

2. **Nathan "Bowmar" Williams:** Age 17. Bubble Butt's best friend. African American certified genius, with an IQ somewhere north of 140. Discovered the White Hole Project time machine with BB. Understands time travel and plans adventures with Bubble Butt.

3. **Brianna "Cleopatra" Williams:** Age 18. Bowmar's sister, a total social butterfly with a high social IQ. Becomes the queen of any social circle she enters. Tries to keep her brother Bowmar grounded. Very independent. Crisco's best friend.

4. **Jimmy "Goondoggy" Blanchert:** Age 17. Bubble Butt's next-door neighbor from early childhood who has absolutely no concept of fear. Loves the outdoors and adventure. Always ready for the next adventure into the unknown, and will try anything at least once. Highly energetic and very smart.

5. **Billy "Willy" Blanchert:** Age 19. Goondoggy's older brother. A pilot, he learned how to fly with Bubble Butt. The polar opposite of Goondoggy. Analyzes Bad Love Gang plans to calculate odds of success. Struggles to overcome caution and fear. Has a gentle spirit, and usually caves into the group's plans. Very smart.

6. **Donny "The Runt" Legrande:** Age 18. French American, shorter in stature than the rest of the Bad Love Gang. Son of a talented aircraft mechanic. A resourceful mechanical genius who can fix or improve any and all internal combustion engines. Not afraid to take on a fight. Loyal friend.

7. **David "Crazy Ike" Eichenmuller:** Age 19. German Irish American who can speak perfect German and English. Covered head to toes with freckles. A bit of a troublemaker who generally ignores rules/laws. Can steal anything and lie his way out of trouble. Smart, always entertaining, and just a little bit crazy. Starting college in journalism school.

8. **Karen "Crisco" O'Sullivan:** Age 15+. Irish-Catholic American and the oldest of eleven children. Overly mature for her age, athletic, and street smart. Interested in nursing and photography. Super cute with blonde hair, blue eyes, mature voice for her age, and a perfect body—other than a slightly disproportionate booty. Cleopatra's best friend.

9. **Frankie "Spaghetti Head" Russo:** Age 17. Italian-Catholic American, a relatively new addition to the Bad Love Gang. Strong Italian family background. Speaks with an Italian accent and adds a Mafia-style touch to the gang. Has incredibly thick, curly, dark hair. Good at calculating damage and destruction.

10. **Gary "The Pud" Jacobson:** Age 16. Great at doing tedious and/ or time-consuming jobs. Understands wireless communication devices backwards and forwards. Got his nickname for being average in every sport as a kid. Resourceful, dependable and reliable—gets the job done. Cynical sense of humor.

11. **Aaron "Meatball" Eisen:** Age 17. From a Jewish-American family. A jack of all trades who can fix anything mechanical or electrical. Always ready to lend a helping hand. Has a true heart of gold. A problem solver and totally street-smart. A great cook. Fell in love with Hannah Lieb and fathered a child (Elijah) with her during time travel in *Bad Love Strikes*.

12. **Paul "Waldo" Thompson:** Age 44. A Korean War Medal of Honor recipient. Works in procurement at Oak Ridge National Laboratory. A gun collector and firearms expert. Loves to camp, play cards, and talk about everything under the sun. Married and devoted to Mary, with no children. Together, they virtually adopted the entire Bad Love Gang and serve as surrogate parents. Their home is always open to the gang.

13. **Mary Thompson:** Age 43. Married to Waldo and surrogate mom to the Bad Love Gang. Incredibly nice, sweet, nonjudgmental and a peacemaker. Worries about the gang's adventures and encourages Waldo to protect their "children." Uniquely, never assigned a nickname by the Bad Love Gang. Devoted to Waldo. Knows how to handle firearms.

14. **Danny "Tater" Ford:** Age 17. A southern boy to his core, from a military family. Born in Columbus, Georgia and moved to Oak Ridge, Tennessee at age eight. The Bad Love Gang's continual

source of southern-fried humor. Terrific sense of humor and uncanny wit. Always entertaining, always ready for adventure.

BAD LOVE GANG ADDED FROM THE *BAD LOVE STRIKES* 1944 RESCUE MISSION

15. **Jack "Bucky" Smith:** Age 27. West Point graduate, 1940. US-AAF Captain and Special Forces WWII pilot. Personally chosen by President Franklin Roosevelt as the first White Hole Project test pilot. Has top-secret clearance to Area 51. Was lost in time on his inaugural time-travel mission until rescued by the Bad Love Gang. Returned with the Bad Love Gang to November 1974 and has become BB's "big brother." Smart, courageous, handsome, great at strategy, and hard to kill.

16. **Darby "Pumpkin" Nelson:** Age 23. British by heritage, from London, England. Adopted, his parents were both killed in a Nazi bombing raid on London. Navigator extraordinaire and trained as a pilot. Joined the Bad Love Gang along with Bucky during the Phantom Fortress mission and returned with the gang to November 1974. Adopted the Jewish orphan boy Benzion "Ben" Kaplan. Great British wit and a total team player. Face turns orange when embarrassed.

17. **Benzion "Ben" Kaplan:** Age 9. Jewish orphan boy on the run from Nazi authorities during the Holocaust. Rescued by the Bad Love Gang in November 1944 and brought back to the future, along with Bucky and Pumpkin. Adopted by Pumpkin. Smart and growing up fast. Inquisitive and good at math. Wants to become a pilot.

THE 13 RESCUED HOLOCAUST SURVIVORS FROM THE *BAD LOVE STRIKES* 1944 RESCUE MISSION

1-3. David, Sarah, and Hannah Lieb
4-5. Vadoma and Barsali Loveridge
6-7. Asher and Avigail Goldberg
8. Benzion "Ben" Kaplan
9-13. Daniel, Mazal, Zelda and Rhoda Roth, and Mazal's mother, Rachel Soros

BAD LOVE GANG ARCH ENEMIES

1. **Borya Krovopuskov:** Russian KGB super-agent bent on stealing the secrets of the White Hole Project. Known in America as "Russ Krovo," he is cagey, effective and deadly, running the oldest KGB spy cell in the United States.

2. **Catherine Krovopuskov:** Borya's American-born devoted wife and mother to their two American-born children, Bobbie and Natalie. Known locally as "Cathy Krovo," she and the two children have all been taught and trained in KGB techniques by Borya.

MAIN CHARACTERS FROM PLANET AZUR

1. **Queen Azur:** The supreme ruler of the Blue Azurians on planet Azur. Her maiden name is Blue Mary Ten. She is married to Blue Max Ten.

2. **Blue Nova One:** The prime princess to Queen Azur. The chief diplomat for the Blue Azurians, second in command to the

queen. Made first contact with the Bad Love Gang in the forests of southern China in *Bad Love Tigers*. Blue Azurian confidant and friend to the Bad Love Gang. Extremely intelligent, intellectually on par with Bowmar. A capable Azurian spaceship captain who explores other galaxies in search of blue exotic matter.

3. **Blue Rhett One:** Drilling engineer of the Azurian spaceship on a blue exotic matter drilling expedition in the German Black Forest. Husband to Blue Nova One.

4. **Blue Max Ten:** Captain of the crashed Azurian spaceship at Area 51 in *Bad Love Strikes* and *Bad Love Beyond*. Co-Captain of the Azurian blue exotic matter drilling expedition in *Bad Love Medicine*. Husband to Queen Azur, father to their two children, Blue Bellatrix "Bella" Ten and Blue Badar Ten (who both befriend Ben). Brother to Blue Zaniah Ten.

5. **Blue Zaniah Ten:** Systems engineer of Azurian spaceship at Area 51 and the blue exotic matter drilling expedition in Germany's Black Forest. Sister to Blue Max Ten and sister-in-law to Queen Azur. Shared assistant to the queen and Blue Nova One.

6. **Blue Electra Seven:** Co-pilot of the Azurian blue exotic matter drilling expedition and wife to Blue Izar Seven.

7. **Blue Izar Seven:** Navigator of the Azurian spaceship sent to Germany's Black Forest on a blue exotic matter drilling expedition, and husband to Blue Electra Seven.

8. **Blue Kamaria Twelve:** A young, attractive assistant to the queen's court who lives and works at the queen's palace guest quarters to meet the needs of visiting guests and dignitaries.

9. **Blue Delta Seven:** Precinct ranger from the Azurian Dinosaur Preserve who rescued Goondoggy following his heroic effort to protect the Troodons and their large clutch of eggs from an attacking Carcharodontosaurus.

10. **Danvinio "Dan" One:** Elected and trusted prime minister of the Republic of Azur and its diverse people, the Gazurians. In year seven of a single ten-year term as Prime Minister. A devoted public servant of the Republic who was faced with an impending cataclysmic, volcanic, extinction event. Loves music and the arts. Six feet tall, he is a handsome, athletic black man with salt and pepper hair in his 50s.

11. **Stareveret "Star" Three:** Elected vice-prime minister of the Republic of Azur and the right-hand diplomat to Danvinio One. A military veteran loyal to Dan and the Republic. A trusted and experienced pilot of Gazurian Helium airships. Captain of the Republic's Titan-One Airship. In her mid-30s, she is a fair-skinned, freckled, redhead with green eyes.

12. **Jadedominic "Jade" Eleven:** The Republic's best search and rescue pilot. Captain of the Helium rescue airship Libero Three. From a small tribe in the Republic, her ancestors were forced to immigrate when their planet faced extinction. A striking green woman with incredibly bright green eyes and black hair. Smart and courageous.

NEW CHARACTERS IN *BAD LOVE MEDICINE*

1. **Klaus Richter:** A seasoned German Nazi SS-Storm squad leader in the Fall of France who becomes a rising star in the Waffen-SS after ambushing the Azurian spaceship in the German Black Forest and discovering blue exotic matter. Personally promoted to the rank of SS Obergruppenführer (lieutenant general) by Adolf Hitler as the head of security for the Black Hole Project.

2. **Gunther Brandt:** A brilliant German theoretical and quantum mechanics physicist. A protégé of German Nobel Prize winning physicist Werner Heisenberg (in charge of Uranverein, the Reich's nuclear weapons program). Personally appointed by Adolf Hitler to develop and build the top-secret Black Hole Project time-travel machine.

3. **Emma Hoffman:** A British Special Operations Executive (SOE) spy whose real name was Ela Hellberg. Born to a Jewish family from Strasbourg, France. She worked for the powerful Nazi, Robert Heinrich Wagner, the "Butcher of Alsace," who recommended her transfer to the Black Hole Project. Became Klaus Richter's trusted lover. Fiercely strongminded but governed by resolve to make a difference for the Allies.

4. **Petra Vogel:** A British SOE spy born to a highly educated Ashkenazi, German Jewish family in Göttingen, Germany. A brilliant physicist in her own right, she trained in quantum mechanics under Nobel prize winning physicists, Max Born and Werner Heisenberg. Heisenberg recommended her to Gunther Brandt. Became Brandt's lover while assisting him to develop and build the Black Hole Project.

TABLE OF CONTENTS

CHAPTER ONE

HITLER'S DARKEST SECRET...1

CHAPTER TWO

REGAL KNIGHTS AND MISCHIEF...17

CHAPTER THREE

HANNAH'S CURE AND ALADDIN'S LAMP...30

CHAPTER FOUR

IN THE MIDNIGHT HOUR, BACK ON EARTH...41

CHAPTER FIVE

BORYA'S REVENGE–DING'S VENGEANCE...47

CHAPTER SIX

BAD LOVE HOMELAND DEFENSE...58

CHAPTER SEVEN

BOWMAR'S HUSH-HUSH...74

CHAPTER EIGHT

THE BLACK HOLE PROJECT...85

CHAPTER NINE

CHURCHILL'S SECRET ARMY...90

CHAPTER TEN

THE HOOKS ARE SET, THE FISH ARE ASLEEP...98

CHAPTER ELEVEN

ESCAPE TO LONDON...111

CHAPTER TWELVE

BAD LOVE MOSQUITOES OVER LONDON...122

CHAPTER THIRTEEN

THE GORING...130

CHAPTER FOURTEEN

HORSES, KNIGHTS, AND THE MONARCHY...139

CHAPTER FIFTEEN

A BLAST FROM THE PAST...148

CHAPTER SIXTEEN

THE BULLDOG'S WAR ROOM...160

CHAPTER SEVENTEEN

OPERATION NO TIME...170

CHAPTER EIGHTEEN
DARK DAYS...180

CHAPTER NINETEEN
BLACK IS BLACK...188

CHAPTER TWENTY
BLUE IS BETTER...201

CHAPTER TWENTY-ONE
THE FIFTH BEATLE...211

CHAPTER TWENTY-TWO
TWO SHOTS...219

EPILOGUE...230

CHAPTER ONE:

HITLER'S DARKEST SECRET

"Make the lie big, make it simple, keep saying it,
and eventually, they'll believe."
—Adolf Hitler

*November 26, 1941, at 5:00 PM local time, The Black Forest,
state of Baden-Württemberg in southwest Germany*

On this day in history, President Franklin D. Roosevelt signed a bill making Thanksgiving the last Thursday in November; a Japanese attack fleet of 33 warships and auxiliary craft, including six aircraft carriers, sailed from northern Japan for the Hawaiian Islands on a top-secret mission to bomb Pearl Harbor; and Blue Nova One suffered an immense, unexpected, personal tragedy in the densely wooded German Black Forest. Second in command and prime princess to Queen Azur, Blue Nova One was a brilliant and capable Azurian spaceship captain who was tasked with exploring galaxies far and wide in the search for blue exotic matter, which was in critical short supply on planet Azur and essential to the blue Azurians' way of life. Nearly seven months prior, after years of exhaustive, intergalactic searching, she had finally located blue exotic matter identical to that of Azur on planet Earth. Much to her and Queen Azur's delight, Earth had evolved in many ways much like Azur, and they had claimed it as Azur's sister planet after discovering the precious blue exotic matter on Earth.

Blue Nova One had pinpointed a rich vein of blue exotic matter—accessible by ultra-sophisticated Azurian deep targeted drilling techniques—in the beautiful Black Forest. The Black Forest Mountain Range in the state of Baden-Württemberg in southwest Germany was oblong in shape, measuring about 100 miles long and 30 miles wide, bounded by the Rhine Valley to the west and south. The area was known for mining and an abundant variety of ore deposits including baryte, fluorite, lead, iron, zinc, cobalt, silver, and uranium. She identified a well-hidden landing zone in the mountain range of the Black Forest, south of the town of Bühl and east of Strasbourg, with a panoramic view to the west across the Rhine Valley into neighboring Alsace, France and the Vosges mountains. She and her drilling team discretely landed on Sunday, May 4, 1941—the same day that Adolf Hitler addressed the Nazi Reichstag, reviewing the Balkan campaign and declaring that the German Third Reich and its allies were far superior to any conceivable competing coalition in the world.

The small but talented crew accompanying Blue Nova One on this drilling and extraction mission included her drilling engineer husband, Blue Rhett One, Queen Azur's husband, co-captain Blue Max Ten, and his sister, systems engineer Blue Zaniah Ten. Also on board were co-pilot Blue Electra Seven and her husband navigator, Blue Izar Seven. All six of the crew were trained to multitask for this mission of vital importance. They had established a secret drilling site hidden in the Black Forest; using their advanced drilling equipment, they reached the vein of blue exotic matter in late July 1941. The extraction process was slow and tedious, and the extricated raw blue exotic matter was placed into specialized cubic containers. The containers were periodically shipped directly to the Queen's Island Space Center on planet Azur, using the spaceship's white hole intergalactic transport unit. They had used the intergalactic transport drive sparingly, as it required the lower and upper hulls of the double decker spaceship to telescope and separate with unavoidable flashing of lights in the process. The crew of six had bonded together like one big family during this mission and were scheduled to depart in December. There had been precious few close encounters with Earthlings in the Black Forest during their covert operation, which may have given them a false sense of security by November 1941.

On this day in late November 1941, twenty-four-year-old Nazi Waffen-SS Storm squad leader Sergeant Major Klaus Richter, a seasoned veteran of the German victory in the Fall of France in May–June 1940, and a rising star in the Waffen-SS, was leading a small squad of Nazi Waffen-SS soldiers to investigate strange lights reported by local deer and elk hunters in the Black Forest. Richter's unit reported directly to the ambitious and powerful Robert Heinrich Wagner, who had stood trial with Adolf Hitler in the November 1923 Beer Hall Putsch, a failed coup d'état undertaken by party leader Adolf Hitler as his political career was beginning to take form. Wagner knew Hitler and became an early and loyal member of Hitler's Nazi Party. After the defeat of France, Germany incorporated Alsace into the Greater German Reich; on August 2, 1940, Wagner became the chief of civil administration for the region. Wagner led an aggressive Germanization campaign in Alsace, proclaiming a ban on speaking French in public and restoring old German place names that had existed prior to 1918. He also embarked on a crusade to rid Alsace of Jews, earning himself the nickname "Butcher of Alsace." Sergeant Major Klaus Richter knew that if he could impress Wagner, he would go far in the Third Reich Nazi Waffen-SS hierarchy.

Born in Stuttgart, Germany in 1917, Klaus Richter was a prototypical product of the Hitler Youth Program. Founded in 1922, the Nazi youth arm was designed to recruit and prepare members for its paramilitary service. In January of 1933, when Adolf Hitler initially came to power as Chancellor of Germany, there were 50,000 members of Hitler Youth; by the end of 1933, there were more than two million members. By the end of 1936, Hitler Youth membership exceeded five million. In other words, as the Nazis became more powerful, their youth arm grew exponentially. In 1936, the Nazis banned all other youth groups, including the Boy Scouts, and forced their members to become part of the Hitler Youth instead. With other scouting organizations completely banned, the only way for Germany's kids to get a scouting experience was to join the Hitler Youth. By 1939, more than 90 percent of German children were part of the Hitler Youth Program. German Jewish children were banned from joining Hitler Youth.

Through the Hitler Youth Program, the Nazi Third Reich removed German children from the influence of their parents and indoctrinated them at their most impressionable age. The Nazi Party knew that families could be an obstacle to their goals. The Hitler Youth was a way to get Hitler's ideology into the family unit, and some members of the Hitler Youth eventually even denounced their parents and/or extended families when they behaved in ways inconsistent with the Third Reich's philosophy. Early on, the Hitler Youth took part in typical scouting type activities like wearing uniforms, reciting pledges, taking summer camping trips, singing, hiking, and telling stories over campfires. But over time, the activities changed and became more militaristic, training young men in everything from survival skills to handling Nazi weaponry. The Hitler Youth propaganda machine encouraged a religious devotion to the Führer, Adolf Hitler.

Klaus Richter could not wait to become a full-fledged Hitler Youth member from his earliest childhood memories and relished the team building, marching, singing, and attending rallies. When he joined the Waffen-SS at age 20 in 1937, he was a handsome, chiseled German athlete, standing six feet tall with blondish-brown hair and piercing blue eyes, and had a burning desire to rise in the ranks of the Nazi Waffen-SS. At age 24, with victorious battlefield experience, he was a celebrated pistol marksman and known for his uncanny scouting abilities, particularly behind enemy lines. He had been brainwashed since his days in the Hitler Youth program and belonged to Adolf Hitler, body, mind, and soul. He could not know that on this day, his life's trajectory would put him on a course to intersect with the Führer himself.

Blue Nova One had landed their Azurian spaceship adjacent to a wooded hillside with a sheer rocky bluff that shielded their eastern flank and had a perfect overhanging cliff, under which they had erected their drilling equipment. A mere fifty yards separated the entrance hatch of the lower hull, where the drilling equipment and spare parts were stored, and the outside drilling site. The crew had carefully camouflaged the ship's upper and lower hulls with pine trees, branches, and pine needles, making it blend in nicely with the surroundings. They had constructed two separate perimeter defenses around their landing and drilling site. The first was a minimum half-mile out and served as a discreet passive warning system that unwanted visitors could be approaching. Once the passive warning system was activated, fixed cameras and drones quickly identified the intruder(s). The second perimeter was an invisible active defense enclosure around the spaceship and drilling site that would electrically disable any trespassers.

Only twice in six months had any humans (local hunters) breached the outer perimeter; the most recent event had occurred three weeks prior. The crew had quickly and efficiently redirected the hunters with clever, drone-manipulated distractions. However, there were quite a few forest animals—including eagles, hawks, deer, foxes, grey squirrels, rabbits, raccoons, wolves, and wild cats—that had been allowed to inhabit the first perimeter, most of which naturally avoided direct encounters with the spaceship and drilling site. The only close call they had experienced was a crazed wild boar who charged the inner, active defense enclosure only to be shocked and temporarily paralyzed into submission, then carefully relocated to safer surroundings by Blue Nova's husband, Rhett.

Blue Nova One had met her husband, Blue Rhett One, ten years prior when they were both postgraduate students at the Azurian Advanced Institute of Technology (AAIT), which could be considered like a hybrid of Earth's Oxford University and Massachusetts Institute of Technology (MIT). It was nearly love at first sight, and a match made in heaven. Nova was beautiful, athletic, truly brilliant, and academically focused on the physics properties and harnessing of blue exotic matter for space and time travel, with the goal of becoming a spaceship captain in the extraterrestrial search for new sources of blue exotic matter. Rhett was very smart, physically and mentally strong, and adventurous but practical; he was at AAIT learning the advanced engineering and physics principles to drill for and to extract blue exotic matter in its natural state. In addition to their common interest in blue exotic matter, they shared a love of the outdoors and a passion for traveling to exotic locations, as well as climbing, hiking, and camping. Nova had a way of getting them to exotic locales, but she loved the way that Rhett could find his way around and discover the hidden gems wherever they went. Where she was impulsive and driven, he was cautious and deliberate. She was hopelessly intellectual, but he was hopelessly romantic, and she found herself in physical and emotional places she could have never dreamed of on her own. They became an unbreakable team.

They celebrated graduating from AAIT with their advanced degrees by getting married. Blue Zaniah Ten, Blue Nova One's best friend from school, was the maid of honor at their wedding. Zaniah's older brother, Blue Max Ten, was married to Queen Azur, and they attended the wedding. The queen was personally impressed with Nova and Rhett, as well as with their skills and passions regarding blue exotic matter. She added the newly married couple to her inner circle and assigned them to explore the universe in a quest to find new sources of blue exotic matter. When Blue Nova One discovered blue exotic matter on Earth after many years of searching, the queen promoted her to the role of prime princess, which meant she was second in command to the queen.

At 3:00 PM, Klaus Richter and his squad of seven men arrived near the outer Azurian passive defense perimeter on a small trail where the local hunters had noticed the strange lights several weeks prior. Growing up in Stuttgart, Richter had spent plenty of time hunting in the Black Forest during his youth and had some familiarity with this area. He knew that sunset would be upon them in 100 minutes. He needed to relieve his bladder and ordered his men to take their rest while he walked a short way up the wooded hillside. On his way up the hill, he noticed a tall, rocky bluff with a large overhanging cliff in the distance to the northeast. Just as he started to unbutton his fly to drain his bladder against a tree, he saw a skinny, vertical sensor apparatus fastened to the side of the tree with a very tiny, blinking, blue light. He looked closer and saw there was a matching device on the other side of the tree; both had been partially concealed with brush and branches. *Holy shit*, he thought, *we may be on to something here.*

Richter returned to his squad and explained what he had accidently discovered. He suspected it was some type of sensor, but it was unlike anything he had ever seen. He picked his two best men, Fritz Meier and Diedrich Fisher, to go with him and ordered the other five men to wait and watch after helping the three of them climb the tree where the sensors were located, avoiding the sensors and jumping to the ground on the other side. The five men were instructed to wait at the hunter's trail unless Richter, Meier, or Fisher radioed for help. On the ground inside the outer defense perimeter and undetected by Blue Nova's crew, Richter led the way slowly, quietly, and covertly toward the large cliff he had seen and was using as a landmark.

At 4:00 PM, Richter, Meier and Fisher got their first view of the Azurian spaceship and the advanced blue exotic matter drilling site. Blue Rhett One was supervising the drilling/extraction process, helped by Blue Elektra Seven and Blue Izar Seven. Looking through his field binoculars, Richter was awestruck by the sight and scope of the double-decker spaceship, its subtle white glow underneath the camouflage, the blue glow of exotic matter trickling from the drilling apparatus into a small cubic storage container, and the blue Azurians dressed in shiny, metallic, skintight outfits with hoods. Fritz Meier was the first to whisper, "Those people are blue in color."

Richter immediately whispered back, "How do you know those are regular people? None of what we are seeing here looks like it is from this world. Normally, I would try to report this sighting up the chain of command. But based on where we are, it would take far too long to get any help. If they leave before we can get help or reinforcements, no one will believe us. We are going to confront them and detain them."

Diedrich Fisher, who was carrying an MP 40 submachine gun with a 32-round box magazine, enquired, "What's your plan, sir? We can see three of them now, but there is no telling how many are in that saucer-shaped vessel."

Richter replied, "That's right, Diedrich. I want you to sneak over to the side and behind the entrance of that ship. You'll have anyone who comes out of that ship easily covered with your machine gun if they fail to comply and surrender. After we see you get into position, Fritz and I will confront the three of them by the drilling unit. None of those three appear to be armed. Now go!"

Fisher stealthily made his way toward the ship's entrance, which was open. He then approached from the side and moved behind the entrance while Richter and Meier watched his progress. When Fisher advanced to about 25 feet from the side of the ship, tragedy began to unfold, and history changed. Fisher walked directly into the invisible active defense enclosure that extended around the spaceship and drilling site. For a brief moment, he stood rigid, shaking as his body was filled with paralyzing electricity. Alarm sirens blared inside the spaceship and around the drilling site. As Fisher's limp body fell to the ground unconscious, the Azurians and the Nazi aggressors alike were all caught off-guard by the unexpected circumstances. Following emergency protocol, inside the ship, Blue Nova One yelled to Blue Max Ten and Blue Zaniah Ten to activate the ship's main computers and launch systems as she made her way toward the exit.

Fritz Meier was carrying a standard issue Karabiner 98k controlled-feed, bolt-action rifle. Klaus Richter was armed with his favorite close combat weapon, a Luger P08 pistol which he handled with deadly accuracy. Richter was temporarily mesmerized by the sight of Fisher's electrified encounter and paralysis, but quickly recovered with a modified action plan. He commanded Meier, "Go directly toward the drilling unit, but not as close in as Fisher went. Lay down your rifle, hold up your hands, and tell them that you come in peace. Then plead to help your injured friend. Once they turn off their barrier and let you in, I will get through with my pistol and arrest them. Don't hesitate; our element of surprise is gone now. We must move quickly! Schnéll, schnéll!"

Blue Elektra Seven and Blue Izar Seven were moving from the drilling unit in the direction of the unconscious Diedrich Fisher as Fritz Meier approached the active defense perimeter. Wearing their Azurian outfits with their Luna artificial intelligence (AI) hoods up and ready for language translation, Elektra and Izar stopped when they saw Fritz moving toward them and laying down his rifle. Blue Rhett One was busy shutting down the drilling unit and activated the remote destruction program. Unfortunately, there were a dozen cubic containers of recently extracted blue exotic matter stacked against the sheer rock face enclosure that protected the drilling site. As Rhett completed the shutdown and remote destruct procedures, he grabbed one of the containers containing the precious blue exotic matter to take back to the ship. In the chaos of the moment, no one saw Klaus Richter on the ground at the edge of the active defense perimeter, waiting to spring into action.

Fritz Meier laid his Karabiner 98k rifle down, held his hands in the air, and put on an Academy Award winning acting performance. With a sad and frightened face, he stated urgently, "I hope you can understand me!"

Elektra, using her Luna AI language translation program, replied, "We can understand you. Why are you here?"

Meier replied, "We were on patrol. We got separated from our group and got lost. The two of us are here by accident. I am so worried about my friend, Diedrich, who hit your barrier. He has a medical condition, and I do not want him to die! Please, let me in to help him!" Meier started slowly moving directly toward Elektra and Izar with his hands held high.

Elektra warned him, "You have to stop, or you will suffer the same fate as your friend."

Meier pleaded as he continued his gradual advance, "I *must* help him! He is my best friend!"

Izar broke protocol and whispered to Elektra, "He is unarmed; I will let him assist his friend." Before Elektra could think to react, Izar addressed Meier, "I will let you through to assist your friend. Come ahead and give him aid." Izar stepped forward into the invisible barrier, and his Azurian suit automatically disengaged the defensive perimeter.

Richter, watching and listening, sprang into action with his Luger P08 pistol drawn and crossed the barrier near the side of the drilling unit as soon as he saw Meier cross the invisible line. At that moment,

Blue Nova One was exiting the ship. Blue Rhett One came from behind the drilling unit, carrying the heavily shielded cubic container of rare blue exotic matter. Nova could see Rhett coming her way and quickly surveyed the surroundings, not sure why an Earthling was inside the active defense perimeter, walking to another Earthling on the ground, unconscious. Her senses sharpened acutely, and a frisson of fear ran through her body. She looked back at Rhett and saw there was a third Earthling approaching him from behind, aiming a gun trained at him. Nova quickly moved directly toward Rhett, simultaneously whispering to her Luna AI, "Luna, make all of our suits bullet-proof and turn on our defensive shields now." Their outfits were already bullet-proof, but this command would make their suits literally repel ballistic projectiles on impact. The only flesh potentially exposed to harm was their faces and hands. Their defensive shields would electrically shock intruders into submission on physical contact.

As Nova hurried toward Rhett, she was experiencing the emotion of fear like never before. Her heart was pounding and despite moving quickly, she felt like she was in slow motion and could not get to him fast enough. Richter had closed to within fifteen feet of Rhett and loudly addressed him from behind. "Stop where you are and turn around!"

Surprised by the voice behind him, Rhett stopped and faced Richter, who had also stopped. Richter had assumed a shooting position, his pistol pointed straight at Rhett. It was all happening so fast. Meier was at Diedrich's side, with Izar watching them, and Elektra had started making her way to the ship's entrance. All of them heard Richter's command and stopped what they were doing, looking at Rhett and Richter facing each other. Nova was nearly there. Richter, trained and seasoned as a Nazi Waffen-SS assassin during the Fall of France, forcefully commanded Rhett, "Drop the box *now*, and put your hands behind your head!"

Rhett, who had been preoccupied shutting down the drilling site, had not activated his Luna AI language translator. He looked confused, holding the cubic container of blue exotic matter tightly and staring back at the man with a gun pointed at him. Richter yelled, "DROP THE BOX!" When Rhett did not immediately comply, Richter thought to himself, *I will make an example of him, and we will secure this area.* He could not shoot Rhett in the chest because he was holding the box, so he raised his aim. Firing a single shot, Richter put a bullet one inch above Rhett's nose, directly through the middle of his forehead and into his brain. At that instant, Nova reached Rhett and he crumpled backwards into her arms.

Nova screamed, "NO, RHETT! NO! PLEASE DON'T DIE!" She gently laid him back on the ground and charged Richter with her head down. Richter wasted no time and fired his seven additional rounds at the oncoming Blue Nova One. All his shots hit her bullet resistant Azurian suit and were deflected as she hurtled toward him. "Maximum defense, Luna!" Nova ordered. When she reached Richter, the shock from her Azurian suit sent Richter flying backwards more than a dozen feet and she took him for dead; he was not, but he was fully incapacitated. She communicated to Blue Max Ten as she returned to Rhett, "Max, program the intergalactic transport unit to send Rhett and I directly to the Space Center. Ready the ship to return to home. Rhett is gravely injured, and I have to get him back to Azur quickly!" She reached Rhett, threw his limp body over her shoulder, and ran for the ship. Izar, witnessing the events and knowing that his Azurian suit defense was activated, ignored using the electrical shock and punched Meier in the face so hard that he broke Meier's nose and knocked him out cold. Izar, Elektra, and Nova, carrying Rhett, boarded the ship and closed the hatch.

Max had readied the intergalactic transport unit and the lower and upper hulls were separating by the time Nova reached the stage of the transport racetrack with Rhett. The second she and Rhett were in place, Max hit the transport button and they were gone. Max and Zaniah then initiated the launch sequence and simultaneously blew the drilling site, the implosion destroying the equipment and the drilling shaft. It was 5:00 PM local time, and twenty minutes past sunset. The spaceship blasted off in emergency mode and turned the early evening into daylight as they departed the area. The five remaining Nazi soldiers waiting on the hunter's trail below, witnessed the spaceship launch in awe and then ran toward their three fellow soldiers.

Traveling through the white hole back to the Queen's Island Space Station with Rhett held tightly in her arms, Blue Nova One whispered in his ear, telling him not to die and how much she loved him. She closed her eyes and dreamt of their honeymoon on Azur, embracing on the beach in soft white sand on a beautiful, sunny day, sharing how excited they were for their future of exploring the universe together. In her momentary dream, Rhett was holding her, and she looked deep into his eyes as he pulled her into a passionate kiss that reverberated throughout her soul. They landed on the intergalactic transport racetrack on Azur which startled her. She was crying and shaking uncontrollably as help arrived. It was too late; Rhett was gone.

March 23, 1942, 1:00 PM local time, at the Berghof:
Adolf Hitler's home in the Obersalzberg of the Bavarian Alps
near Berchtesgaden, Bavaria, Germany

Other than the top-secret, heavily guarded "Wolf's Lair" military headquarters in East Prussia (Poland) built in 1941 for the start of Operation Barbarossa, the German invasion of the Soviet Union, Hitler spent more time at the Berghof (meaning "mountain court") than anywhere else during World War II. Located in southeast Germany, with a commanding view to the snowcapped mountains of his native

Austria, Hitler purchased the chalet in 1933 with money from the sale of his politically motivated book, *Mein Kampf*. The chalet-style holiday home was then refurbished and significantly expanded during 1935–36 and renamed the Berghof. A landing strip and many buildings for security and support staff were constructed in close proximity to a large complex of mountain homes for Nazi leadership. Following the encounter and raid on the Azurian spaceship, and his "heroic" actions leading to the classified Nazi discovery of blue exotic matter, Klaus Richter had been elevated to Hauptsturmführer, or the Waffen-SS equivalent of captain. Richter had been summoned by the Führer and had arrived at the nearby landing strip by private plane. He was then shuttled directly to the Berghof.

The Berghof had a large outdoor terrace that featured big, colorful, resort-style canvas umbrellas. The chalet was bright and airy, with a light jade green color scheme. The entrance hall was lined with a display of plants in decorative glazed pots. The dining room was paneled with very costly cembra pine. There was a great hall furnished with expensive Teutonic furniture, and an expansive fireplace with a custom red marble mantel. Behind a wall in the great hall was a projection booth for evening screenings of films (many of them Hollywood productions that were otherwise banned in Germany). Hitler's large study had a telephone switchboard room. The library contained books about history, painting, architecture, and music. The house was operated like a small resort hotel by a dedicated staff of housekeepers, gardeners, cooks, and other domestic workers.

Richter took mental notes as he arrived and had noticed Wehrmacht mountain troop units when they got close and Reich Security Service (RSD) SS men patrolling the grounds around the Berghof. Once inside the Berghof, Führerbegleitkommando (Führer Escort Command, FBK) were present, providing personal security protection for Hitler. One of the FBK guards escorted him to the great hall, where

Adolf Hitler and another man were seated in front of the impressive fireplace. Richter noticed a large globe of the world and oddly, a cage with some type of bright yellow canary with dark brown markings. Both Hitler and the other man stood as Richter and the guard saluted. The guard announced, "SS Captain Klaus Richter as requested, Mein Führer." Richter's heart was pounding as Hitler waved the guard off to a seating area in the corner and began to speak.

Hitler started, "Captain Richter, I want you to meet Gunther Brandt, a brilliant theoretical and quantum mechanics physicist who has previously reported to our German Nobel Prize winning physicist, Werner Heisenberg." Richter shook hands with Brandt and Hitler had them take their seats. He continued, "Heisenberg is focused on atomic power generation and the Reich's nuclear weapons program, known as Uranverein, but Brandt is now focused on using the blue exotic matter that you discovered when you thwarted the invading aliens in the Black Forest. I want you to tell Gunther and I the details of exactly what happened on November twenty-sixth."

Richter spent the next 25 minutes detailing everything that happened that fateful day. When he finished, Hitler was silent for a few minutes. He stared coldly and deliberately into the eyes of first Brandt, then Richter. When he spoke again, Hitler's firm, low, methodical voice chilled Richter's spine to its core. "Gunther believes that the blue exotic matter can be used to create a machine that will function as a portal for time and space travel. I have selected a small, devoted group of scientists to work with Gunther and I am appointing you, Richter, as the head of security for what we are calling the Ein Schwarzes Loch Project. As of this moment, I am promoting you to the rank of SS Obergruppenführer." Richter was stunned by his promotion to lieutenant general of the Black Hole Project. The Führer continued, "This is a secret that stops here in my house!" His mesmerizing intensity was growing palpable. "No one can know of it! Not your families, not other

Reich officers or officials, not anyone but me. You will report only to me!"

Hitler stood and took a few steps to the large globe on display. He spun the world on its axis and proclaimed, "When my work is done here, I will take *Mein Kampf* to the future. This is my life, and this is my destiny; you two will make that certain and have this time machine successfully prepared when I am ready to use it!"

CHAPTER TWO:

REGAL KNIGHTS AND MISCHIEF

"I believe in kindness. Also in mischief. Also in singing,
especially when singing is not necessarily prescribed."
—Mary Oliver

Saturday, December 20, 1975: early evening,
the Queen's Palace, planet Azur

A classic, strong Azurian thunderstorm had blown across Queen's
Island during the day, giving way to a clear and peaceful late after-
noon. There was a planned historic gathering of Queen Azur's Royal
Court, governmental dignitaries, and workers to celebrate the Bad
Love Gang's successful intervention to save the Republic of Azur from
volcanic disaster, as well as to mark the opening of peaceful relations
between the Blue Azurians and the Republic of Azur. The Republic of
Azur's Prime Minister, Danvinio One, had assured the queen and Blue
Nova One of the rights for the blue Azurians to drill for blue exotic
matter on the island of the Republic.

Getting dressed and ready for the event, I mused about how the
day after Thanksgiving, the same day our Oakridge Wildcats had beat
the odds to win the 1975 Tennessee State Football Championship,
I had shared with the entire Bad Love Gang what my time-traveling,

62-year-old self had said to me. He or I had said, "You and the Bad Love Gang will make history in 1975. Don't blow it, Bubble Butt!" I did not understand what the older me meant then, but now I knew. During the past week, we had made history on two accounts. First, we had succeeded with intergalactic space travel; second, we had managed to effectively redirect the eruption of a major volcano, the Republic of Azur's Mount Pelorius, averting certain disaster for millions of people and saving the Republic. In addition to reflecting on the events of the past week, I was also imagining meeting with President Gerald Ford for a very private celebration with the Bad Love Gang, and Ford making a new entry in the *Book of Presidents*.

I had briefly spoken with Blue Nova One earlier in the day to request that the Bad Love Gang be allowed to provide some Earth-style music for dancing and entertainment during the night's festivities. We had not yet met the queen and I asked Nova if the queen would tolerate some Earth music, dancing, and a little good-natured teasing. I also enquired as to the queen's real name since she had only been referred to as Queen Azur. Nova reassured me that the queen definitely had a sense of humor and enjoyed music, but she could not promise that the queen would do any dancing. Her name before becoming Queen Azur was Blue Mary Ten; I told Nova I could work with that.

Nova assigned Blue Kamaria Twelve, who had been living and working with us while we stayed at the Queen's Palace in the guest quarters, to help me with the music arrangements and make sure that it could be heard perfectly on their sound systems in the palace. I shared with Nova that we wanted the celebration to be fun for everyone attending. She encouraged me and said, "We are all greatly relieved by the turn of events these past few days, and very much look forward to having some amusement in the Queen's Court after quite a dry spell. As they say on Earth, knock yourself out, BB! After dinner tonight, we will need to discuss a few things privately before you head back to Earth."

Blue Kamaria Twelve had become quite busy at the palace guest quarters because in addition to the Bad Love Gang, more guests had arrived for the night's celebration. The Republic of Azur's Prime Minister Danvinio One and Republic Vice Prime Minister Stareveret Three, along with their extended staff, were staying there as well. In addition, they had also brought Republic rescue pilot Jadedominic Eleven, along with her family and TBM Avenger pilot Charlie Taylor. With a little group social pressure, we successfully recruited Stareveret Three and Jadedominic Eleven to join the nine of us Bad Love Gang members as we practiced a few entertainment ideas with the accompanying music from my collection. Blue Kamaria Twelve also danced and joined in the fun, working with me on getting the proper sequence of music ready to play over the palace sound system. We had a rather diverse ensemble with a total of twelve black, blue, green, and white members rehearsing together.

Kamaria took all of us staying at the palace guest quarters to the Queen's Palace in a large Azurian Flashback at the appointed time. On the way over, Kamaria called Blue Nova One and let her know things would be a little different than the typical protocol, with the Bad Love Gang's roguish mischievousness and lightheartedness at play. She also told Nova that she had become a willing participant as she smiled and winked at me.

The evening started in the Knight's Hall of the Queen's Palace, which had a cathedral-type feel to it due to the beautiful tall, arched, multicolored, stained-glass windows. The center aisle, leading to a large throne in the front of the hall, was lined with ornate columns leading to a high, arched, ornamental ceiling. Gigantic elaborate chandeliers hung from the ceiling. Both sides of the center isle were lined with Blue Azurians and the Republic of Azur staff, along with Jadedominic's family members, all anxious to see the intrepid guests from Earth and the Republic come down the aisle and for the night's festivities to begin. Kamaria had notified the palace trumpeters that there would be some "unusual music" playing between their opening trumpeting and the trumpets to announce the knighting ceremony.

After entering the Knight's Hall, the twelve of us—Bucky, Bowmar, Cleopatra, Crisco, the Pud, Goondoggy, Pumpkin, Ben, me, Stareveret, Jadedominic, and Kamaria—gathered in the rear of the hall. The Republic of Azur's Prime Minister Danvinio One was seated in an opulent chair to the left of the throne; Blue Nova One and Blue Max Ten were seated in identical chairs to the right of the throne. Charlie Taylor was seated in the front row facing the throne. The trumpeters sounded their opening stanza, and Kamaria had us start slowly walking down the center aisle as everyone stood. When the trumpeters stopped, the lead trumpeter loudly announced, "The queen of Azur!" as the queen entered from the right side, walking to the throne in regal attire.

It was quiet in the hall for a moment as the queen made her way to the throne, but on Kamaria's cue, Earth music blared over the sound system. The song was **"Along Comes Mary,"** by the Association. Released on the Association's debut album, the song spent eleven weeks on the charts and was their first big hit, reaching number seven on the US Billboard Hot 100 in July 1966. It was one of my all-time favorite 60s songs; rhythmic clapping throughout the song made you want to stand up, clap, dance, and sing about Mary, who made everything seem better. I saw the Association sing **"Along Comes Mary"** live on the *Smother Brothers Comedy Hour* in 1967 and they were a hoot, introducing and describing the band members as music robots and the group as the "Association Machine" before they started playing.

The twelve of us clapped and danced down the center aisle, lip syncing the refrain as we went. The music was contagious; the crowd looked briefly confused, but quickly started joyfully clapping their hands to the beat of the song with us and dancing in place. I looked to the front and could see Danvinio One clapping his hands and tapping his right foot. Blue Nova One and Blue Max Ten were rocking their heads and bumping shoulders with big grins on their faces. But most importantly, the queen was standing in front of her throne with a wide smile, clapping her hands to the music. As the song ended, our group stood before the queen. Stareveret and Kamaria sat down in the front row, and Charlie Taylor stood and joined us.

The trumpeters again sounded their instruments in a glorious melody that signaled the knighting ceremony to begin. As the trumpeters completed, Danvinio One stood to the left of the queen. Two royal attendants brought beautiful shining swords adorned with precious jewels, first to the queen and then to Danvinio One. The queen announced, "Tonight we honor the Bad Love Gang, along with Jadedominic Eleven and TBM Avenger pilot Charlie Taylor for their extraordinary courage and bravery in diverting a volcanic disaster of untold destruction on the Republic of Azur. Because of their actions the Republic is safe, and our peoples have been reunited in peace and prosperity for the future. Prime Minister Danvinio One and I, for the first time in Azurian history, will jointly hail these heroes as knights of Azur and knights of the Republic!" The hall was filled with an overwhelming, deafening roar of applause, with shouts of joy from all those attending.

We had Jadedominic and Charlie go first. Then one by one, the Bad Love Gang approached Queen Azur and Danvinio One and took a knee in front of them. The queen and Danvinio crossed their swords as they tapped each person's shoulders to officially knight them. Goondoggy was directly behind me as we stood in the line, watching Bucky and Bowmar get knighted. Goondoggy's original left hand had been chomped off by an angry *Carcharodontosaurus* earlier in the week, then medically rebuilt using advanced Azurian bioengineering. He put his rebuilt left hand on my left shoulder and whispered, "I gotta hand it to you, Bubble Butt; I got to play with dinosaurs and get knighted on this adventure. How are you gonna top that?"

I put my right hand on top of his left and whispered, "You know what, Goondoggy, next time we go time traveling it's gonna be all hands on deck to get that cancer medicine to Hannah. So you'd better hope that new hand of yours is securely fastened!" We giggled at each other, trying to be quiet.

Cleopatra and Crisco were directly ahead of me. Both simultaneously turned their heads, shushing me with index fingers to their lips. They whispered, "Be quiet, Bubble Butt! We are about to be made queens!"

I murmured, "You say you wish you had new jeans? No knights in white satin for you two; it's denim all the way." They scowled back at me.

The Pud, standing behind Goondoggy overheard our exchanges and whispered his two cents. "For being such an average guy, I'm pretty excited about this ceremony. You are all calling me 'Sir Pud' from now on, after this is over."

Ben and Pumpkin brought up the rear behind the Pud. Ben nudged the Pud from behind and teased, "You're being knighted Sir *Dud*, not Sir Pud. Didn't they tell you?"

The Pud smirked at Ben, smiling as he whispered to Pumpkin, "Tell that boy to respect his elders."

Pumpkin leaned forward and breathed his response. "Blimey! That boy is brilliant, don't you think?" The three of them quietly chuckled to each other.

We were all sequentially knighted; coming up last, Pumpkin and Ben knelt side by side and were knighted together by the queen and Danvinio. Then we all faced the crowd to another rousing round of applause and cheers. The eleven of us who were knighted stood there with ear-to-ear smiles and clapped along with everyone else. We eleven knights then turned and bowed to Queen Azur and Danvinio One, and the loudest cheers of the night erupted in their honor. It was a celebration ceremony for the ages, one that we would never forget.

The lead trumpeter loudly proclaimed, "A royal feast is now served for all in the Queen's Banquet Hall!" Massive, extra-wide, tall double doors along one of the inner walls of the Knight's Hall swung open, and we all adjourned to the adjoining banquet hall. Seated at the head table with the queen were her husband, Blue Max Ten; her sister-in-law, Blue Zaniah Ten; her two children, Bella and Badar, along with our Ben; and Blue Nova One. Invited guests at the queen's table were Republic of Azur's Prime Minister Danvinio One, Republic Vice Prime Minister Stareveret Three, and Republic ace rescue pilot Jadedominic Eleven. Jadedominic had deftly plucked Charlie Taylor, the Pud, Crisco, and me from the Azurian Sea two days earlier, when we had been forced to ditch our heavily damaged TBM Avengers after successfully bombing the cryptodome of the volcano Mount Pelorious and redirecting the volcano's eruption out to sea.

Seated at the first table at a right angle to the queen's table were us other eight members of the Bad Love Gang, Avenger TBM pilot Charlie Taylor, and Blue Kamaria Twelve. There was also a surprise guest at our table who had contacted Kamaria and requested to be present: Blue Delta Seven, the precinct ranger from the Azurian Dinosaur Preserve who had rescued Goondoggy following his heroic effort to protect the Troodons and their large clutch of eggs from the attacking Carcharodontosaurus. It appeared that she and Goondoggy had hit it off. She surprised Goondoggy as his "date for the night," and he was on cloud nine. During dinner we reminisced about our amazing week on Azur, Goondoggy's otherworldly dinosaur adventure, and the epic rescue mission to the Republic. We also talked through and verbally rehearsed our planned musical entertainment again, planning to get our Blue Azurian and Republic of Azur friends up on their feet and dancing.

Blue Kamaria Twelve had ordered a sizable dance floor prepared in the banquet hall, with standing microphones on an elevated stage in the middle of the dance floor that could be turned on to make announcements or used as props. As dinner was winding down, Kamaria went over to the dance floor stage and stood in front of one of the microphones. As she started to speak, I was impressed by the quality of the sound system for such a large room. Kamaria enthusiastically declared, "I hope everyone has been enjoying their dinner!" Everyone clapped, whistled and howled their approval. She continued, "Our guests of honor from planet Earth, the Bad Love Gang, brought some Earth music with them and would like to play a few tunes to get us all dancing. They managed to cajole Republic Vice-Prime Minister Stareveret Three, Republic rescue pilot Jadedominic Eleven, and me to join in their entertainment plans. We haven't danced much around here for a while, so tonight is our chance to maybe try something a little different and a little far out—like 11.5 billion light years away far out! So, Bad Love Gang, Stareveret, and Jadedominic, get on up here and let's give this a whirl!"

We all joined Kamaria on the stage. I took the microphone and announced, "Hey, everybody! I'm called 'Bubble Butt' by the gang here, and back on Earth, I grew up with what they call a 'music brain.' So we are going to share a few Earth songs with you, and we want all of you to let this music seep into your bodies and down into your legs; come on up here and dance with us! This first song is a celebration of the Republic and the Blue Azurians coming together in peace. Everyone should be out **"Dancing in the Streets,"** by Martha and the Vandellas!" The song blared over the sound system and up on the stage we all started dancing to the music, lip syncing the words and clapping as the Vandellas did during the song. I loved this tune from my youth; recorded by Martha and the Vandellas in 1964, it reached number two on the Billboard Hot 100 chart and peaked at number four in the UK Singles Chart. It was a Motown classic and the group's premier signature song, guaranteed to get you dancing. In my mind's eye, I could see my two sisters, Kathy and Denise, dancing with their friends to this song in front of our jukebox back on Earth. It worked great for our plan to get them dancing! By the end of the song, roughly half the people had made it up to the dance floor to give their legs a chance to move with the music.

As the music faded, Cleopatra, Crisco, and Kamaria stepped up to the mics on the elevated stage, all wearing their shiny silver Azurian suits with high-heeled, black boots. They were joined by Stareveret and Jadedominic, both dressed in Republic fighter pilot jumpsuits and wearing the same footwear. Cleopatra, standing in the center of the five women, took the microphone and boldly declared, "I *love* this planet! The utterly amazing women here are running the show!" The applause was deafening. "Back on Earth, we have some catching up to do, let me tell you!" She put her arm around Crisco and continued, "So Crisco and I plan to take the torch from you back to Earth and march to the beat of our newfound Azurian sisters! Join us in marching and dancing to **"These Boots Are Made for Walkin'."**

Released in December 1965, this Nancy Sinatra song took off like a rocket in early 1966. By late February 1966, it topped the US Billboard Hot 100 chart and made its way to number one in Australia, Canada, Ireland, New Zealand, the UK, and South Africa. Cleo, Crisco, Kamaria, Stareveret, and Jadedominic put on quite the coordinated dance routine as they pointed to their boots and then to various men in the audience while lip syncing the words. Crisco and Cleopatra double-teamed, pointing at me, and I shook my head in complete denial as I danced with them. Stareveret first singled out Bucky, who was still awkwardly trying to dance more modernly. Then she and Jadedominic doubled down on Danvinio One, who gladly danced with the two of them. The queen and Blue Nova One were clearly enjoying the show with ear-to-ear grins, pointing out various dignitaries and friends who were up and dancing.

When the music ended, we all heard the young voice of our nine-year-old Benzion "Ben" Kaplan, who had grabbed the live microphone. Ben pointed to his two new best friends—the queen's children, Blue Badar Ten and Blue Bellatrix Ten—and broadcast, "I'm new at this modern Earth music, but I have a fun song for Badar and Bella to join me on, up here on the stage, and to get the rest of you dancing!" As Badar and Bella made their way up to the stage, the next song, **"ABC"** by The Jackson Five, started to play. **"ABC"**, considered one of The Jackson Five's signature songs, was the title track to the group's second album, released in February 1970. It successfully knocked The Beatles' "Let It Be" off the top of the US Billboard Hot 100 and was number one on the soul singles chart for four consecutive weeks. Despite its release in early 1970, it was considered by some to be one of the first disco songs. It was also billed as soul music and bubblegum pop music. Whatever genre you wanted to call it, it made you want to move your feet and get dancing.

Ben had secretly prepared Badar and Bella for the song and dance routine earlier in the day; the three of them completely hammed it up, dancing together on the stage to the entire crowd's amusement. Many other children in attendance joyfully joined them. The queen and Blue Max Ten were a bit flabbergasted, but totally delighted watching their two children dance and sing in front of such a large and distinguished crowd. They looked at each other, shook their heads, shrugged and rose together from their chairs. The pair held hands as they walked to the dance floor and began to dance with the children and the crowd. There was a loud roar of approval and clapping from all those attending, and virtually everyone was on their feet dancing to the end of the song. Blue Nova One had also made onto the dance floor and finished the song dancing with Bowmar.

I took the microphone and announced, "I am going to slow it down just a tiny notch to play a tune dedicated to all these fierce rainstorms that you have here on Azur. This is one of my beloved rainy-day songs from Earth, and I thought of it earlier today when that big thunderstorm blew through here. I give you **"Here Comes That Rainy Day Feeling Again,"** by The Fortunes!" Released in May 1971, the song reached number fifteen on the US Billboard Hot 100 and number eight on the Cash Box Top 100. It was also a hit in Canada, charting in the UK and Australia as well. It was a mellow, dreamy '70's tune that made me want to close my eyes and rock my head and shoulders to the sounds. We all had rainy day feelings from time to time, but this song took the edge off and made you feel good. Crisco came and danced with me, and we reminisced about watching the raging storm from my bedroom window in the middle of our first night on Azur. By the end of the song, everyone was singing the refrain together.

Goondoggy had picked out a song for the event too, not even knowing that Blue Delta Seven was coming as his surprise date for the night. He took the microphone and before he could speak, the entire Bad Love Gang from their various locations on the dance floor, simultaneously screamed at the very top of their lungs, "GOONDOGGY!" Unexpectedly, the audience joined in, yelling "GOONDOGGY!" With his left arm around Blue Delta Seven and the microphone in his right hand, Goondoggy proclaimed, "I gotta song to play for all of you and you're gonna love it! This one is new on Earth; it just came out this year. When I was in big trouble fighting a *Carcharodontosaurus* in the Dinosaur Preserve, my Luna sent out a SOS and Blue Delta Seven came to my rescue. I owe this woman my life, big time!" He held up Delta's right hand in his left and shook it to everyone's pleasure and applause. Then he snatched Delta's left hand, pulled her into an embrace, and kissed her, right out of left field. We were all stunned, but the audience was cheering uncontrollably, and that made the kiss go even longer. Coming out of their long kiss, Goondoggy announced on the microphone, "Here it is: **"SOS,"** from Abba on planet Earth!"

"SOS" was the third single and a huge global hit song from the Swedish pop group ABBA's self-titled album, released in the US in September 1975. The song was ABBA's second Top 20 hit in the United States, peaking at number fifteen. But around the world it did better, reaching number one in Belgium, France, West Germany, Australia, New Zealand, and South Africa. It was a top five hit in the Netherlands, Norway, Austria, Italy, Mexico, Rhodesia, and Switzerland. The Bad Love Gang loved the song; we had played it and danced to it in the White Hole Project vault. I saw ABBA perform **"SOS"** watching *American Bandstand* with my sisters in November 1975. It was a perfectly fresh and electric sound with a great performance, and of course they started dancing to the music in front of the TV, instant fans of Abba. I noticed Bucky dancing with Stareveret, Pumpkin with Jadedominic, the Pud with Zaniah, Bowmar with Nova, Cleopatra with Danvinio, Goondoggy with Delta, and Ben with Bella, Badar, and the other children, along with the queen and Max. Crisco and I danced together, and I thought *what a remarkable sight to behold, everyone dancing and having so much fun!*

As the music faded, Pumpkin stepped up to the microphone with Jadedominic in tow and announced, "I was worried that we were gonna pop our clogs bombing that volcano, but we managed to wangle our way out of there. And this woman wondrously plucked some of us from the sea!" He bowed with his arms out and palms up, honoring Jadedominic, and she received a hearty ovation from the crowd. "We're done gallivanting through the universe for now. This party would not be bloody fit for the queen without some Beatles' music to make you move your feet. It was a hard-fought battle against Mount Pelorius and the forces of nature, but we prevailed. So I offer to you **"A Hard Day's Night,"** by The Beatles!"

The song was the fifth of seven songs by the Beatles to hit number one in a one-year time frame, and that was an all-time record on the US popular music charts. It was written by John Lennon, with some collaboration from Paul McCartney. The recording session in the studio took them less than three hours, selecting the ninth take as the final one to be released. So many of the Beatles' songs were my "favorites," and this was one of them. When the music started, I mused about going back in time to attend Beatles' concerts. *Now,* that *would be a fun use for the White Hole Project!* We all started dancing, Blue Nova One walking over to dance with me. I had fun showing her some jitterbug moves along the way. As the song was coming to its end, she firmly took my right hand and briefly pierced my eyes with hers as she said, "Come with me, Bubble Butt; we need to talk."

CHAPTER THREE:

HANNAH'S CURE AND ALADDIN'S LAMP

"Like so many things, it is not what is outside,
but what is inside that counts."
—Aladdin

Saturday, December 20, 1975, mid evening,
a private meeting room in the Queen's Palace, planet Azur

B lue Nova One led me to a private meeting room upstairs in the Queen's Palace. The focal point of the room was a stunning fireplace, which interestingly was built with stones embedded with what appeared to be precious jewels of various radiant colors. Above the mantle was a recent portrait of the queen with her husband, Blue Max Ten, and their two children Bella and Badar. Graceful arched windows lined the outer wall with gorgeous, spectacular views out to the moonlit Azurian Sea. A matching doorway led out to a balcony. There were comfy, cozy chairs and a sofa placed around the fireplace where several logs were burning, creating a warm, amber glow in the room. We sat down on the sofa together, and one of the queen's servants asked us what we wanted to drink. We were both parched from the dancing extravaganza. We shared a pitcher of ice water, drinking from beautiful crystal glasses as we embarked on a fascinating discussion.

Blue Nova One started the conversation. "Bubble Butt, the first thing I have to tell you is how much it has meant to me, and by extension to the queen, to work with you and the entire Bad Love Gang this past week. You all have restored our faith in our own future here on Azur and in our ability to work with the Republic of Azur, as well as other alien societies—first and foremost, planet Earth. Trust is something that is earned, and we consider it to be sacred here on Azur. We have not detected any ulterior motives or hidden agendas from the Bad Love Gang." She smiled, then said, "Other than perhaps Goondoggy's determination to go explore the Azurian Dinosaur Preserve and play with the dinosaurs!" We both laughed and she continued, "We are most impressed that all of you would risk your lives coming here and then tackling the mission to save the Republic of Azur from extinction, just so that you could save the life of one person, your friend Hannah Lieb."

I explained, "When we first met Hannah, we had gone back in time from November 1974 to November of 1944 on a rescue mission to try and save a small group of Jews and Gypsies from the World War II Holocaust on Earth. Hitler and the Nazis were in the process of committing genocide, and as a group, we had determined that saving even a single life from the Holocaust would be worthwhile. We managed to save thirteen lives, but something else unexpected happened along the way. Our Bad Love Gang member Aaron Eisen, whom we call 'Meatball', fell head over heels in love with one of the people we rescued, Hannah Lieb. In the emotions and heat of the moment, they made love by a pond in Poland, and Hannah got pregnant. She bore a son and named him Elijah. Bowmar and I tracked the people we rescued in 1944. When we caught up with the Lieb family living in Jerusalem in 1975, we discovered that Hannah was forty-nine years old and afflicted with terminal breast cancer. Meatball, only one year older at age seventeen, went to see her in Jerusalem and met his thirty-year-old son,

Elijah. How crazy is that? Hannah is too young to be dying of breast cancer! She never got married, and Meatball is still madly in love with her. He literally *just* got to meet his son. So saving Hannah's life from breast cancer actually impacts much more than the life of one person."

Nova reached into one of her pockets and placed three items on the table in front of the couch where we were sitting. There were two small, clear, glass vials containing what I suspected was some form of liquid medication. The third object was black, metallic, polished, and shiny, about the size of a lipstick tube with what looked like a button on the top. The first vial contained clear liquid, and she handed it to me. As I held it and looked at it, she said to me, "Your friend Hannah Lieb is an Ashkenazi Jew, which refers to Jewish settlers who established communities along the Rhine River in western Germany and northern France, dating back to Earth's Middle Ages. I find this very curious or fateful because I have more to tell you about that area of Germany later in this discussion. In the late Middle Ages, the Ashkenazi population, under the pressure of religious persecution, moved out of the Holy Roman Empire into the areas comprising parts of Poland, Russia, Slovakia, Ukraine, Belarus, Estonia, Latvia, Lithuania, and Moldova. The Ashkenazi ancestors of the Lieb family had immigrated to Poland. Two-thirds of European Jews died in the Holocaust of the Second World War, and this decimated the Ashkenazi Jews. In 1930 the Ashkenazi comprised about ninety percent of Earth's Jews; after the Holocaust, the Ashkenazi Jews made up sixty-five percent of Jews worldwide."

"Why does it matter that Hannah Lieb and her family are Ashkenazi Jews?" I enquired.

Nova responded, "I am going to teach you some medical facts that are not yet known on Earth in 1975 but are necessary to provide the cure for Hannah. Remember that we all talked last week about how DNA is the molecular blueprint for biologic life comprising individual genes?

There are two different genes that impact a person's chances of developing breast cancer: breast cancer genes 1 and 2, abbreviated BRCA1 and BRCA2. Every human is living with both the BRCA1 and BRCA2 genes; normally these genes play a big role in preventing breast cancer. They help repair DNA breaks that can lead to the start of cancer and uncontrolled growth of cancerous tumors. Because of this, the BRCA genes are known as tumor suppressor genes. However, in some people these tumor suppression genes become altered or broken; this gene mutation causes them to not function correctly. When a BRCA gene is mutated, it may be ineffective at repairing broken DNA and helping to prevent breast cancer. People with a BRCA gene mutation are more likely to develop breast cancer, and more likely to develop cancer at a younger age. It also increases the risk for ovarian and other cancers. One in forty Ashkenazi Jewish women has a BRCA gene mutation, which is ten times higher than the rest of the population. About sixty percent of women with the BRCA1 mutation and forty-five percent of women with the BRCA2 mutation will develop breast cancer by age seventy. Hannah Lieb carries the BRCA mutation, and that is why she developed breast cancer at such a young age.

"The first vial that you have in your hand is a treatment that we have developed here on Azur called *gene therapy*. While we cannot yet cure all genetic mutations, we have learned how to repair BRCA1 and BRCA2 mutations and many others. Since you need to get this to Hannah at a point in time when she knows and trusts you, it will have to be after you all met her, and when she is pregnant with her and Meatball's child. It will be necessary that you wait until after her first trimester of pregnancy, or a little more than thirteen weeks after the day she and Meatball were at the pond in Poland together. Any time after that first trimester has passed will be okay. You will need to administer this vial to Hannah as an intravenous injection. She may experience a day or two of flu-like symptoms, but it will be safe for her and the baby. Giving Hannah that first vial of medicine will prevent her from developing inherited breast cancer at such a young age."

I looked into Nova's eyes and expressed with sincerity, "Thank you, Nova. Getting a cure or prevention for Hannah was the main motivation for us to come to Azur. Now all we have to do is figure out how to find Hannah and get it to her in early 1945, during the midst of World War II." I put the first vial back on the table and picked up the second. It was an identical clear glass vial, but the liquid contents had a subtle bluish glow. As I examined the second vial, I queried, "So, Nova, this second vial looks different. What is its purpose?"

Nova answered, "When you and the Bad Love Gang met with me at my home the second day after you arrived here, we discussed the biology of aging. Bowmar enlightened us about telomeres, the so-called 'protective caps' at the ends of our DNA strands. Those protective caps get shorter every time our cells divide during our lives. Eventually, as we get older, the telomeres get too short to do their jobs and our cells begin to age and malfunction. I love how Bowmar described it when he said, 'As the clock of life ticks, the candlestick telomeres burn themselves down to the ends of the DNA.' Then I told you about our newborn vaccination formula. For centuries, we have used an infinitesimal amount of blue exotic matter in that formulation, and that has been largely credited as having a stabilizing effect on our DNA telomeres to increase our longevity. We Blue Azurians live an average of one hundred twenty Earth years and tend not to show our age until the end of that spectrum.

"I have an idea about how to help equalize the age difference between Meatball and Hannah so that when they meet again in 1975 or early 1976, their overall life expectancies would be roughly equal. Let's just say that at age seventeen, Meatball has another sixty to seventy-five years to live, depending on how well he takes care of himself. At age forty-nine, if Hannah could expect to reach age one hundred twenty, she would have another seventy years to live. The vial that you hold in your hand now is an adult form of our Azurian vaccination formula. If you administer it to Hannah in her second trimester of pregnancy, it will vaccinate her and at least partially vaccinate her baby, Elijah. Like Blue Azurians, it will stabilize their telomeres and extend their natural longevity to about one hundred twenty Earth years. So I would propose to you that this second vial is optional for Hannah and Meatball. When the Bad Love Gang and Meatball find Hannah in early 1945, she and Meatball can decide if Hannah taking this second vial is what they want. It would give them an opportunity to live their lives together with similar lifespans, from 1975 or 1976 until death do they part."

I reacted to Nova's remarks with amazement. "Excuse my French, but holy shit, Nova! How did you come up with that idea? That is really wild! What about Elijah? How does that work? Will he be a blue baby?"

"Well, Bubble Butt, I guess Hannah and Meatball will have to tread on some new ground, having a son who is thirteen years older than his father, but stranger things have happened in this universe. Plus, the age difference thing will become less noticeable and less of an issue as they all grow older together. They will just have to keep their story straight, at least for a while. Oh, and you Earthlings would have to use the vaccination formula for a couple of generations to start turning blue in color."

"Wow, this time and space travel business just keeps getting more intriguing every day!" I declared. "So what is this sleek and shiny black trigger mechanism thing on the table?" I asked as I put the second vial down and reached for the final item sitting on the table.

I noticed that the expression on Nova's face became more somber and serious as she started to answer me. "I had that made especially for you and the Bad Love Gang, because it is hard to know how we could ever repay you for what you have done here on Azur. We do not have a name for it yet, but maybe we should call it a 'Blackback.'" She started to tear up as she spoke. "This brings me back to my earlier comment about the Rhine River in western Germany, and the darkest day in my life. The story that I tell you next may in some way impact your upcoming time travels to find Hannah. Please know that I have not purposely hidden this story from you; it is just that it did not come up or seem to matter until now."

I could tell that Nova was feeling some emotional pain at this moment. "You know, Nova, trust is a two-way street. I trust you, and I know that you are not intentionally hiding things from us. So whatever it is, you can just get it off your chest and we'll talk it through," I said.

She replied, "Okay BB, this is *hard*, but we'll get through it." She let out a big sigh and continued, "Years ago, I was happily married to the love of my life. His name was Blue Rhett One, and we met in graduate school. My goal was to become an Azurian starship captain to discover extraterrestrial sources of blue exotic matter; Rhett was an engineer, trained to drill for and to extract blue exotic matter. He was cautious and deliberate, whereas I am impulsive and driven. I tend to be hopelessly intellectual, but he was hopelessly romantic. We mutually loved traveling, the outdoors, and adventure. Our opposite personalities and shared common interests created an amazing bond. I loved him so much!

"My best friend in school was Blue Zaniah Ten, Max's sister. Max and the queen attended our wedding. The queen liked us, and our joint skill set. She assigned Rhett and I to explore the universe in the quest to find new sources of blue exotic matter. After many years of searching, I discovered blue exotic matter on your planet, Earth. Following that discovery, the queen promoted me to the role of prime princess, second in command to the queen. I then planned a mission to Earth to extract enough blue exotic matter to make up for our shortage."

I interjected, "Sure, I know all about it. That is when I met you for the first time in the forests of southern China, when the Bad Love

Gang were operating as the Bad Love Tigers, and we fought off the Japanese army and air force long enough for you to get out of there."

"That statement is not totally correct, BB. You met me on our second mission to Earth in June of 1942." I looked at her with surprise on my face and she continued, "I first discovered blue exotic matter in May 1941, in the mountain range of the German Black Forest, south of the town of Bühl and east of Strasbourg in the southwestern state of Baden-Württemberg, Germany. Other than Rhett, you know our crew for that mission: me, Rhett, Blue Max Ten, Blue Zaniah Ten, Blue Elektra Seven, and Blue Izar Seven. We established a secret drilling site well hidden in the Black Forest with panoramic views to the west across the Rhine Valley into neighboring Alsace, France. Thanks to Rhett and his skillful drilling tactics, we reached the vein of blue exotic matter in late July 1941. The extraction process was slow and tedious, and we periodically shipped blue exotic matter back here to Azur using the spaceship's white hole intergalactic transport unit.

"Everything about our mission was going perfectly and we were planning to depart Earth in December 1941. On Earth date November 26, 1941, disaster struck, and my life changed forever. Three Waffen-SS Nazi soldiers, Klaus Richter, Diedrich Fisher, and Fritz Meier managed to ambush our drilling site. Fisher and Meier created a diversion while Richter, the leader, snuck up behind my husband Rhett with a gun in his hand, planning to try and detain us. We all had our bulletproof suits on, but when Richter surprised Rhett from behind, Rhett turned and faced him. I ran toward Rhett, knowing in my heart something bad was happening, but I couldn't get to him fast enough." Nova was sobbing by this point, and I scooted over to give her a hug as she spoke. "Richter pulled the trigger and shot Rhett in the one place he was exposed, between the eyes. Rhett fell backwards, dying in my arms; I was too late."

"Did you kill those Nazi bastards?" I sternly asked as I scooted back.

"I charged Richter with my head down and told my Luna AI to give him the maximum shock. It threw him back and knocked him out, but he somehow survived. We did not kill the other two just for the sake of revenge. We left in a hurry...but there is one detail that has me worried to this day."

"From my current perspective time on Earth in December 1975, that was thirty-four years ago. Why are you still worried?" I enquired.

Nova responded, "There were eleven carefully packed containers of blue exotic matter stacked adjacent to the drill site, and Rhett was carrying a twelfth box that we left behind. We destroyed the drill site and drilling equipment as we departed, but we did not know whether Rhett had included the crates of blue exotic matter in the demolition charges or not. So I have worried about the possibility that the Nazis got their hands on a dozen crates of blue exotic matter."

"Why didn't you try to go back in time and reverse it all?" I asked.

"It's complicated, BB. Rhett was already dead; going back in time to Earth to change that and what we had done, or to encounter more Nazi resistance, was felt to be too risky on multiple levels. We had effectively extracted and transported a good quantity of blue exotic matter back to Azur, so the mission was partially a success—at the incredible expense of Rhett's life and my own future.

"However, all that said, we learned a lot from that event. During our analysis of that mission, we did come up with the concept of the thirty-second flashback in time that we use in our Azurian Flashback vehicles to potentially change some time continuum outcomes without disrupting time or history as a whole. Which brings me to the device in your hand."

I had forgotten that I was holding the gizmo that she had called the Blackback. I said, "Oh, yeah; by the way, we did use the blue flashback button on our trip to the Republic of Azur, or else we would have been a tasty meal for Meggy the megalodon. The Bad Love Gang is living proof that flashback function saves lives! So, what does this Blackback do?"

Nova answered, "We wanted to do something extra special to show our gratitude, and our engineers came up with this device. If you and the Bad Love Gang ever get into a major jam in your time travels, one where you feel like there is no hope or solution, then just hit this button. It will contact me directly and I'll be there, thirty seconds prior to the time you hit the button to do what I can to help you out."

My music brain went crazy, immediately playing **"Reach Out I'll Be There,"** by the Four Tops. Written by Lamont Dozier and brothers Brian and Eddie Holland, famously known as Holland-Dozier-Holland. The trio composed, arranged, and produced many songs that defined the Motown sound in the 1960s. **"Reach Out I'll Be There,"** considered The Four Tops' signature song, was from their fourth studio album, called *Reach Out*, in 1967. It hit number one on both the US Billboard Hot 100 and Rhythm and Blues charts and reached number one on the UK Singles Chart.

"Bubble Butt, did you hear me?" The question slowly registered in my head as coming from Blue Nova One.

"Oh, sorry, Nova; my music brain was going nuts there for a minute! I think that I might want to call it the Reach Out button instead of the Blackback.'"

"That's fine," she replied. "You can call it anything you want, BB. Just know it is a bit of a last resort, and I hope that you actually do not ever have need to use it. I do want to remind you that when you first danced up to me in the forests of southern China, you were singing the song 'Stand by Me.' I hope you know that I have taken that to heart." I could tell that we were getting to the end of our discussion as Nova leaned toward me. Our eyes met and she said, "There's one last thing, Bubble Butt."

"What's that, Nova?"

"I did some checking earlier today and it's almost midnight on Saturday, December 20, 1975, at your home in Oakridge, Tennessee on planet Earth. Your nemesis, Borya Krovopuskov, is about to wreak havoc on your friend Ding and his team of FBI men. But perhaps even worse, he has sent others to your house and Waldo's house. I can use our White Hole Transport Unit to get the nine of you there by midnight. The rest is up to you. It is time for you and the Bad Love Gang to head home."

CHAPTER FOUR:

IN THE MIDNIGHT HOUR, BACK ON EARTH

"We should come home from adventures, and perils,
and discoveries every day with new experience and character."
—Henry David Thoreau

Saturday, December 20, 1975, approaching midnight,
Eastern Standard Time on planet Earth

Nova and I made our way back downstairs to the Queen's Banquet Hall and the party was winding down. We gathered up the Bad Love Gang and bade the queen, Max, Bella, and Badar farewell, thanking them for the unforgettable night and regal celebration. We then said goodbye to Danvinio, Stareveret, Jadedominic, and Charlie, promising to return someday to spend more time at the Republic. I did notice that Goondoggy and Delta were still an item; Bucky was still hanging with Stareveret, and Pumpkin with Jadedominic. Fortunately, we did not have to physically pry any of them apart to get underway. Ben asked if Badar and Bella could ride along to see us leave, and we were fine with that. Nova walked up to Bowmar, embraced him, and whispered something in his ear. She then asked Kamaria to take us to quickly gather up our things from the guest quarters and said that she would meet us all at the Queen's Island Space Center to personally send us off to the location of our choice on Earth, using the Azurian White Hole Transport Unit.

It only took a few minutes to get to the guest quarters and grab all our stuff. Once our entire group was back in the Flashback for the twenty-minute ride to the Space Center, Cleopatra asked, "OK, Bubble Buster; why the big rush to leave paradise? I was just getting ready to enjoy my vacation and have a little time at the beach here on Azur. You better have a good reason, or Crisco and I are going to pin you to the ground and drool in your face!" Everyone chuckled.

"At midnight tonight in Knoxville, Borya and Catherine Krovopuskov are coming for their children, Bobby and Natalie, with a KGB team," I answered. "A separate KGB squad is headed to my house, and another to Waldo's house. It sounds like Borya is out for revenge on multiple fronts, and our Bad Love Gang has been split in two during this past week. We need to come up with a quick plan for how we are going to respond. I am pretty freaked out that KGB agents are headed to my house! When Borya had a gun pointed at the back of Bucky's and my head at the Smithsonian, he threatened to have my sisters, Kathy and Denise disappear if he and Catherine didn't get their children back. Both my sisters are home from college now; it's semester break."

Cleopatra's lips momentarily turned down in sadness, then she pressed them thin with anger. She said, "Sorry, BB. That's some serious shit, so we'd better get our act together and crush this rebellion. What's your plan?"

"The first thing we need to decide is where best to land to take action and defend our own. It is one thing for Borya and Catherine to try and penetrate the FBI perimeter in Knoxville, attempting to get their own children. It's totally another thing to attack our childhood neighborhood in Oak Ridge. We need to make it loud and clear to Borya and those Russian KGB buttheads that messing with the Bad Love Gang's homeland is much worse for them than playing Russian roulette with all the chambers loaded! Nova said she can send the nine of us to any coordinates that we want to give her, but we are getting there just as the action is getting underway. Does anyone have any good ideas?" I enquired.

Goondoggy was the first to respond, showing us his left hand. "If anyone hurts either of your sisters, I'm going to take my new bionic hand and squeeze their neck until their head pops!" We all cried "*Goondoggy!*" He continued, "No, in all seriousness, we should have Nova zap us to Crazy Ike's backyard and start there. He and his old man have a helluva gun collection, with all the hunting that they do with Ike's uncle. We need Crazy Ike, and we need guns, and that location puts us squarely in our own neighborhood to mount our defense."

Bowmar chimed in, "I like that idea, Goondoggy. I just happen to know the coordinates for all our homes. I did that one day, thinking of various contingency plans."

The Pud interjected, "Of course you did, brainy boy. Once we get to Crazy Ike's, we should use his phone and try to call BB's sisters, Waldo, and Ding to warn them. Then I recommend we get ahold of Spaghetti Head and have him meet us at Waldo's with some of his family. You know how Spaghetti Head is always saying his family takes care of their own problems and doesn't need the authorities. Let's give Tater a call too; that southern boy is armed to the teeth as well."

"Shit!" I exclaimed. "I almost forgot about Ding. Good idea, Pud! We may not get to him quickly enough, but we should try. We'll have to depend on the FBI and Ding's men to fend for themselves out at the Krovopuskov home in Sequoyah Hills. That is what they have prepared for these past few months and are trained to do, after all. They have every room in that home bugged, and surveillance cameras everywhere around that house.

"The Runt lives closest to Waldo, just three houses away. We'll call him so he can get a head start checking out the area around Waldo's house. Those Russians have a burr up their butts about Waldo, but they are playing with fire there. He and Mary sleep with loaded guns, and their house has guns hidden everywhere. I'm sorry to say, I think our neighborhood is going to hear and light up with some early New Year's fireworks tonight.

"Bowmar, how about you start making all the phone calls as soon as we get to Ike's house? We will have to split into two groups, one going with me to my house and one going to Waldo's house. I'll take Bucky, Pumpkin, Ben, Goondoggy, and Crisco with me. Pud, you take Crazy Ike and Cleopatra, and meet the Runt, Spaghetti Head, and Tater at Waldo's house. Let's leave Meatball and Willy out of this danger tonight. We have a time-travel mission back to 1945 to get Meatball and the breast cancer medicine safely to Hannah once we deal with Borya and the KGB."

Badar and Bella jointly exclaimed, "We want to help out!"

Kamaria, driving the Flashback and approaching the Space Center, responded to that sternly. "Not on your young lives are you going to Earth for this adventure!" Badar and Bella pouted together.

We arrived at the Space Center and made haste to get to the White Hole Transport Unit with our backpacks and the Black Box. Blue Nova One was waiting for us at the Transport Unit, and Bowmar gave her the coordinates for Crazy Ike's backyard in Oak Ridge, Tennessee. Ike had a black Labrador retriever named Sam who pretty much lived in his back yard, and I briefly mused about Sam's reaction to the nine of us and the Black Box suddenly appearing out of thin air and into his domain. We all hugged Blue Nova One, Kamaria, Bella, and Badar as we climbed onto the circular racetrack of the White Hole Transport Unit. To a person, the nine of us were glad to be going home to Oak Ridge, anxious about the action awaiting us there and sad to be saying goodbye to our Azurian friends. The nine of us sat in a circle together and once we were all situated and in place, Blue Nova One said, "Good luck, my friends," as she hit the *Send* button on the White Hole Transport Unit.

When Nova pressed the send button, my thoughts were shifting to our history with our KGB arch nemesis, Borya Krovopuskov. He had first come into our lives when he ambushed us at the White Hole Project at the stroke of midnight nearly one year prior, on New Year's Eve 1975. Now, with ten days to go in 1975, he was striking again at midnight to try and get his children back, as well as take some revenge on those he blamed for putting him on the run. I was just starting to ponder this evolving pattern of midnight attacks and thinking about my two sisters being in potential peril. Then my world turned white as we were transported through the worm hole, 11.5 billion light years back to planet Earth, Oak Ridge, Tennessee. All I knew was that my brain had seized on the word *midnight* as we entered the white hole and the funniest thing happened next, considering that we were headed squarely into midnight danger.

My eyes were closed, and I had a vivid daydream that I was watching my sisters, Kathy and Denise, dancing in front of our family jukebox to the song **"In the Midnight Hour,"** by Wilson Pickett. Released in June 1965, the song was composed by Wilson Pickett and Steve Cropper (who played the guitar for this amazing tune) at the historic Lorraine Motel in Memphis, Tennessee. Three years later, the Lorraine Motel was the site of the assassination of Martin Luther King Jr. when he was shot and killed by James Earl Ray on April 4, 1968. **"In the Midnight Hour"** was Pickett's breakout hit on Atlantic Records; it reached number one on the US R&B Singles chart, peaking at number twelve in the UK and number twenty-one on the Billboard Hot 100 chart. In my dream, Kathy and Denise were singing, dancing and rocking out. I was laughing at them when I hit the ground in Crazy Ike's back yard, coming to my senses. Sam the black Labrador was barking in my face.

Sam was shocked by our arrival and could not quit barking at the nine of us. Crazy Ike was watching the Saturday night late movie in his back porch. Hearing the commotion, he came running out to check on Sam, only to see nine people sitting in a circle in his back yard. He stared at us briefly then loudly exclaimed, "Holy mother of god! What the hell is going on here?!"

CHAPTER FIVE:

BORYA'S REVENGE, DING'S VENGEANCE

"Revenge is an act of passion; vengeance of justice.
Injuries are revenged; crimes are avenged."
—Samuel Johnson

Saturday, December 20, 1975, 11:55 PM local time, the Krovo/
Krovopuskov family home in the Sequoyah Hills neighborhood
of Knoxville, Tennessee

Bobbie and Natalie Krovo (AKA Krovopuskov), along with their Aunt Nancy Royer, had all gone to bed for the night at the Krovo family home in Sequoya Hills. It was Natalie's nineteenth birthday; the three of them had a relatively muted celebration earlier in the evening, given the fact that they were locked down under FBI surveillance. The FBI was trying to entice Borya and Catherine Krovopuskov to rescue their two children. The birthday party had consisted of Aunt Nancy's famous lasagna for dinner and a homemade chocolate birthday cake with brownie fudge frosting and vanilla ice cream for dessert, followed by a movie on TV. Of course, Natalie got to pick the movie on her birthday (much to her brother's chagrin); they had watched the 1968 award-winning movie *Funny Girl*, based on the 1964 Broadway musical. The plot was built on the life and career of Broadway star, film actress, and comedian Fanny Brice, underscoring her stormy relationship with entrepreneur and gambler Nick Arnstein. Starring twenty-two-year-old Barbara Streisand, *Funny Girl* became the highest-grossing Hollywood film of 1968, bringing in $58,500,000. The movie received eight Academy Award nominations; Streisand won the award for Best Actress for her performance. Natalie loved the song **"Don't Rain on My Parade"** from the soundtrack (which went certified Platinum in the US and certified Gold in Canada), and when that track played, she put on her own entertaining song and dance routine in front of the TV for Aunt Nancy and Bobbie.

The various surveillance devices installed throughout the home were under active watch by Ding's FBI team. FBI agents Allan Turnbull and Jim Franklin were taking their turn at the Saturday night shift in the home. Nancy was sleeping in the main level master bedroom, Bobbie and Natalie in their own rooms upstairs, and Turnbull and Franklin were free to use the fourth bedroom upstairs. Turnbull was relaxing in the guest bedroom, guarding the upstairs, and Franklin was watching late night TV on the main level. They were connected to each other and the rest of the FBI team by closed-circuit radio. Ding's FBI team had rented the house two doors to the southwest; three agents were there, monitoring the remote cameras mounted inside and outside the Krovo home. Finally, there were two additional FBI agents stationed in an unmarked car parked on Cherokee Boulevard, to the northeast of the Krovo home. The seven-man FBI surveillance teams rotated every twelve hours and had been on active duty for exactly two months, since October 20, 1975: when Royer, Bobbie, and Natalie had moved back into the Krovo family home. There had been no FBI or CIA network leads, no indications of Borya and Catherine Krovopuskov's whereabouts the entire time, until this night.

In the summer of 1962, when building a pool in the back yard for his growing family, Borya Krovopuskov (Russ Krovo) had clandestinely constructed an underground escape tunnel leading out of their base-ment, around the pool, and out to a bluff overlooking the Tennessee River. The tunnel entrance from the basement was very well concealed behind a false wall, and the exit near the bluff was covered with earth and sod. Through the years, Borya had planned many routes of escape to leave his house in Sequoya Hills in a hurry. Tonight, he, his wife Catherine, and two KGB agents (Alec Antonov and Pavel Orlov) had covertly used the Tennessee River to approach their home undetected. They had used a new, 1975 Zodiac model 2245 inflatable boat, with a wooden floor and a specially modified and muffled twenty-five horsepower Evinrude outboard motor. Arguably, it was a small KGB intrusion force, but the boat could only carry six adults and they were coming for Bobbie and Natalie. Given the element of surprise and the secret tunnel leading to the basement of their home, Borya and Catherine were confident in their extraction plan and the strength of their actual force.

Knowing an armed conflict with the FBI and law enforcement was inevitable, and at Borya's obsessive planning and insistence, they all carried American M16A1 assault rifles with 30-round clips, Colt .45 caliber ACP pistols with 8-round box magazines, Gerber Mark II fight-ing knives, and M67 fragmentation grenades. Borya and Catherine each carried two pistols. Borya knew the terrain and details of the bluff behind his house like the back of his hand, and soon after arriv-ing, the four of them were huddled around the secret tunnel hatch covered with sod. Borya and Catherine methodically used their knives to swiftly unearth the entrance hatch to the tunnel. With the hatch exposed, Borya, concerned about potential FBI surveillance cameras around their home, ordered Alec and Pavel to go outside the perimeter of their property and check the street in front of the house, as they had planned. Their coordinated strike would begin at midnight. Within a few minutes, Borya and Catherine had used the tunnel to make their way to the secret doorway in the basement concealed by a false wall, and Alec and Pavel were combing Cherokee Boulevard looking for active surveillance. It was 11:55 PM. At that moment, the FBI did not know that anything was amiss. That would change in the next few minutes.

FBI agents David Jackson and Brett "Yank" Yankovich were in a 1975, black, unmarked Ford LTD Crown Victoria, parked on Cherokee Boulevard a block to the northeast of the Krovo home. They had an unobstructed view of the street and the Krovo driveway. It was a perfectly clear night, with a waning full moon. The temperature was a Knoxville, Tennessee "cold," 34 degrees Fahrenheit. Jackson and Yankovich had just finished eating sandwiches and poured cups of black coffee from their shared Thermos bottle. Both were enjoying after-meal cigarettes, with their windows temporarily rolled down. Alec and Pavel had identified their target and had stealthily crossed Cherokee Boulevard to the north, behind Jackson and Yankovich's parked Ford. A lone random car was approaching from behind and the two KGB agents knew this was their opportunity to initiate the assault. Inside the car, Jackson commented, "God, I love ham and Swiss cheese on rye. *That* was a good sandwich. Hey, Yank, there is a car coming up behind us."

Yank responded, "Yeah, that sandwich was probably our highlight for this shift." They both turned to their left to observe the vehicle coming up the street. As the innocent auto approached the FBI agents, Alec and Pavel swiftly made their move in coordinated fashion. They each took one of their M67 fragmentation grenades, pulled the pins, and released the safety levers (AKA spoons) as they approached Yank's open passenger side window from behind on the run. Releasing the spoons activated the spring-loaded strikers, which initiated the grenade's fuse assembly. The M67 grenade fuse delays detonation between four and five seconds after the spoon is released. Two seconds had ticked off the clock when Alec lobbed his grenade past Yank's lap onto the front floor of the Ford LTD, and Pavel tossed his grenade into the back seat.

While looking to his left at the passing car on Cherokee Boulevard with two seconds of life remaining and the first fourteen-ounce M67 grenade glancing off his left thigh onto the front floor of the Ford, Yank shouted, "What the hell?!" Jackson got off one word: "What?" The two M67 grenades blew, killing the two FBI agents instantaneously and turning the 1975 unmarked Ford LTD Crown Victoria into an exploding fireball as the car and its gas tank all detonated with a roar. On the closed-circuit radio, Turnbull, Franklin, and the other three FBI agents heard in their earpieces, "What the hell?!" followed by "What?" followed by a thunderous explosion.

It was midnight when special FBI agent Chuck "Ding" Brooks' phone rang at his rented home in Oak Ridge, Tennessee, waking him in the middle of a dream. Ding answered, "Chuck Brooks here."

"Ding, it's Bowmar. I need you to be awake and listening carefully."

Ding deeply inhaled, exhaled, and shook his head clear. "Bowmar, you guys made it back from deep space!" he exclaimed. "How'd it go?"

"Ding, we are under attack by Borya Krovopuskov and the KGB! BB's house and Waldo's house are prime targets, and we are responding here with force. Borya, Catherine, and a KGB team are assaulting your FBI unit at the Krovopuskov home in Knoxville, planning to somehow extract their children."

Ding enquired, "Do you need my help there?"

"Send an FBI cleanup crew here. I don't think the KGB will make it out of our neighborhood alive, but if they do, they will be wrapped in duct tape and headed to jail. Our guys are really pissed, and they know we are under attack. They are probably engaging the KGB as we speak. We have the element of surprise; they have no idea that we are onto them. They are in our neighborhood, and nobody knows our neighborhood like we do. You need to alert your men and get to the Krovopuskov home before it's too late."

"All right, Bowmar. I can get there in twenty-five minutes or less, with the pedal to the metal. I'll alert all of our forces in Knoxville to descend on the Krovopuskov home while closing off the roads in and out of the Sequoya Hills neighborhood. We have planned for this moment. I'll catch up with you and the gang after the dust settles tonight. Good luck!" As Ding hung up the phone, his emergency alert pager went off and confirmed Bowmar's warnings. Ding was on the move.

The three men at the FBI-rented home, two houses away from the Krovopuskov home, were Greg Jenson, Tyrus Simmons, and Nate Durham. The five surviving FBI men on site had all heard Yank's and Jackson's last words on closed-circuit radio, followed by the loud explosion. Neither Yank or Jackson answered calls to their radios and were presumed dead. Standing at the false wall entrance to their basement, Borya and Catherine heard the explosion outside and made their move. Bobbie and Natalie Krovo and their Aunt Nancy Royer had all been awakened in their bedrooms by the explosion outside, and they could hear FBI agents Allen Turnbull and Jim Franklin talking to each other and their remaining team. Franklin, on the home's main level, and Turnbull, on the second floor, both went to peek out of windows facing the front of the house and could see the burning car wreckage up the street. Borya and Catherine quietly and quickly ascended the stairs from the basement of their own home with pistols drawn. Borya took the main level, while Catherine headed up the back stairs to sweep the second floor.

It all happened too fast, unfair to the FBI agents who thought they were ready for this night. They were unaware of the secret basement entrance from the escape tunnel, and Borya's and Catherine's home intrusion had occurred without the slightest warning in the midst of their partners' car blowing up in the street of the otherwise quiet Sequoyah Hills neighborhood. They were both actively talking on their radios, which gave away their positions within the house. As Jim Franklin turned from looking out the front window, he found himself staring at Borya Krovopuskov and down the barrel of Borya's Colt .45 ACP pistol. Borya emotionlessly pulled the trigger, instantly slaying Franklin with a head shot. Allen Turnbull, hearing the shot downstairs, radioed the other three FBI agents, saying, "Shot fired downstairs," as he drew his pistol and exited the guest bedroom. Catherine was waiting for him; kneeling in the hallway in a shooting position, she put a bullet through the side of his head, dropping him straightaway. Greg Jenson, Tyrus Simmons, and Nate Durham all tried to radio both Allen Turnbull and Jim Franklin, to no avail. Jenson, Simmons, and Durham had already placed the emergency page to Ding. They quickly made their plan to confront the attackers while radioing for even more backup.

After assassinating Franklin, Borya went to the master bedroom and found Nancy, crouched on the bed with her head between her legs, quietly sobbing. He knew that the rooms were bugged. He went to her, hugged her, and whispered in her ear, "We're here to get our children. Someday, maybe you will understand."

She responded through the quiet, copious tears flowing down her cheeks. "I'll never understand; you've stolen my sister's heritage and torn our family apart."

Upstairs, after Catherine dropped Turnbull, she yelled, "Bobbie, Natalie, it's your mom and dad! We have to get out of here!" Bobbie and Natalie came out of their rooms and ran into their mother's open arms. As they hugged, Catherine proudly looked at Natalie and declared, "Happy birthday, sweetheart. This time next year, we'll make it a 'Russian birthday!'" The three of them headed downstairs and joined Borya and Nancy.

Catherine hugged a reluctant Nancy, who remained semi-paralyzed on the bed. Nancy looked her sister in the eyes and begged her, "Please don't do this Cathy! You can tell them all you know and come back to our family!"

Catherine replied, "Nancy, I will always love you, and thank you for caring for Bobbie and Natalie, but my heart is set; we are leaving for Russia. Borya, Bobbie, and Natalie are my family, and Russia is our home."

Jenson, Simmons, and Durham had surreptitiously made their way to the front of the house with pistols drawn and ready. Jenson and Simmons faced the front door and Durham had their backs covered, facing the long front yard and street beyond. Simmons yelled out through a bullhorn, "Overwhelming force will be here in minutes! Let the children and their aunt go! No harm needs to come to them!" Bellowing sirens could be heard, approaching from all directions and growing louder.

Listening inside, Borya and Catherine handed the two extra Colt pistols they were carrying to Bobbie and Natalie, hugged them both, and said, "You know what to do. Make it quick, and then we are leaving." Nancy looked at the four of them with wide eyes and Borya told her, "I am gagging you and tying you up. When they get to you, try to keep your mouth shut for a while."

Bobbie opened the front door with his elbows up and his hands behind his back. Natalie was directly behind him, acting like she was gently pushing him and guiding him. Bobbie loudly announced, "We are coming out, but our parents will never give up!"

Simmons answered, "Okay, you two come to us. More help will be here any minute." When Bobbie and Natalie were ten feet away, Simmons stated, "It's good to see you kids safe and sound."

Bobbie replied, "It's a shame that we don't feel the same way about you." He pulled the Colt .45 from behind his back as Natalie came from behind him with her Colt .45, and they opened fire on the three agents. Totally unprepared, Jenson and Simmons took the brunt of Bobbie's and Natalie's gunfire as they unloaded both their clips. Durham reflexively dove to the side at the sound of gunfire and simultaneously saw the shadows of Alec and Pavil, approaching from across the street with assault rifles drawn. Peeking out a front window, Borya could see an unmarked car with its lights out, speeding up behind Alec and Pavil as they started firing at Durham. Durham got behind a tree and saw Bobbie and Natalie rapidly retreating through the front door of the house, rejoining their parents. With Nancy tied up and isolated in the master bedroom, the four of them made haste to use the secret basement tunnel and close the false wall behind them. Hurrying through the tunnel, Catherine asked, "What about Alec and Pavil?"

Borya replied, "They will have to fend for themselves. They know the network if they can get away in time." Borya knew they were being sacrificed. The Krovopuskov family speedily made it to the Zodiac inflatable boat and quickly got underway, heading down the Tennessee River to a getaway car. They would then drive to the McGhee Tyson Airport, where a private plane was waiting to take them on the first leg of their long journey back to Mother Russia.

As the Krovopuskov family was making their escape, Alec's and Pavil's gunfire kept Durham pinned down, making it nearly impossible for him to return fire. They brazenly strode across the street toward him as they kept firing, planning to walk their gunfire directly into him when they got close enough.

It was Ding's car that Borya had seen arriving. Ding was speeding to the scene in his unmarked 1975 police-package, high-performance Chevrolet Nova 9C1 with the headlights turned off. Ding knew the neighborhood, his fellow FBI teammates, and the Krovopuskov property well from all their training and preparation on these premises over past few months. He could see Alec and Pavil in the moonlight marching across the long Krovo front yard toward Durham while firing their assault rifles.

Ding knew that he had to act fast or lose another man. He aimed his Nova at the backs of the two Russians and accelerated. Alec and Pavil could not hear and did not notice Ding approaching them from behind over their deadly focus and the noise of firing their assault rifles at Durham's position. Ding sped through low-lying hedges in the Krovo front yard and rammed Alec and Pavil from behind, sending them both flying. Ding then slammed on his brakes and spun out, striking a tree with the passenger side of his Nova and coming to an abrupt stop.

Ding, known for his pistol marksmanship, was carrying his favorite Browning Hi-Power P35 9mm pistol with 13 round-clip. He hurriedly exited his damaged Nova and made his way toward Alec and Pavil. Ding had viewed the burning wreckage of Yank's and Jackson's Ford LTD as he drove by, and he had observed the slain bodies of Agents Jenson and Simmons near the front door. He could now see that Durham was alive but injured. He was feeling no mercy toward the KGB killers. Pavil's back was broken; he couldn't feel or move his legs, but his M16A1 assault rifle was within reach. As he got his hands on the rifle and started to swing it around, Ding fired six rounds into Pavil's upper torso, ending his life and night of terror. Alec had been jettisoned into a tree trunk, fracturing his pelvis and right femur. His assault rifle was ten feet away. Ding was approaching him, and Alec reached for his pistol with his right hand. Ding put a 9mm round into Alec's right elbow, ending that endeavor. Then Alec reached for his Gerber Mark II fighting knife with his left hand. Ding put another round into Alec's left forearm, preventing that effort, and he cursed loudly at Ding in Russian.

Ding could see Durham's injured and bleeding body and face to his left as he reached Alec. Durham looked at him, quietly nodding his head in angry affirmation. Ding acknowledged Durham and then stepped hard on Alec's broken right leg, sending pain and retribution through Alec's body. "Where are the Krovopuskovs going?" he demanded.

Alec smirked through his pain and said, "You'll never catch them."

Ding leaned harder on Alec's broken leg and again asked, "Where are they going?"

Alec grimaced in agony and gritted his teeth. With fire in his eyes he bellowed, "They are going home to Mother Russia, and I am going with them!"

Ding fired his last five rounds directly into Alec's torso and flatly said, "Yeah, you're going with them...in a plywood box."

Durham, the only surviving FBI agent of the team of seven, faintly smiled. Then he passed out, just as emergency vehicles began arriving from all directions.

CHAPTER SIX:

BAD LOVE HOMELAND DEFENSE

"We shall defend our island, whatever the cost may be,
we shall fight on the beaches, we shall fight on the landing grounds,
we shall fight in the fields and in the streets,
we shall fight in the hills; we shall never surrender."
—Winston Churchill

Saturday, December 20, 1975, 11:47 PM local time
in Oak Ridge, Tennessee

The nine of us Bad Love Gang members returning from planet Azur had landed in a circle in the middle of Crazy Ike's back yard, thanks to Bowmar's precise coordinates that he had given to Blue Nova One. Sam the black Labrador was barking non-stop in my face as Crazy Ike came out of his back porch, where he had been watching TV, flabbergasted to see the nine of us sitting in his back yard. After hearing Ike curse a bit at the situation, I yelled at him, "Get this barking dog out of my face before I kick him in the chops!"

Crazy Ike was quick to recover and respond, trying to command his dog, "Sam, bite Bubble Butt in the balls right now! Do it, Sam, you hear me?"

Ben joined in, "No Sam, bite Goondoggy, he has balls of steel!"

Everyone laughed with relief at being back on Earth with our typical banter. Sam quit barking as he looked up at Ike. I started scratching around his ears, which he loved. I looked at Ike and said, "The KGB has sent agents to our neighborhood, specifically to my house and to Waldo's house. Borya and Catherine Krovopuskov and a KGB team are coming for their children at their house in Sequoya Hills. Bowmar needs to use your phone to call Waldo, my house, and Ding to warn them, and then he needs to call the Runt, Spaghetti Head, and Tater to bring them up to speed to help us defend our homeland. We needed guns and a launching point for our defense, so we picked you and your house."

Ike replied, "Before we go kick some KGB ass, how the hell did you land here and not have to use the White Hole Project to get back?"

"Blue Nova One and the Azurians have a White Hole Transport Unit that can send people one way to coordinates on Earth," I explained. "I'm not sure it would work for any old planet, but we are Azur's sister planet. Anyway, Nova had done some checking and seemed to know there was trouble brewing here tonight. She tried to get us back here in time to intervene. We should have a bit of the element of surprise here on our own turf, but I am afraid Ding's FBI team is in for a rough night on their side of town."

Ike said, "Lucky for us, my parents are out at a Christmas party tonight...and you definitely came to right place for guns. We have three thirty-aught-six rifles; one is a Remington Model 788 with a scope, and the other two are Winchester Model 70s, one with a scope. Then we have about a dozen different shotguns and Magnum shells for all of them; my old man loves shotguns! We have a nice collection of pistols, too; a couple are semi-automatics, but most are revolvers. I know from our experience fighting the Colorado Vodka Cowboys back in April that I'm giving Cleopatra and Crisco a couple of pump-action shotguns."

Cleo crowed, "You got *that* right, white boy!" She loved teasing Ike that way because he was so fair complected and absolutely covered with freckles. "We are pumping the fires of hell out on any KGB asshole messing with our neighborhood."

Ike responded, "I don't know who they're sending, but they're frickin' crazy to come to this neighborhood! We know every nook and cranny, every bush, tree and pothole, every yard, fence, and sewer pipe. Besides that, if they're going to Waldo's house, that's like walking into an ambush on the Korean War battlefield. That crazy old bald bastard will send them to the next life, sure as shittin'!"

Everyone was chuckling at Ike's bravado as I enquired, "You got any duct tape?"

Ike looked insulted as he answered, "Holy shit, Bubble Butt, are you flipping kidding me?! We fix everything that goes wrong at my house with duct tape! Who needs to pay for repairs? It's good for plumbing problems, roof leaks, cracked windows, broken chairs, holding parts in place on the cars, you name it... I think it basically holds our whole goddam house together. What do you have in mind there, Bubble Shit for Brains?"

"I'd like to capture as many of these KGB intruders alive as possible, then tape 'em up and give them to the authorities. Let's not make our neighborhood a killing field if we can help it. That said, let's not any of *us* get dead tonight."

Everybody replied together, "Live dangerously, have fun, don't die!"

Ike helped us all get armed and Bowmar started making phone calls. We split into two groups: Bucky, Pumpkin, Ben, Goondoggy, and Crisco were going with me to my house, and the Pud, Crazy Ike, and Cleopatra were going to meet the Runt, Spaghetti Head, and Tater at Waldo's house—assuming Bowmar was successful in getting ahold of everyone with his phone calls. The Pud grabbed some walkie-talkies out of the Black Box, distributing them to the two groups. Our two groups moved out on foot, knowing that we could cut through yards and across our well-known-since-childhood neighborhood terrain on the run, reaching our destinations without delay. We realized that we had to check the streets for strange cars, and also knew that no strangers should be just standing around twiddling their thumbs in our neighborhood at midnight.

With the natural Bubble Butt related strength in my legs, I was a fast runner at age seventeen. I led our group on the dash to my house. I was thinking about engaging these KGB bastards who had no business being here on Saturday night and my music brain started playing **"Saturday Night's Alright for Fighting,"** by Elton John while we were on the run. Elton John composed this classic '70's rock song with his long-time songwriting partner Bernie Taupin. It was the only song recorded during Elton and the band's time in Jamaica. It was super high energy with long-time Elton collaborator Davey Johnstone on guitar. The band had put their tracks down first, and Elton overdubbed his rapid-fire piano afterward. Elton John was absolutely on fire in the 1970s; this song went to number seven in the UK and number twelve on the US Billboard Hot 100.

Saturday, December 20, 1975, at midnight,
Bubble Butt's home on Hemlock Lane

At 11:50 PM, two cars, each with two Russian KGB agents, had discreetly pulled up near my house on Hemlock Lane. Two of the agents, Sergei Chernoff and Rolan Zima, went to my front door while the other two went to cover the outside of the house, with Ivan Utkin in the front and Karlin Sobolev watching the back yard. Whether needed or not, all four of the Russians had their pistols drawn. My parents, who never missed a good cocktail party while we were growing up, were also out, at a work-related holiday party. My sisters, Kathy and Denise, were at home from college, watching a late-night movie together on TV. The Russians were planning to kidnap my sisters and use them as bait to get Waldo out of his house; then Borya planned to use them to get to me and Bucky. Sergei rang the front doorbell at 11:57 PM.

Denise was the first to get up to answer the doorbell. Kathy looked at her and said, "That can't be Mom and Dad ringing the doorbell. And besides, it's too early for them to be home. Maybe it's Kevin and he forgot his key. Ask before you open the door."

Denise made her way to the front door and Kathy stood up, following her. Denise loudly enquired, "Who is it?"

Sergei responded in perfect English, "This is Sergeant Black from the police department. I need to talk to you about your brother, Bubble Butt."

Denise unlocked the door and looked over her shoulder at Kathy, saying, "Oh, crap. It sounds like Kevin is in some kind of trouble again; that's just what we need." Denise was starting to slowly open the door and Kathy, standing six feet to her right, commented, "Tell him that we don't know anyone named Bubble Butt, or Kevin, and let's get on with watching the movie. Let Kevin fend for himself, the little shit."

Astutely looking out to the front porch as the front door cracked open, Denise saw two men in black trench coats with guns drawn. She tried to slam the door on them with her left hand and screamed at Kathy in a panic, "Kathy, run to the back! *Get out!*"

Sergei forced his left foot into the opening in the front door and shoved the door open with such force that Denise was thrown back into the living room sofa. Kathy was on the move toward the back door; Denise tried her best to spring up from the sofa and follow her sister. Sergei was through the front door in a heartbeat and caught Denise from behind. Despite her shrieking and struggling,

Sergei swung her around and handed her off to Rolan Zima, who very quickly bound and gagged her. He led Denise out to the closest parked car with the help of Ivan Utkin in the front yard. Sergei pursued Kathy toward the back of the house and radioed Karlin Sobolev to be ready to nab her as she came through the back door. Sobolev and Sergei weren't quite prepared for all that happened next.

Bucky, Pumpkin, Ben, Goondoggy, Crisco, and I approached my house at midnight, going through Goondoggy's and Willy's backyard next door. We stopped and spied on a shadowy figure standing at the ready in my back yard, Karlin Sobolev. Before I could even think, I saw that Goondoggy was taking his shoes and socks off, and he wasn't doing it because the weather was warm. He started moving silently toward Sobolev, apparently fearless. I whispered to Crisco, Pumpkin, and Ben to sneak around to the front of the house. No sooner had they made their move to the front when we saw Kathy burst through the back door, frantically screeching for help. Sobolev was focused on nabbing Kathy and did not notice that Goondoggy was already halfway to him, and now in a full-speed sprint.

I punched Bucky's right shoulder, pointed at Goondoggy approaching Sobolev and Kathy coming out of the back door, and declared, "Cover me, Bucky! Let's go!" Bucky and I ran headlong into the fray.

At that moment, Sobolev was ready to grab Kathy with his out-stretched arms, but he sensed someone approaching to his right and looked in that direction. Goondoggy leapt from the midst of his full-on sprint and tackled Sobolev head-on. The force and momentum of Goondoggy's gallop slammed Sobolev to the ground, and Goondoggy immediately pistol whipped him across the side of his head. Goondoggy looked at his unconscious prey and declared, "If I can fight a giant shark-toothed lizard named *Carcharodontosaurus*, you didn't stand a chance, mister."

Kathy saw me coming and ran into my arms just as Sergei burst through the back door with his gun drawn. It did not totally register with him what he next saw, with Goondoggy on top of Sobolev in the back yard to his right and Kathy in my arms to his left. Bucky was right behind me carrying an Ithaca double-barrel 12-gauge shotgun with Magnum loads, pointed at the exiting Sergei. Crazy Ike had given me a Smith & Wesson Model 12 six-shot .38 special revolver, which I now had in my right hand pointed at Sergei while hugging Kathy tightly with my left arm. Despite wanting to try and take the KGB perpetrators alive, Sergei reflexively pointed his pistol at me; with Kathy in my arms, he gave Bucky and I no choice but to react without hesitation. I fired my pistol while Bucky unloaded both barrels of his shotgun at once. The force of the combined shots blew Sergei clear off the back porch and he landed in the back yard, dead.

Those were the first shots fired, and they came just as Rolan Zima, and Ivan Utkin had transferred the bound and gagged Denise into the back seat of their car. When they heard the gunfire, they immediately radioed both Sergei and Sobolev but got no response. They needed at least one hostage to take to Waldo's house, so they hastily made their getaway and headed to join the rest of the KGB team at Waldo's house. From a distance, Crisco, Pumpkin, and Ben barely had time to witness the bound and gagged Denise being shoved into the black sedan and Zima and Utkin getting away with her as their hostage.

We thoroughly duct taped the slowly waking, partially conscious Sobolev; so he wasn't going anywhere. I covered the dead Sergei with a blanket and had Crisco and Ben stay with my emotionally shaken sister, Kathy. Bucky, Pumpkin, Goondoggy, and I headed to Waldo's house, where Denise was being used as live bait to lure Waldo into the open.

Saturday, December 20, 1975, at midnight,
Waldo's house on Griffith Drive

The Runt got the call from Bowmar and said he would take a walkie-talkie and use the "sewer rat method" to spy on Waldo's house without being detected. When we were little kids, we played whiffle ball in the streets in front of our houses and had temporarily lost many balls down the narrow, street-level openings of the sewers that drained rainwater from our streets. Not only did we learn how to open the sewer lids and retrieve our swallowed whiffle balls, but we also explored the connecting network of sewer system pipes and access lids. Waldo's house, positioned close to the street corner, had a sewer opening directly across the street. The connecting sewer pipe went under the street into his front yard, made a right turn, and continued to the end of the street. There was a sewer lid in his front yard where the pipe made the turn. The Runt said he would radio the group as soon as he was in position.

After hanging up with the Runt, Bowmar tried to call Tater, but no one answered at his home. He then called Spaghetti Head, who happened to be sitting close to the phone and immediately answered. Bowmar quickly explained the evolving scenario and Spaghetti Head reacted with a hint of his Italian Mafioso accent. "Well, Bowmar, you know my family; we take care of our own predicaments, no questions asked, brother! Most of the family is out tonight, but my older twin brothers Louie and Tony are here. They just happen to have a couple of M1921 Thompson submachine guns with vertical foregrips, and the 100 round C-type drum magazines. I'll get them and we'll take some real firepower to Waldo's party."

Bowmar replied, "Bubble Butt said he did not want to make our neighborhood a total killing field tonight. So let your brothers know that we want to take some of these KGB agents alive, if possible."

"Got it, Bowmar. You know I am good at calculating destruction. I'll try to tone it down a bit tonight. Let the others know that we are on the way, and I'll grab a walkie-talkie as we are headed out the door."

Parked just beyond Waldo's property near the street corner was a black 1966 Pontiac GTO XS coupe, driven by KGB agent Nikolai Kozlov (Nick Kolo), with Maxim Meknikov (Max Miller) in the passenger seat. Waldo had outsmarted and outmaneuvered the two of them six months prior, on June 30th. The GTO was red then, and Bucky and I had pumped that car full of lead from Waldo's .44 Magnums, causing them to crash and abruptly ending their pursuit of us. When Nick got the car repaired, he had it painted black. He and Max had burrs up their butts about getting even with Waldo, so they had eagerly accepted this assignment. They were waiting for the other portion of the KGB team to arrive with my sisters, whom they planned to use as hostages.

Four other KGB agents had arrived and parked up the street from Waldo's house in a nondescript black Ford sedan. The driver, Denis Balaken, stayed with the car while the other three positioned themselves around Waldo's house, two (Andrey Zorken and Ludis Poletov) in the back and one (Sacha Kamenev) in the front. More team members would arrive at the front of the house with my sister soon.

At midnight, Waldo's phone rang. "Paul Thompson here," he answered.

Bowmar anxiously described the situation. "Waldo, it's Bowmar, and I have to talk fast. Your home and Bubble Butt's home are being approached or attacked by KGB agents. Borya and Catherine Krovopuskov are in Sequoya Hills right now with a separate KGB team, going for their two children. It seems all coordinated to happen at midnight, which is...now." Bowmar's walkie-talkie barked at him. "Hold on, Waldo; listen to the walkie-talkie." Bowmar held the handset close to the phone.

It was me on the other end of the walkie-talkie, talking rapidly to Bowmar and the rest of the Bad Love Gang carrying walkie-talkies while Bucky, Pumpkin, Goondoggy, and I were on the move to Waldo's house. "It's BB; my house is secure now, but the KGB has my sister Denise as their hostage. We think they are taking her to Waldo's to use her as bait, luring him out so they can kill him or take him. We cannot, I repeat, *cannot*, allow them to take my sister out of this neighborhood, or let them have their way with Waldo."

Bowmar responded on the walkie-talkie. "Everybody listen, it's Bowmar; the Runt is a 'sewer rat' in front of Waldo's house. Spaghetti Head and his twin brothers are en route with 100-round Thompson machine guns, and Tater is not answering his phone."

Waldo, already pissed and ready to fight, yelled into the phone loudly enough that those of us on the walkie-talkies heard him. "Tater's family is out of town, and he is spending the night here with Mary and me. He's sleeping out in the Airstream." Waldo and Mary loved to go camping, and they had a 1973 Airstream Safari Land Yacht 23 parked in their expanded driveway. "Don't let that Southern-fried little shit get hurt if he wakes up and sticks his head out of that Airstream door!" Bowmar repeated Waldo's words to the group.

The Pud crackled in on his walkie-talkie. "It's the Pud here; hi, everyone. Crazy Ike, me, and Cleopatra are all in position. There is a guy waiting in a black sedan up the street from Waldo's, and Cleo is going to stick her shotgun in his face as soon anyone makes a move or takes a shot. There are two guys in Waldo's back yard. Crazy Ike went into the woods behind Waldo's house with his thirty-aught-six; those guys are *toast* if this goes bad. There is another guy hiding behind the Airstream in the driveway; I've got him covered."

The Runt broke in, a bit muffled. "Hey, it's the sewer rat, and it stinks like shit down here! There's a jacked-up 1966, black GTO goat with two guys sitting in it near the corner. I could easily pop up through the sewer lid in Waldo's front yard as a stinky surprise for these bastards! I live on this street, and I'll be damned if these guys think they can cause trouble here!"

Spaghetti Head then entered the chatter. "Louie, Tony and I are almost there. You want us on foot or driving straight in?"

We had just arrived on the run in the back yard of the house across the street from Waldo's. I could see a black sedan slowly rounding the corner at the bottom of the street, lights out. It was Rolan Zima and Ivan Utkin, with my sister Denise in the back seat of their car. They had radioed and warned their team that shots were fired in Bubble Butt's backyard, and Sergie's and Sobolev's status was not known. Nikolai Kozlov (Nick Kolo) and Maxim Meknikov (Max Miller) got out of their GTO and started deliberately moving toward the front of Waldo's house.

I rejoined the dialogue. "Spaghetti Head, when the action starts, you and your brothers come to the corner and block the front of the black GTO. Take those Thompson machine guns and incapacitate that GTO, and then the black sedan carrying my sister and parking directly in front of Waldo's house now. Those cars aren't leaving here. Pumpkin will cover Tater if he comes out of the Airstream. Runt, when we yell your name, pop up out of that sewer lid in Waldo's front yard and go for the guy holding my sister. Me, Bucky, and Goondoggy will join you, going for my sister as well. There will be so many of us they won't know which way to look. Try to get 'em alive, if possible...but do what you have to do. Can Waldo hear me?"

Bowmar confirmed that Waldo could hear us, so I said, "Waldo, you get the two jackasses coming toward the front of your house from that black GTO down the street. I think they are the same guys we fought off on I-81 North on the way to see President Ford last summer. They must think they're gonna get back at you."

"Coming to my house has got to be the world's dumbest way to try and get back at me. I'll take care of those two shitheads, Bubble Butt," Waldo replied. *That's the Waldo we know and love!* I thought. Bowmar, who was holding the phone, could hear Waldo telling Mary, "Honey, take your special shotgun and cover the back door. If anyone tries to come through, don't hesitate."

Hiding in the woods behind the house, a mere fifty yards away from the KGB agents watching the back of Waldo's house (Andrey Zorken and Ludis Poletov), Crazy Ike had his Winchester Model 70 .30-06 with scope and 24-inch barrel resting on a log. First, he aimed at Zorken's kneecap, then moved the crosshairs up to his right hip. He had been rehearsing how he was going to wing these two, without necessarily killing them once the battle started. The Pud had the Remington Model 788 with the scope pointed at Sacha Kamenev, who was hiding behind the Airstream. Cleopatra had her pump-action 12-gauge at the ready and had managed to sneak behind a large oak tree less than ten feet behind the KGB driver Denis Balaken, waiting in the parked sedan up the street with his motor idling.

Only seconds remained before we had to act. I advised the Runt to get in place, ready to pop out of the sewer lid in Waldo's front yard. He acknowledged that he was ready. Rolan Zima and Ivan Utkin pulled up to the curb in front of Waldo's house and quickly exited the car, pulling the bound and gagged Denise out of the back seat. Ivan was holding Denise with his right hand around her arm and had a pistol in his left. Rolan was leading the way, headed straight to Waldo's front door. Nikolai Kozlov and Maxim Meknikov were closing in, moving toward the left of the front door with guns drawn. I could tell they must have thought Waldo was dangerous; all their guns were pointed at Waldo's front door.

Rolan Zima reached Waldo's front door, rang the doorbell, and stood back. My last words on the walkie-talkie were to the Runt. "The guy holding Denise has a gun in his left hand. Go for that gun! *Now GO!*" Until that moment, the Russians were on the alert, but nothing seemed amiss. Everything changed in a millisecond; the mêlée precipitously ensued, lasting only a few minutes.

Ivan, holding my sister, was facing the house. He stood five feet in front of the opening sewer access lid with his back to it. The Runt stealthily moved the sewer lid to the side, a hatchet in his right hand. He moved so fast! He buried the blade of the hatchet into the back of Ivan's left shoulder, then grabbed Ivan's left arm and pulled it back. Ivan could not hang onto Denise but managed to pull the trigger of his pistol once, sending a wild shot into the air, and the battle was on. I rushed to Denise with the .38 special in my right hand and yelled for Bucky and Goondoggy to cover me. Spaghetti Head and his brothers had heard me shout "*Now GO!*" and pulled their car directly in front of the black GTO at the end of the street, blocking it. All three then jumped out of their car with their Thompson machine guns, firing steadily into the GTO and rendering it unusable. The machine guns got everyone's attention real fast. Spaghetti head and his brothers had managed to put some fear into the KGB team, who suddenly realized that they were now the hunted.

Waldo had grabbed one of his assault rifles and had Nikolai Kozlov and Maxim Mekinov in his sights through a slit in the curtain over the front corner window of his house. The second that Ivan's first shot rang out, Waldo fired right through the glass and cut Nikolai and Maxim down, sending them both to the ground. The two KGB agents were out of commission, seriously injured and writhing in pain. In the back of the house, Crazy Ike shot Andrey Zorken in the right side of his pelvis, and he went down. Ludis Poletov, a large muscular man, went for Waldo's back door. Ike, blocked by a tree as Poletov made his move, couldn't get a clear shot at him. Poletov, with his adrenaline rushing, managed to kick the back door open; that was a mistake.

Mary had positioned herself in the corner of the back den, facing the back door with a sawed-off, double barrel 12-gauge shotgun that Waldo had made for her for home protection. Magnum shells with steel pellets were loaded in both barrels. Mary saw the door fly open and the dark shadow of a large man with a gun start to come through. She fired both barrels at once at a range of ten feet, blowing Poletov away from the door and into the backyard. Crazy Ike heard the blast and saw the flash of the shotgun through the windows and watched Poletov's lifeless body slam backwards into the ground. Ike murmured to himself, "Holy shit, that guy just bit the dust big time!" Waldo ran to the back yelling, "MARY, ARE YOU OKAY?" He got to her swiftly and she firmly answered, "I'm okay, but whoever I just shot is not!"

Waldo went into the backyard and confirmed one man dead and one man alive, but down and injured badly. Crazy Ike announced himself coming out of the woods behind the house to avoid a similar fate. Up the street, Denis Balaken, waiting in the parked sedan, saw the combat was going badly for his comrades and decided to use his car as a weapon. Cleopatra had just begun to make her move behind his car as Balaken started to take off down the street. She got a shot off that took out Balaken's back window, but that did not stop him. At the same time, Spaghetti Head and his twin brothers, Louie and Tony, were methodically moving up the street on foot, getting ready to destroy Rolan's and Ivan's black sedan with their Thompson machine guns. Balaken saw the three of them in the street and accelerated directly toward them, not knowing the fire power in their possession. Seeing the speeding car coming at them, Spaghetti Head, Louie, and Tony opened fire. All three Thompsons blazing created a virtual wall of .45 caliber bullets that flew into Balaken and his car. He and the car were riddled with lead, and he lost control, crashing into Rolan and Ivan's sedan.

Goondoggy had helped the Runt finish subduing Ivan Utkin while I was freeing my sister Denise and watching over her in every direction, my .38 special at the ready. Bucky got the drop on Rolan Zima with his double barrel shotgun and Rolan surrendered, releasing his gun and falling to his knees with his hands behind his head at Bucky's stern command. That left Sacha Kamenev hiding behind the Airstream, armed with a West German Heckler & Koch P9S semi-automatic 9mm pistol. The Pud had him in the crosshairs of his scoped Remington Model 788, but Kamenev had seemed to freeze up when all hell had broken loose. The rapidly evolving clash was winding down when Kamenev suddenly snapped out of his self-imposed restraint and decided to try and be a hero for his comrades. He dashed out from behind the Airstream and the Pud took a shot at him that missed but punched through the wall of the Airstream and into one of the dish cabinets inside. That noise made the waking Tater hit the floor inside the trailer, cursing to himself.

We all heard the Pud's rifle shot just as Kamenev came from the behind the Airstream Safari trailer, running and shooting his pistol on the move. Tony, Spaghetti Head's brother, was turned sidewise in the street and caught a bullet coming across the front of his left shoulder. It grazed the left side of his chest, just missing going into his lung. Louie, his twin, ducked down as Spaghetti Head swung his Thompson machine gun around to open fire; he later swore that he felt a bullet whiz right by his nose while he was turning. As Spaghetti Head let loose with his machine gun, those of us in front of the house with guns—me, Goondoggy, Bucky, and Pumpkin—simultaneously turned and fired at Kamenev, who went down in a blaze of crossfire hell. The KGB did not fare so well coming to our neighborhood with bad intentions.

After Kamenev went down, Waldo, Mary, and Crazy Ike came around to the front of the house as the Pud and Cleopatra arrived from up the street. For a very brief moment of time, we were all silently staring and glaring at the battlefield and the devastation from defending our homeland. We were all startled when the side door of the Airstream Safari flew open and Tater loudly exclaimed, "Good God *almighty*, I guess this neighborhood is going to hell in a handbasket. I'd say y'all were throwin' a hissy fit with a tail on it out here! I thought I was waking up to New Year's fireworks, somehow! I guess old Waldo, Mary, and I will be dancing at all your weddings for keeping us safe tonight!"

It was a moment of relief that we all needed!

CHAPTER SEVEN:

BOWMAR'S HUSH-HUSH

"It's not enough that we do our best;
sometimes we have to do what's required."
—Winston Churchill

Sunday, December 21, 1975, 8:00 PM local time
at the White Hole Project in Oak Ridge, Tennessee

Ding's FBI force, with a little help from the CIA and local police, had managed to clear the Oak Ridge, Tennessee battleground known as Waldo's house by the time the sun came up on Sunday morning. I told the Bad Love Gang that I had the cure for Hannah Lieb's breast cancer from Blue Nova One in my possession, and that we needed to meet ASAP to make plans for our next steps to get the cure to Hannah. We all agreed to meet on Sunday night at the White Hole Project to catch up as a group and talk through a mission to go back to World War II Europe in early 1945 and find Hannah. Ding was the only one who couldn't make it; he was fully immersed in his FBI reporting of the prior night's events.

I got there a little early, so I went through the Black Box and organized my music collection while sitting on the soft central floor of the lower White Hole Project time machine racetrack. Everyone soon filtered in and some of the guys were standing in a circle, talking about how much fun they had with the Azurian women at Saturday's epic Queen's Palace celebration on planet Azur, before we were transported back to defend our homeland. Bucky reminisced about dancing with Stareveret, Pumpkin with Jadedominic, the Pud with Zaniah, Bowmar with Nova, Goondoggy with Delta, and Ben with Bella.

Half-watching and listening to them, my music brain kicked into action, and I shuffled through my collection finding the perfect song to enhance the moment. I fired up the new Sony cassette player with Marantz components and Klipsch Heresy speakers that I had recently installed in the White Hole vault and announced to the boys, "I just can't help myself listening to you guys talk about the Azurian women, so here is a little background music for you." The song **"I Wonder What She's Doing Tonight,"** by Tommy Boyce and Bobby Hart, blasted through the White Hole Project vault. The song was a mix of pop rock and bubblegum pop that struck a chord with the conversation at hand and got everyone out on the racetrack, dancing and lip syncing. It had entered the Billboard Hot 100 at number 87 just before Christmas 1967. The tune became a true hit in early 1968, reaching number seven on the Cash Box chart and number eight on the Billboard Hot 100 chart. The music and associated carrying on got everybody loosened up and we all sat down to have a chat about our next adventure, to find Hannah in early 1945 and get the medicine to her.

I got the ball rolling, but I knew I would be putting Bowmar on the spot for information that only he was privy to at this moment. I looked at Meatball as I started the discussion. "Meatball, we have terrific news," I said, holding up the vial of clear liquid medicine that Nova had given me. "This vial contains a futuristic treatment developed on planet Azur called gene therapy, and it will prevent Hannah from getting breast cancer."

Cleopatra pointed at the frayed slits and holes forming in the front thigh and knee areas of Crisco's blue jeans. "Crisco needs some *jean* therapy, big time! What do say we experiment on her first?" Crisco stood up and flaunted her frayed fashion for all of us to see.

Meatball, looking at Cleo and Crisco anxiously interjected, "You both need therapy, but the kind that starts on a couch with 'Doctor Shrink' presiding."

Pumpkin jumped in, saying, "I think we need that Doctor Shrink to check in on the Runt for anger management. Did you guys see how he buried the head of that hatchet in that KGB agent's shoulder last night?!"

The Runt protested, "Well, I wasn't gonna say 'peace, love, and granola' to that son-of-a-bitch. When Goondoggy arrived and put his gun to the guy's head, then saw that blade buried in his shoulder, he did ask him, 'Hey buddy, can you dig it?!'"

We all yelled, "GOONDOGGY!" He stood and took a bow, with a shit-eating grin on his face.

Meatball, more than anxious to hear about Hannah's cure, tried to get us back on track. "Come on, Bubble Butt; give us the lowdown on Hannah's medicine and what we have to do to get it to her."

I continued, "Nova told me about two different genes called breast cancer genes one and two, abbreviated BRCA1 and BRCA2. Normally these genes muffle or prevent breast cancer by fixing DNA potholes that could cause breast cancer. However, in some people, like Hannah, these BRCA genes get damaged. It's called a gene mutation, and then they forget what they're supposed to do to fight off breast cancer. Hannah has one of these BRCA mutations. She and her family are from a particular historic Jewish tribe called the Ashkenazi Jews. One in forty Ashkenazi Jewish women has a BRCA gene mutation, which is ten times higher than the rest of the population. About sixty percent of women with the BRCA1 mutation and forty-five percent of women with the BRCA2 mutation will develop breast cancer...and they tend to get it at a much younger age."

Crazy Ike with a mischievous grin observed, "Hey, Butt Bubbles, you're starting to sound a bit like brainiac boy Bowmar, trying to teach us genetics class or some crap like that. I would prefer reproductive biology."

I countered, "No reproduction for you, my horny sister Ike; I snuck an Azurian neutering medicine into your drink last night. Your balls are going to turn into raisins by sunrise tomorrow, and you'll be singing the high notes with the Supremes!" I couldn't help myself; I grabbed a Supremes' cassette that I had seen in the Black Box and plugged it into the Sony deck. The song **"Love Child"** from Diana Ross & the Supremes started to play, and Cleopatra and Crisco were all over Crazy Ike, dancing around him and singing to him while the rest of us grooved to the tune.

I vividly remembered watching Diana Ross and the Supremes sing **"Love Child"** on The Ed Sullivan Show in September of 1968. Diana was wearing a yellow sweatshirt with the words *Love Child* printed boldly in cursive across the front, along with cut and frayed black jean shorts. I recalled that TV appearance because the Supremes were not dressed up all glamorous as they usually were when they performed, and I liked seeing them that way. **"Love Child"** was a huge success, hitting number one on the Billboard Hot 100 in early December 1968, selling 500,000 records in its first week and two million copies by the end of the year.

As everyone settled down from enjoying the song and laughing at Crazy Ike, I continued with my story. "Blue Nova One stressed that we need to wait until after Hannah's first trimester of pregnancy, or a little more than thirteen weeks after the day she and Meatball were at the pond in Poland together. The gene therapy medicine in this vial must be given to Hannah as an intravenous injection. Crisco, that means you are going on this mission. Hannah may experience a day or two of flu-like symptoms after getting the medicine, but it will be safe for her and the baby after the first trimester. Giving Hannah this vial of medicine will prevent her from developing inherited breast cancer at such a young age."

Crisco responded, "I'll be honored to give Hannah the injection, but how on Earth are we gonna find her in early 1945 Europe, three months after dropping off her, her family, and the other Holocaust victims we rescued at that airbase in Belgium?"

That was my cue to put Bowmar on the spot. "So Bowmar, I know that you are holding onto some secrets imparted to you by Blue Nova One. I saw you dancing with her before she and I went to talk, and I watched her whispering sweet somethings into your ear right before we left the palace and headed back to Earth." My music brain started playing again, and I knew that I had to tease Bowmar just a bit about his little crush on Blue Nova One—and/or hers on him. "Hey, wait a minute Bowmar! Before you answer that, I'm playing a song that I think I might have heard you singing about Blue Nova One." Bowmar was already looking at me a bit cross-eyed, and I had tipped off Crisco and Cleopatra about this moment so they could dance and torment Bowmar a bit to try and embarrass him. However, Bowmar turned the tables and surprised us all.

I switched cassettes in the Sony deck and played **"She's a Lady,"** by Tom Jones. My mom, Gloria, *LOVED* Tom Jones and loved this song; I'm sure she imagined he was serenading and dancing to this song just to entertain her! If he had come to our front door and asked my mom out for a date, she would have turned, smiled at my dad Larry, shrugged, and said, "See you later, honey!" Bowmar was at my house so much that he had heard my mom play this song many times, and he had seen Tom Jones perform on TV. When it started playing, Bowmar didn't wait to be teased. He stood up and took the bull by the horns, dancing and lip syncing into his invisible microphone. He did a very believable impersonation of Jones on stage, while Cleo and Crisco went along as his dance partners. It was Jones' highest-charting single, reaching number one on the US Cash Box Top 100 and number two on the US Billboard Hot 100. It was also a number one hit in Australia and Canada. We all laughed and thoroughly enjoyed the unexpected, not-so-shy stage show from Bowmar.

Bucky commented, "Now, that's the kind of self-confidence that will have the ladies flocking to you, Bowmar! The next time we see Blue Nova One, we're gonna have you put on the 'Bowmar Jones' song and dance routine for her."

"We'll have to see about that, Bucky Boy," Bowmar said. "I'd rather win her over with my sexy science than with my Elvis pelvis." He then shared with us what Blue Nova One had revealed to him about our upcoming adventure. "When we were dancing together, Nova told me that she was meeting privately with BB to go over the details of Hannah's medicine and the timing to get it to her. I was thinking the same thing that Crisco just wondered about; how are we going to find Hannah? I asked Nova that very question. What she told me was a real shocker, not at all what I was expecting..." He briefly paused, staring upward in thought.

Meatball, already impatient and on pins and needles, declared, "Well, *shit*, Bowmar! Are you just gonna stand there and pontificate for a while, or will you tell us what the hell she said so we can make some plans?!"

Cleopatra added, "Oh yeah, he goes into his own little world like that at home sometimes. I have to kick him in his ass or slap him silly for a bit to bring him out of it. You need me to come over there and give you a little whoop ass, little brother?"

"Shut-up, Cleo, and hold your horses! I'm still here, just cogitating about this. Nova said, 'Don't worry about finding Hannah. Have

Bucky use his new presidential connection with Harry Truman to arrange a meeting with Winston Churchill in London on Sunday, April 22, 1945. Compare notes with BB after I talk to him. You two can figure it out.' When we were on our time-travel mission and road trip across 1945 America this past spring, after meeting President Roosevelt, Bucky spoke to President Truman the night we were all in St. Louis: April 16, 1945. That means Bucky is going to have to go back and get through to Truman to set up our meeting with Churchill for April 22nd."

"As you'll recall, I have direct lines to Vannevar Bush and Colonel Carter Clarke during that time frame," Bucky pointed out. "I can get through to Truman and get that done, but President Truman will know that we are time travelers because of the overlap in time with our mission last April."

"Truman already knows you oversee the Denver Project, and that it is more secret than the Manhattan Project. It'll give him something to write about in that *Book of Presidents* in his desk drawer in the Oval Office," I said. "Besides, President Truman also gets briefed on the Denver Project by Bush and Clarke, so he knows about the White Hole Project and its connection to Area 51."

Meatball was almost in panic mode, "How is meeting with Winston Churchill gonna help us get the medicine to Hannah?! I thought this next mission was all about finding Hannah."

"Hold on, Meatball," I responded, "this is just getting interesting. Going back to London in April 1945 gets us there five months into Hannah's pregnancy, well past her first trimester, to give her the medicine safely. What else did Nova say to you, Bowmar?"

Bowmar responded, "While we were dancing, she asked me if Bucky knew how to fly a de Havilland Mosquito."

I started laughing, because Bucky was always getting asked if he could fly this or that WWII airplane—so much so that it generally pissed him off whenever he was asked. But this time Bucky answered, "It's a legendary British twin-engine bomber nicknamed the Wooden Wonder. It had a frame of wood and a skin of plywood, glued and screwed together. It was also called the Mossie, known as the fastest bomber of World War II and known for its bombing, pathfinder, and precision low-level strike capabilities. It could outrun the famous British Spitfire fighter plane by twenty miles per hour. I've never flown one, but I have always wanted to."

Pumpkin interjected, "The Mossie was bloody brilliant, and I happen to have flown a few missions in that rascal. The Brits could assemble those things like crazy, using furniture factories and piano makers for various wooden parts. I've skimmed a few treetops in that plane, and it struck fear in the hearts of the Germans. In fact, Reichsmarschall Hermann Göring, the commander in chief of the German Luftwaffe during the World War II, was giving a radio address in Berlin in January 1943. His radio show was taken off the air by a low-level bombing attack from the famous Royal Air Force Squadron number 105 Mosquitos. Afterwards, Göring was quoted as saying 'It makes me furious when I see the Mosquito; I turn green and yellow with envy! The British, who can afford aluminum better that we can, knock together a beautiful wooden aircraft that every piano factory over there is building. They have the geniuses, and we have the nincompoops. After the war is over, I'm going to buy a British radio set; then at least I'll own something that has always worked.'"

"I love that quote, Pumpkin. Three cheers to British ingenuity! What did Nova whisper in your ear as we were getting ready to leave?' I asked Bowmar.

Bowmar answered, "She said, 'I forgot to mention to you, the Goring is tough to beat!' I really didn't know exactly what she meant by that. I don't think she was talking about Nazi Reichsmarschall Hermann Göring."

"Well fashion that. Since I'm from London, *I get to tell Bowmar the answer for once!*" Pumpkin exclaimed. "The Goring Hotel is a posh, absolutely *smashing* place to stay. It's located next door to Buckingham Palace, and an easy walk to 10 Downing Street! It has been lovingly run by the Goring family since its inception, and reportedly was the first hotel in the world to offer a bathroom for every bedroom and central heating. During the First World War, the Goring became the command center for the chief of the Allied Forces. Since we are talking a bit about Winston Churchill, his mother, Lady Randolph Churchill, an American-born British socialite, moved into The Goring Hotel for a time. Winston was known to hold meetings with allied leaders in the hotel during World War II."

With a wall-to-wall grin on her face, Cleopatra blurted, "Now you guys are *talkin'*! Crisco and I can stay at that posh London hotel at night and hunt for Hannah during the day, while you all go do your save-the-world-secret-military shit." We all laughed along with Cleo.

"Cleo may have something there but let me start to put this puzzle together for you all," I said. "Blue Nova One told me an important story that none of you know about. We met Nova in the forests of southern China on her *second* mission to Earth, in June of 1942. She actually first discovered blue exotic matter on Earth in May of 1941 in the mountain range of the German Black Forest, in the southwestern state of Baden-Württemberg, Germany. At that time, Nova was happily married to a guy named Blue Rhett One who was an engineer, trained to drill for and extract blue exotic matter. They had established a secret drilling site concealed in the Black Forest, and thanks to Rhett and his expert drilling tactics, they had reached a rich vein of blue exotic matter in late July 1941. They intermittently shipped blue exotic matter back to Azur using their spaceship's intergalactic white hole transport unit and had planned to depart Earth in December 1941.

"On November 26, 1941, three Waffen-SS Nazi soldiers managed to ambush their drilling site. Rhett was shot and killed by a Nazi soldier named Klaus Richter. There were eleven containers of blue exotic matter stacked against a hillside by the drill site, and Rhett was carrying one when he was killed. As the Azurians hastily departed, the crew destroyed the drill site and drilling equipment, but they did not know whether Rhett had included the crates of blue exotic matter in the predetermined placement of demolition charges or not. Blue Nova One has worried about the possibility that the Nazis got their hands on a dozen crates of refined blue exotic matter since then. After comparing notes here tonight with Bowmar, I suspect that Churchill knows something about this problem and Nova is sending us to him for a reason."

"BB, how is this all working together for us to find Hannah and give her the medicine?" Meatball asked.

"Thanks for bearing with me, Meatball," I responded. "We dropped off Hannah and the group we rescued from the Holocaust at Belgium's Chièvres Air Base in November 1944. The base was used by Allied air forces, with regular flights going back and forth to England's air bases. I am betting that the group we left there were taken to England because of General Waldo's strongly worded orders to take care of them and get them to safety promptly." Waldo nodded his bald head in affirmation, making everyone smile. "If they did go to England, who better to locate them than Winston Churchill, with his intelligence and military resources? We will ask Churchill to help locate Hannah for us. We are getting rather good at exchanging favors with folks in power as we travel through time!"

Meatball breathed a big sigh of relief and said, "I'm all in! Let's light this candle and get that medicine to Hannah." Everyone agreed, and Meatball looked much relieved—and happier than he had been in a while. I decided not to tell Meatball about the second vial of medicine that Nova had given me until he and Hannah were together in person. Nor did I share with the group anything about what I had called the Reach Out flashback gadget that Nova and her engineers had developed. I planned to always carry that emergency gadget, but I hoped we would not ever need to use it.

CHAPTER EIGHT:

THE BLACK HOLE PROJECT

"If you win, you need not have to explain...
If you lose, you should not be there to explain!"
—Adolf Hitler

Sunday, January 21, 1945, 3:00 PM local time, the Führerbunker in Berlin and the top-secret Black Hole Project Command Center in the town of Berchtesgaden in Bavaria, Germany

By early 1945, Hitler's Nazi Germany was on the verge of total military collapse. Poland had fallen to the advancing Soviet Red Army to the west of Berlin, British and Canadian forces had crossed the Rhine into the German industrial heartland of the Ruhr to the east, and US forces in the southwest had captured Lorraine and were advancing. German forces in Italy were withdrawing northward as they were hammered by the US and Allied forces. Hitler retreated to his Führerbunker in Berlin on January 16, 1945, and it was becoming obvious to Nazi military leadership that the battle for Berlin would be the final battle of the war in Europe.

The Führerbunker, located 28 feet below ground, had a roof made of reinforced concrete nearly ten feet thick. It enclosed about thirty small rooms that were protected by approximately thirteen feet of concrete. Exits led to the nearby Reich Chancellery buildings above ground, as well as an emergency exit up to the garden of the Reich Chancellery. The underground bunker complex was self-contained but located below the water table, making conditions distastefully damp; pumps were kept running continuously to remove groundwater. Diesel generators supplied electricity, and the water supply was pumped from a well. Hitler's outside communications systems included a telephone switchboard run by Nazi SS Sergeant Rochus Misch, an army radio set with an outdoor antenna array, and a telex machine.

In the lower level of the Führerbunker, Hitler's personal accommodations were decorated with the finest furniture taken from the Chancellery, along with several framed oil paintings—including a large portrait of Frederick the Great, one of Hitler's heroes. After descending the stairs into the lower Führerbunker and passing through a steel door, there was a long corridor with a series of rooms on each side. Located on the right side of the hall were generator and ventilation rooms, as well as Sergeant Misch's telephone switchboard. On the left side was Hitler's soon-to-be-bride Eva Braun's bedroom and Hitler's sitting room, which led into his private office. Another door from Hitler's sitting room led into his private bedroom, and it shared a wall with the conference or map room, also known as the briefing or situation room.

At 3:00 PM, Hitler was walking out of his personal office to the conference room when he was interrupted by switchboard operator SS Sergeant Rochus Misch. "Mein Führer, Obergruppenführer Klaus Richter and Herr Gunther Brandt are calling on your private line, requesting to speak with you immediately. They say it is a matter of highest importance."

Hitler responded, "Thank you, Sergeant. Put that call directly through to my desk phone and tell the others that I am delayed." He turned and went back into his office, shutting the doors leading to his sitting room and the conference room. He sat down at his office desk, crossed his arms, and quietly stared in serious thought at the phone for a minute before taking the call. He picked up the receiver and said, "I hope you have good news for me."

Gunther Brandt, the brilliant theoretical and quantum mechanics physicist secretly in charge of developing the Black Hole Project, was the first to answer. "Mein Führer, I do bring you worthy news on this day. The racetrack apparatus has been completed and successfully tested. We are now working on the computers necessary to link the transport unit with time, space, and global geographical coordinates. As you required, I have designed the machine to transport you to the future. If I had enough additional construction time, I believe that I could design the controls to transport you anywhere on Earth at any time in the future—or the past, for that matter. But that would take me another six to twelve months, minimum, to accomplish. The blue exotic matter is both fascinating and mysterious—I could spend the rest of my life studying its attributes. I need two things from you today, Mein Führer: I need to know how much time I have left to make this machine fully operational, as well as the time and exact place that you want to be transported to."

Hitler answered, "The machine will need to be fully operational and ready for my departure in the next eight to twelve weeks. I will take *Mein Kampf* to the New World of South America in the future. We already have connections in Santiago, Chile. When I arrive at the Black Hole, you will send me exactly thirty years into the future to the Pontifical Catholic University of Chile in Santiago. In 1930, Pope Pius declared it a pontifical university. In 1931 it was granted full autonomy by the Chilean government, and it has strong and close relationships with the Vatican. I was raised Catholic, but I despise the religion. However, I have learned that I can work certain religions to my advantage. The University will be a safe starting place for me to reconnect with the German community there and begin to execute my plans for the future. I will take gold and civilian clothing. Will you be ready, Gunther? Not a day later than three months from now?"

"Based on the parameters you just outlined, I guarantee we will be ready for you, Mein Führer. We will call you again the moment we know that preparations are completed."

Hitler continued, "Obergruppenführer Richter, I trust that security has been airtight under your watchful eyes."

Klaus Richter replied, "Yes, absolutely impermeable, Mein Führer! Anyone even suspected of treason or spying has been eliminated, by me personally."

"I expected nothing less from you, Klaus," Hitler replied. "I have two requests of you. First, at a time of my choosing, I will have my personal pilot, Standartenführer Hans Baur, reach out to you for the coordinates of your secret landing field. He will arrange for a test flight from here to there to deliver the gold and my packed clothing. Baur has been with me for many years, and I trust him. Treat him well and show him around the facility that he may report back to me personally. Second, I want you, Hans, and Gunther to accompany me to the future. Gunther, can you make that happen and prepare some blue exotic matter to bring with you into the future?"

Gunther replied, "I have the Black Hole Project machine configured to send one person at a time. I can send you first, then Klaus, and Hans Baur after Klaus. Sending me will be trickier; I would need to automate that process, but I believe I can do that. Is there anyone else we need to be prepared to send with you?" Gunther was wondering if Eva Braun would be going.

"Gunther, it will be me, Klaus, Hans, you and enough blue exotic matter and gold for the future—that is all. You will make that happen, and you and Klaus will work together to wire the Black Hole Project time-travel machinery to self-destruct after we are transported out of there. I do not want the Black Hole to fall into the hands of our enemies after we are gone or give them any clues to follow us or our whereabouts. Do we understand each other?" Hitler demanded.

Gunther and Klaus simultaneously exclaimed, "Yes, Mein Führer!"

CHAPTER NINE:

CHURCHILL'S SECRET ARMY

"Generally speaking, espionage offers each spy an opportunity
to go crazy in a way he (or she) finds irresistible."
—Kurt Vonnegut

*Tuesday, March 6, 1945, the Black Hole Project near the
shoreline of the picturesque Lake Königsee in the Malerwinkel
forest of Bavaria, Germany*

The Berchtesgaden Alps are a mountain range of the Northern
Limestone Alps, named after the German market town of Berchtesgaden, located centrally. The range includes the Obersalzberg
slope east of Berchtesgaden. Dating back to the 1920s, Adolf Hitler
began vacationing in the Berchtesgaden area. His home and southern headquarters, the Berghof was built on the Obersalzberg above
the town of Berchtesgaden. Many other notorious top Third Reich
officials of Hitler's inner circle—such as Hermann Göring, Heinrich
Himmler, Joseph Goebbels, Martin Bormann, and Albert Speer—also
established neighboring homes in the Obersalzberg. The entire area
was saturated with well-trained Wehrmacht, mountain troop units,
and Nazi SS security forces. The Black Hole Project architect and chief

physicist, Hans Gunther, and Nazi SS Security Chief, Obergruppen-führer Klaus Richter, had established a covert "administrative plan-ning office" as a front for their Black Hole Construction Command Center in the town of Berchtesgaden. Emma Hoffman, an attractive but unassuming woman in her late twenties, had worked as the cleri-cal secretary at the front desk of that office since it opened in August 1942.

The Black Hole Project had been built using engineering techniques similar to those used to build Hitler's underground Führerbunker, about four miles south of Berchtesgaden and set into a steep hillside near the shoreline of the picturesque Lake Königsee, in the Malerwin-kel forest. Lake Königssee, Germany's third deepest lake, was located at a Jurassic rift formed by glaciers during the last ice age. The lake stretched almost five miles in a north-south direction and was about one mile across at its widest point. Except at its outlet at the village of Königssee (just north of the Black Hole Project), the lake was similar to a fjord: surrounded by the cliffs of mountains rising to 8,900 feet. Gunther and Richter believed that the Black Hole was well protected from the possibility of a motorized or coordinated ground attack. Also, there were no military ships on the lake and an air assault would be fruitless, with the steep surrounding mountains. They were correct on two of three counts.

Petra Vogel, a brilliant physicist and strikingly beautiful woman in her mid-thirties, had joined Gunther Brandt's Black Hole Project physics team in September of 1942 at the personal recommendation of German Nobel Prize winning physicist Werner Heisenberg, Gunther's mentor and one of the key German pioneers of quantum mechan-ics. Gunther Brandt and Klaus Richter had bonded in friendship and worked well together since meeting with Hitler at the Berghof in March of 1942, starting construction on the Black Hole Project in June 1942. Both had worked long, hard hours under a stressful timetable and knew without a doubt that they could not and would not disappoint the Führer. Gunther was estranged from his wife, who lived in Cologne, Germany; Richter was single. Richter was dating and had fallen for Emma Hoffman within three months of her taking the job at the front desk at the construction command center in Berchtesgaden. After six months of working together on the theoretical physics and proposed quantum mechanics of the Black Hole Project, Gunther Brandt was having an affair with Petra Vogel. Neither Klaus nor Gunther had the slightest clue or suspicion that both Emma and Petra were working for Churchill's secret army, the British Special Operations Executive (SOE).

The Special Operations Executive (SOE) was a top-secret British World War II espionage enterprise. It was formally established on July 22, 1940, under British Minister of Economic Warfare, Hugh Dalton, by the merging of three other existing secret organizations. It was designated and charged with conducting reconnaissance, espionage, and sabotage in German Nazi-occupied Europe—as well as in Japan-occupied Southeast Asia—against the Axis powers and intended to give aid and support to local resistance movements. The SOE's London headquarters was located on Baker Street. and the SOE was variously referred to as the "Baker Street Irregulars," "Churchill's Secret Army," or the "Ministry of Ungentlemanly Warfare." The organization directly employed or supervised more than 13,000 people, about 3,200 of whom were women.

Charles Henry Maxwell Knight, also known as Maxwell Knight, was a British spymaster who later became the prototype for the James Bond character M. He played major roles in surveillance of the early British Fascist and Communist parties. In a memo in connection with having women of the SOE serve as secret agents, Knight tackled the subject of women spies seducing men to extract information. He ventured that not just any woman could manage this, but only those who were not "markedly oversexed or undersexed." Like the proverbial and famous British porridge, an effective female agent could be neither too hot nor too cold, but just right. Knight surmised that what was needed was, "a clever woman who could use her personal attractions wisely." Both Emma Hoffman and Petra Vogel were quite capable in this regard and had extracted invaluable information from Klaus and Gunther.

On this early March 1945 day, the effort to reveal Hitler's darkest secret—his plan to use blue exotic matter and time travel through the Black Hole to escape the failing German Nazi Third Reich and take his evil agenda of world domination to the future—was in the hands of the two beautiful and cunning SOE agents Emma Hoffman and Petra Vogel. Emma's real name was Ela Hellberg; she and her Jewish family were from Strasbourg, France, located at the border with Germany in the historic region of Alsace. After the Fall of France to Nazi Germany in June of 1940, anti-Semitic laws started to come into force in both the occupied and unoccupied zones of France that summer. By October 1940, Vichy, France, introduced the Statut des Juifs, which required all Jews in France to register with the authorities and banned Jews from their professions, such as lawyers, university professors, medical and public service positions. Jewish businesses were "Aryanized" and placed in the hands of Aryan trustees who engaged in the most flagrant acts of corruption. Jews were banned from cinemas, music halls, fairs, museums, libraries, public parks, cafes, theatres, concerts, restaurants, swimming pools, and markets. Jews could not own radios or bicycles, were denied home phone service, could not use phone booths, and could not geographically move or relocate without first informing the police.

Emma's father, Adam Hellberg, was from a long family line of police detectives. Adam's older brother (Emma's favorite uncle), Seth Hellberg, was living in London and working for the SOE. After Adam learned that Paris had fallen to Hitler's forces in June of 1940, he had spoken to Seth in July; Seth urged him to get the family and extended family to Spain and join the French Resistance. Emma, age twenty-four at the time, was fiercely independent and working as a law clerk at a local Jewish law office. She spoke to her uncle Seth and told him that despite her father's objections, she desperately wanted to play a role in helping the Allies to fight Nazi Germany. After much cajoling and convincing on her part, her father relented, and Uncle Seth assigned her to the SOE. Her law firm assisted in changing her identity from the Jewish Ela Hellberg to the German Emma Hoffman. Her father, Adam Hellberg, became a leader in the French Resistance and established two faux family phone contacts for Emma to use in the event she ever needed to flee Germany. One of the contacts was in Switzerland, the other in France.

In August 1940, the powerful Nazi Robert Heinrich Wagner, personally acquainted with Hitler since the beginnings of the Nazi regime, became chief of civil administration for Alsace and subsequently led an aggressive Germanization campaign for the region. He embarked on a crusade to rid Alsace of Jews, earning himself the nickname the Butcher of Alsace. Emma, ambitious and unafraid to dive headlong into allied espionage, landed a job "with the devil himself," as she put it, in Wagner's office in the spring of 1941.

Klaus Richter had risen in the ranks after discovering Blue Nova One's alien drilling expedition and blue exotic matter in the German Black Forest in late November of 1941 and had a distinguished military record serving under Wagner. When Hitler promoted Richter to the rank of SS Obergruppenführer (lieutenant general) and made him the head of security for the top-secret Black Hole Project in March of 1942, Wagner recommended to Richter that Emma Hoffman be among his first hires to his new office in Berchtesgaden. Given this high-level recommendation, Emma had managed to embed herself as a trusted "German" civilian assistant to what became the most secretive project in the history of Nazi Germany. On this day in March 1945, Emma had set a plan in motion for both her and Petra Vogel to daringly escape by air to her father in France. From there they would travel to London, where they could warn the SOE of Hitler's dark plan of escape to the future.

Petra Vogel was from a German Ashkenazi, Jewish family and was born in Göttingen, a university city in Lower Saxony, Germany, in 1907. Her family was highly educated; both her parents taught mathematics at the University of Göttingen, which was a leading center of mathematics by the turn of the 20th century. Her older brother Karl Vogel, a mathematician and physicist, had taken a position at Cambridge University in Britain in 1930. Petra, also drawn to the science of physics, had trained under Max Born, a German physicist and mathematician who was instrumental in the development of quantum mechanics. In May 1933, after the Nazi Party came to power in Germany, Max Born, who was Jewish, was suspended from his professorship at the University of Göttingen. He emigrated from Germany to the United Kingdom, where he initially worked at St John's College, Cambridge. In October 1936, he became a distinguished professor at the University of Edinburgh. Petra raved to her brother about Max Born, and Karl managed to follow him in joining the faculty at Edinburgh. In 1940, Karl was recruited by the SOE, given his strong physics background and family connections in Germany.

Petra and her parents were incredibly careful and successfully concealed their Jewish heritage from the Nazi Party. Werner Heisenberg was awarded the 1932 Nobel Prize in Physics "for the creation of quantum mechanics [...]." After Max Born left Göttingen, Petra, interested in quantum mechanics, went to work as a research associate under Heisenberg, who was professor of theoretical physics and head of the department of physics at the University of Leipzig. As fate would have it, Heisenberg was also a principal scientist in the German nuclear weapons program during World War II. In early 1941, Karl Petrov managed to recruit his brilliant and beautiful sister Petra to spy for the SOE. She had become a close, trusted associate of Werner Heisenberg, and accompanied him to a scientific conference at the Kaiser Wilhelm Institute for Physics in February 1942. Heisenberg presented a lecture to Nazi Third Reich officials on energy acquisition from nuclear fission. The lecture, entitled "The Theoretical Basis for Energy Generation from Uranium Fission," espoused the enormous energy potential of nuclear fission, stating that 250 million electron volts could be released through the fission of an atomic nucleus. Heisenberg stressed that pure U-235 had to be obtained to achieve a nuclear chain reaction and that future nuclear machines (reactors) could be used in practical ways to fuel vehicles, ships, and submarines. Heisenberg emphasized the importance of financial and material support for this scientific endeavor from Germany's Army Weapons Office.

Gunther Brandt, a protégé and respected colleague of Werner Heisenberg, had regularly communicated with Heisenberg regarding quantum mechanics theory after the March 1942 meeting, when Hitler assigned him to develop the Black Hole Project using the captured alien blue exotic matter. Heisenberg, not knowing the specifics of Brandt's top-secret project but impressed with Petra Vogel's grasp of quantum mechanics theory, recommended her services to Brandt in August 1942. Petra joined Brandt's team at the Black Hole Project in September 1942; by both chance and destiny, she too was an SOE agent embedded into the most secretive and guarded project in the history of World War II Nazi Germany.

By January 1945, Heisenberg, and most of his staff, had moved from the Kaiser Wilhelm Institute for Physics to facilities in the German town of Hechingen and its neighboring town of Haigerloch, on the edge of the Black Forest, where they were working on the development of an experimental nuclear reactor. As the war was drawing to its conclusion, Heisenberg's nuclear reactor project was only 275 miles west from Brandt's Black Hole Project. Winston Churchill had been appraised of the clandestine German atomic activities at Hechingen and Haigerloch and was taking steps to intervene. However, the existence of the Black Hole Project was wholly unknown and would become an ominous and worrisome revelation to Churchill in the final days of World War II in Europe, while Hitler held on to dark aspirations for the future hunkered down in his underground, Berlin Führerbunker.

CHAPTER TEN:

THE HOOKS ARE SET, THE FISH ARE ASLEEP

"If you want to catch little fish, you can stay in the shallow water.
But if you want to catch the big fish, you've got to go deeper."
—David Lynch

Tuesday and Wednesday, March 6–7, 1945,
the Black Hole Project near the shoreline of Lake Königsee
in the Malerwinkel forest of Bavaria, Germany

On March 6, 1945, Germany launched Operation Spring Awakening, which was the final major German offensive of World War II. The operation aimed to secure the last significant oil reserves still available to the Axis powers and prevent the Russian Red Army from advancing towards Vienna. It took place in Western Hungary on the Eastern Front and lasted from March 6 until March 15, 1945. Operation Spring Awakening was a failure for Nazi Germany, and the allies were relentlessly closing in from all sides with the goal of taking Berlin and ending the war in Europe.

Emma was sleeping with and virtually living with Klaus Richter. She had convinced him that her love for him was passionate, unconditional, and for all eternity. They had been sexually intimate with each other for two years and four months, since November of 1942. The two of them were best friends with Gunther Brandt and Petra Vogel, who had been bonded in secret love for two years. The four of them viewed each other as an inseparable team to complete the Black Hole Project on time for the Führer's upcoming departure to the future.

Petra Vogel arrived at the Black Hole Project in September 1942, and straightaway gained the respect of Brandt and the small group of physicists helping him. Known in German physics circles as a sleepless workaholic, Brandt constructed the Black Hole Project time machine vault with reasonably comfortable living quarters and a well-equipped kitchen, knowing that he would practically live there until his work was completed. Being estranged from his wife since March of 1942 and working with Petra for six months, she had gradually and deliberately fed his ego as only a fellow physicist could. Petra had inherited her family's intellectual competence; she was also undeniably beautiful. She was slender but shapely, five feet eight inches tall, with luminous, pale skin and thick, curly red hair. As was pushed by Hitler's Nazi regime, she wore dresses or skirts exclusively. Pants for women were frowned on by the Führer.

One night in March 1943, while working together well past midnight at the Black Hole and exchanging subtle compliments and references of veiled affection towards each other, Petra made her move and "accidently" spilled her cup of coffee on the floor. As she got on her hands and knees with a towel to clean up the spillage, Gunther grabbed a towel and joined her on the floor to assist. Starting at opposite ends of the circle of spilled coffee on the floor, they moved towards each other on hands and knees as they soaked up the mess. When they met in the middle, they were face to face and only inches apart. Petra pursed her feminine lips ever so slightly and said, "I'm sorry, Gunther, for being so clumsy tonight..." He put his hand behind her head and pulled her into a long and heavy kiss, which sent Gunther deep into the world of quantum physics love. From that moment on, the Black Hole Project and its living quarters frequently served as a second home *to* both Gunther and Petra.

Emma Hoffman's and Klaus Richter's affair started in a more Neanderthal or carnal fashion, as might be expected given Klaus's macho Nazi stormtrooper reputation. After Emma had taken the job at the front desk of the Construction Command Center in Berchtesgaden, arriving in August 1942, she quickly learned that Nazi SS Obergruppenführer Klaus Richter was the head of security for the top-secret Black Hole Project. She determined that he would be her target for information related to this top-secret Nazi project. Her office was extremely busy and hectic in the early days of the Black Hole construction, ordering and tracking a myriad of construction materials and construction workers coming and going. Klaus would come and go from her office, ensuring airtight security in the flow of materials and manpower. Emma was five feet five inches tall with a medium, curvy build and had natural long blonde hair paired with blue-green eyes—physical traits that had protected her from ever being suspected of having a Jewish background by the Aryan Nazis she worked for and spied upon. She was an absolute firecracker inside, fiercely strong-minded but governed by resolve to make a difference for the Allies. As such, she portrayed herself as unassertive and slightly vulnerable while flirting with Klaus amid his busy daily schedule.

One day in late November 1942, there was an early heavy snow in Berchtesgaden. Emma had the wood-burning stove glowing with heat, but work had come to a standstill, and she was alone in the office. She was getting ready to close early and go home, but Klaus showed up unexpectedly, coming through the front office door with a bouquet of fresh flowers in his hand. He said, "These are for you, my dear!" He handed them to Emma with a smile and a tip of his hat as he took it off and threw it and his coat on the chair. He then turned, locked the front door, and pulled the window curtains shut as he stated, "The office is now closed."

Emma, smiled warmly and somewhat shyly said, "Thank you, Obergruppenführer, these are beautiful."

"Not nearly as beautiful as you and call me Klaus whenever we are alone together from now on," Klaus replied. He swept his right arm across her desk, aggressively brushing everything off the desk and crashing onto the floor. He reached under her arms, effortlessly lifted her off her feet, and placed her sitting on the desk. He said, "It is time that we got to know each other, Emma." From that day forward, Emma made certain that she continually caressed Klaus's ego and met his needs while garnering his complete trust, learning everything about the top-secret Black Hole Project in the process.

It was now early March 1945 and Emma, and Petra were fully aware of the details of Hitler's scheme to escape to the future using the Black Hole Project. The time had arrived for Emma and Petra to make their escape to London, taking the news and secrets of the Black Hole Project to the British SOE. Emma had used the faux family phone contact that her father (Adam Hellberg) had preemptively established for her to call in France when she needed to flee Germany. France had been liberated by the Allies, and her father was a hero of the French Resistance. It was Emma who planned the details of their escape to London, with the help of her father and his SOE contacts.

Emma had taken a classified call from Hitler's personal pilot, SS-Gruppenführer (major general) Hans Baur, to Klaus Richter ten days prior, requesting the coordinates to the Black Hole Project's secret landing field. Following the Führer's direct orders, Bauer had chosen the timing and arranged for a test flight from Berlin to deliver Hitler's gold and packed personal items. He was scheduled to arrive mid-morning on Wednesday, March 7, 1945. Hitler had previously told Klaus to treat Bauer well and show him around the Black Hole Project, so that he could report back to Hitler personally about the status and readiness of the facility. Emma saw this upcoming visit by Baur as the best opportunity to orchestrate a daring getaway attempt and deliver the details of Hitler's escape plan into the hands of the British SOE.

After he became chancellor of Germany in 1933, Hitler was the first head of state to have his own personal pilot and airplane. Hans Baur was a nine-victory ace pilot in World War I and became a Lufthansa flight captain in the postwar period. In 1933, he was selected to be Hitler's personal pilot and commander of Hitler's personal transport squadron, the Fliegerstaffel des Führers, or F.d.F. Based at Berlin's Tempelhof Airport, Baur's F.d.F. was a separate government organization and not part of the German Luftwaffe. Baur was commissioned by Heinrich Himmler in October 1933 as a colonel in the Nazi SS and appointed a police major so that he could be responsible for the Führer's security in connection with his flying duties.

The Führer's personal flight squadron had a special insignia that was painted on the nose of all planes: a black eagle's head on a white background, surrounded by a narrow red ring. Hitler was provided with a personal Junkers Ju 52/3m (registration D-2600), named Immelmann II after Germany's World War I fighter pilot ace Max Immelmann. The Ju-52/3m was equipped with robust landing gear that enabled it to take off and land on dirt or grass strips as short as 1,300 feet (400 meters) that other aircraft could not use. What is more, its metal structure and corrugated aluminum alloy skin could withstand considerable punishment. As his power and position grew, Hitler's personal air force grew to nearly 50 aircraft made up mainly of Junkers Ju 52s. In September 1939, at Baur's suggestion, Immelmann II was replaced by a Focke-Wulf Fw 200 Condor, a large four-engine aircraft with much better performance and capacity; it was called Immelman III. However, Immelman II remained as Hitler's backup aircraft for the rest of the Second World War.

Hans Baur, as his private pilot and personal friend, was in Hitler's presence nearly every day from 1933 to 1945. In June of 1937, Hitler held a 40th birthday celebration for Baur at the Reich Chancellery. Even though Hitler was a vegetarian, he served Baur his favorite meal of pork and dumplings for his birthday and gave him a new Mercedes Benz to replace his Ford. On January 31, 1944, Baur was promoted to SS-Brigadeführer (brigadier general) and major general of the police; and on February 24, 1945, he became an SS-Gruppenführer (major general) and lieutenant general of the police. Baur was one of very few people truly close to Hitler, and during these last days of the war, he was with Hitler in the Führerbunker. Baur was charged with the details of the plan to enable the Führer's escape from the Führerbunker and the Battle of Berlin and get safely to the Black Hole Project. Given the relatively short length of the secret Black Hole Project runway at 2,300 feet (700 meters), Baur had told Klaus Richter that he would be arriving in Hitler's personal Junkers Ju 52/3m, named Immelmann II, and that it could handle the short runway.

When Emma learned that Baur was planning to arrive on a test flight on Wednesday morning, March 7, 1945, using Hitler's personal Junkers Ju 52/3m named Immelmann II, she was able to get that information to her SOE contact along with the coordinates to the secret landing field. Emma and Petra had been to the secret landing field many times with Klaus and Gunther, greeting visiting engineers and physicists who had flown in to help with various technical aspects of the Black Hole Project. She let her contact know that there was no landing control tower, only two guards protecting the access gate to the rather small top-secret landing field. She and Petra had gotten to know the guards at the entrance gate.

When they talked again three days later, Emma's contact informed her that the SOE had arranged for an exact replica of the Führer's Junkers Ju 52/3m (Hitler's plane had been filmed and photographed on many occasions), piloted by British Special Operations agents, to land at the Black Hole Project runway just after sunrise on Wednesday morning March 7th. The airplane would land and circle at the end of the runway with its engines running. Emma and Petra would need to be waiting there at that time and run to the plane. The entrance door to the Ju 52 was behind the wing on the port side of the aircraft, and they would see the door open when it was time for them to dash aboard. The British commandos would be armed, but the plane itself had no armament. The plan was to spend as little time on the ground as possible and get back into the air as fast as possible with Emma and Petra onboard.

Tuesday, March 6, 1945, at 10:00 PM local time,
the Black Hole Project near the shore of Lake Königsee
in the Malerwinkel forest of Bavaria, Germany

Gunther Brandt and Klaus Richter had been notified ten days prior that Hans Baur would be arriving with Hitler's gold and a packed suitcase of his personal items on Wednesday, March 7, 1945. Baur, who had been recently promoted to SS-Gruppenführer, would be directly inspecting the Black Hole Project and reporting back to the Führer. Gunther knew his schedule for completing the Black Hole Project, meant having it operational no later than April 21, 1945, based on his earlier conversation the Führer. After that discussion, Gunther had created a timetable to be fully operational ahead of schedule on Friday, April 13, 1945. Gunther had jokingly shared with the group that Friday the 13th was the perfect day to have a project called the Black Hole ready to go, challenging any perceived fate of superstition or bad luck. With Hans Baur arriving five weeks before the date of planned operational integrity, Gunther was a bit apprehensive about Baur's visit and making a favorable impression that would then be shared with the Führer.

The night before Baur's visit, it was all hands on deck at the Black Hole Project. Gunther, Petra, Klaus, and Emma had been there all day, working hard to tidy up loose construction debris and to clean and polish all the machinery, control panels, and hard surfaces. Emma and Petra had dubbed this Black Hole Beautification Day; they had built up expectations with Gunther and Klaus that once all the work was completed, they would have an on-site date night with music, food, and drinks to celebrate being prepared for the Führer's proxy (Hans Baur) to visit. During the day on Tuesday, Gunther had successfully tested the upper and lower cyclotron racetracks connected by the blue exotic matter lined time tunnel and planned to demonstrate their function-ality to Baur on Wednesday as a show of readiness. Klaus had visited the secret landing field and explained to the guard detail that Grup-penführer Hans Baur would be landing there Wednesday morning in Hitler's personal Junkers Ju 52/3m airplane, named Immelmann II and bearing the flight numbers D-2600.

Petra and Emma had conspired together to make a late but fabu-lous dinner after the work was done, accompanied by plenty of drinks and music. The two of them were deeply embedded spies, but they were not killers. After finishing all the clean-up work, they planned to keep Gunther and Klaus active and awake late, then drug them to sleep so that they could flee to the secret landing field at sunrise to meet the plane and make their escape. Petra had managed to obtain chloral hydrate tablets from a local pharmacy and had dissolved 2,000 milligrams each in two small vials of the popular WWII German drink called Jägermeister. The drink was created by Curt Mast, the son of Wilhelm Mast: a vinegar manufacturer and wine trader in the city of Wolfenbüttel, Germany. In 1934, at the age of 37, Curt took over his father's business and devised the recipe for the famous Jägermeister.

Jägermeister's ingredients included 56 herbs, roots, fruits, and spices, including licorice, anise, citrus peel, poppy seeds, saffron, ginger, juniper berries, and ginseng. All the ingredients were finely ground, then steeped in water and alcohol for two to three days. This mixture was then filtered and stored in oak barrels for about a year. After that, the liqueur was filtered again and mixed with sugar, caramel, and alcohol. The name *Jägermeister* in German literally means master of the hunt. Reichsmarschall Hermann Göring was famous in Nazi Germany as head of the German Luftwaffe (air force) during WWII. Following Goring's appointment to Reichsjägermeister (reich hunting master) when a new hunting law was introduced in Nazi Germany, Jägermeister became known as "Göring-Schnaps," which propelled its popularity within the German military and social culture.

Chloral hydrate was first synthesized in 1832 by German scientist Justus von Liebigand and was introduced into medicine in 1869 by German pharmacologist Oscar Liebreich. It was Liebreich who discovered and described its effectiveness in inducing sleep. It was easy to synthesize, and widely used for sedation in mental asylums and in general medical practice, but also became a popular drug of abuse in the late 19th century. A therapeutic dose produced a deep sleep lasting four to eight hours. The so-called "Mickey Finn" of popular lore was most likely named after the manager and bartender of the Lone Star Saloon and Palm Garden Restaurant in Chicago from 1896 to 1903. Chloral hydrate was the primary ingredient, along with alcohol, of the Mickey Finn knockout drops. Petra had done some research on dosing and had prepared the two vials to induce deep sleep in Gunther and Klaus within forty minutes of getting it into their systems, along with plenty of German beer and shots of Jägermeister. She and Emma needed to leave the Black Hole at 5:00 AM sharp to be comfortably through the guard gate and waiting at the secret airfield by sunrise at 6:40 AM. She was hoping that the two-gram dosing would keep Gunther and Klaus asleep well past that time frame.

Petra and Emma prepared a German feast in the kitchen of the Black Hole Project. The centerpiece of their meal was beef Sauerbraten. They had marinated a large rump roast in a mixture of vinegar, red wine, water, herbs, and spices for nearly a week before this night. They made a hearty gravy from roasting the beef and served it with potato dumplings. As an alternative to Sauerkraut, they made a traditional local Bavarian favorite called Bayrisch Kraut (literally Bavarian cabbage). Made of shredded cabbage, it was cooked in their beef stock with some pork lard, onion, and apples, then seasoned with vinegar. They also baked some fresh bread and made apple strudel for dessert. The aroma from their cooking extravaganza was enchanting. As they made the late dinner, they served Gunther and Klaus shots of Jägermeister and tall glasses of German wheat beer from nearby Erding, Germany.

Nearly two years prior, Petra had installed a German gramophone with a large-enough horn speaker to fill the black hole vault with sound. The gramophone played 78-rpm shellac records, and on this night, she was playing the song "Lili Marleen." The song, originally written in 1915 as a three-verse poem by Hans Leip, a schoolteacher from Hamburg, Germany, was named by combining the nickname of his friend's girlfriend, Lili, with the name of another friend, Marleen, who was a nurse. The poem was later published in 1937 with two more verses added. It was set to music in 1938 and recorded by Lale Andersen for the first time in 1939. Andersen was a German singer-songwriter and actress and by 1941, her version of song "Lili Marleen," which was a German love song, had become popular with both the Axis and the Allied forces. The song transcended the conflict to become World War II's biggest international hit. Petra and Emma came out of the kitchen with more shots and beer and to dance with Gunther and Klaus. As they played the song a second time, Petra announced that she needed to finish her work in the kitchen and get dinner served. Emma stayed with Klaus and Gunther. It was midnight.

Back in the kitchen alone, Petra became apprehensive about her next move as she fumbled through her purse to pull out the two vials of chloral hydrate and Jägermeister mixture that she had prepared. She pulled them out together with her right hand and as she did, she lost her grip on one of the vials and it dropped to the floor, broke and spilled. She quickly placed the other vial in her pocket. She grabbed a towel to clean up the spillage and as she did, Gunther came into the kitchen. Shaken and trying to regain her composure, she stayed down on her knees with her back to Gunther. He placed his hand on her back and she jumped a bit with surprise. Gunther enquired, "There you go, being clumsy again, what did you spill?"

"Oh, Gunther, you know me, just a little of the broth I'm using for the gravy. Sorry I jumped; I didn't know you were in here," she responded softly.

"Remember the night that you spilled your coffee and we first kissed? Maybe I should join you down there and see if I can get lucky again."

Nearly panicked but still sounding normal she replied, "No need for that, Gunther. You'll get lucky for sure after dinner tonight." She finished her clean-up, stood, and gave Gunther a hug and a kiss, careful not to allow any of the small glass shards from the broken vial to fall from her cleaning towel. "Now you go in the other room while I finish this surprise feast that we have prepared."

Gunther smiled, kissed her once more and complied by leaving the kitchen. Petra muttered to herself, shaking her head, "Shit, shit, shit! You can build a quantum physics time machine, but you can't hold onto a Mickey Finn!" She recovered and collected herself as she finished the dinner arrangements, then prepared four shots of Jägermeister, dividing the remaining vial of chloral hydrate mixture into two of the shots. She then placed those shots on the table in front of Gunther's and Klaus's plates. When she was ready, she called everyone in to eat. Petra and Emma had been very clever and careful to give the appearance of drinking a lot, but really minimizing their alcohol intake to remain stone sober. Halfway through the meal, with everyone laughing, drinking beer, and joyful to be fully ready for next day's visit by Hans Baur, Petra and Emma proposed a toast. "To the Führer, to the Black Hole, and to the Third Reich in 1975!" It was 12:30 AM on Wednesday, March 7, 1945, as Gunther and Klaus drank their Mickey Finn shots laced with chloral hydrate—in addition to all the alcohol they had consumed in the past two and a half hours.

Thirty minutes later, as they were eating dessert, both Gunther and Klaus were noticeably yawning, blinking heavily and starting to nod off just a bit. Petra and Emma took this as their cue to also pretend to be tired and served the men one more large shot of Jägermeister—which Gunther and Klaus gladly consumed, but Petra and Emma did not. At 1:15 AM, they guided their men to the bedrooms, got them into bed and undressed them. They took the two men's clothes into the Black Hole vault and scattered them on the lower racetrack, thinking that when the men woke up, they might be a bit disoriented and wonder just how the wild the night had gotten, once they found their clothing strewn about.

Petra made a strong pot of coffee and the two women dressed warmly in layers of clothing, anticipating their jaunt to the secret airfield at sunrise, when the temperature would be hovering in the mid-thirties (Fahrenheit). When they sat down to drink their coffee, Petra explained to Emma that she had dropped one of vials containing chloral hydrate, shattering it. Emma enquired, "What does that mean?"

"There were two grams dissolved in each of those vials which is on the high-end of the dosage range. As it turned out, Gunther and

Klaus each got half that, or a one-gram dose," Petra explained. "It was enough to get them to sleep, but maybe not enough to keep them asleep for a full six hours."

Emma declared, "Let's go tie them up, we can't take a chance on them following us!"

"We can't take the chance of them waking up while we are tying them up," Petra protested. "That could be disastrous! Besides, when they do wake up, it will take them a bit to get their bearings. And how would they know where you and I went? For all they know, you went to open the office in Berchtesgaden, and perhaps I went into town with you on an errand of some kind."

Emma answered with a mix of anxiety and determination, "Petra, you and I *have* to get to London. Our secrets could change the course of history. Let's get just a touch of rest now. We need to leave here at five AM."

CHAPTER ELEVEN:

ESCAPE TO LONDON

"It sometimes requires courage to fly from danger."
—Maria Edgeworth

Wednesday, March 7, 1945, at 6:15 AM local time,
the Black Hole Project top-secret landing field,
southwest of Salzburg, Austria

Guarding the entrance gate to the secret Black Hole Project landing field were Nazi Staff Sergeant (SS-Oberscharführer), Burnard "Bear" Faust, and Nazi Corporal (SS-Rottenführer) Seigfried "Sigurd" Haagan. Their guard shift started at midnight and ended at noon, and it was by far the most boring duty related to the entire Black Hole Project since its inception. At most, there had been one to two landings per month over the past two and half years, and there were only two twelve hour shifts of two men; a six-man rotation provided one-third time off for the guards selected for this task. Burnard's nickname "Bear" betrayed his physique, as he was a six-foot three-inch tall, burly man in his mid-thirties, weighing about 265 pounds and having thick, dark brown hair. Seigfried, called "Sigurd" was a blond haired, blue-eyed, slightly built man at five-foot nine, weighing 165 pounds, and in his early twenties. Their guard "shack" at the entrance gate for the landing field was actually a twenty-foot by twenty-foot cabin with a kitchenette, bathroom, wood-burning stove, sofa, chairs, and a working desk with three phones. One of the phones was a direct line to the Black Hole, the second was a direct line to Klaus's (and Emma's) office in Berchtesgaden, and the third was a general phone line.

The secret Black Hole Project landing field was just inside the Austrian border, due north of Berchtesgaden and southwest of Salzburg, Austria, which had been occupied and annexed by the Third Reich in March 1938. It was a leisurely thirty-minute drive from Emma's office in Berchtesgaden to the landing field under normal driving conditions. Emma and Petra had lucked out on this morning because the sky was mostly clear with scattered clouds, and it was a "balmy" forty-one degrees outside. Sunrise would occur at about 6:40 AM.

Emma and Petra arrived at the landing field's guardhouse and entrance gate at 6:15 AM, driving Emma's office car: a 1939 Mercedes-Benz 230 four-door sedan. Emma rolled down her window and greeted Nazi SS Staff Sergeant Burnard "Bear" Faust as he approached the car. "Good morning, Bear, we have a big day today! Gruppenführer Hans Baur is flying in here this morning with the Führer's personal airplane, Immelmann II, bearing the flight numbers D-2600. He is scheduled to land at sunrise, and we are here to pick him up and take him to the Black Hole."

Bear responded, "Good morning, Emma. Good morning, Petra. You know the drill; I have to inspect the car before I can let you through the gate."

Emma nodded. "Be our guest, Bear. If you find any loose food, it's yours!"

"Very funny," Bear replied as he looked in the front seat at the two of them. Then he glanced at the back seat, and finally, he opened and inspected the trunk. As Bear was inspecting the trunk, Nazi Corporal Seigfried "Sigurd" Haagan came out of the guard house and approached Emma's car window. "Hi, Emma. Hi, Petra. What are you two doing here so early this morning?"

Emma answered his question with a question. "What do you mean by 'so early this morning' Sigurd?"

Well, Obergruppenführer Klaus Richter was here early yesterday afternoon to tell us and the rest of the guard detail that Gruppenführer Hans Baur was flying in here about mid-morning today, and that he would be personally coming to pick him up."

Emma's heart started to race, but she managed to stay calm and appear confident. "Oh, yes, of course. We received notice late yesterday afternoon that Gruppenführer Baur changed his schedule to arrive earlier, at sunrise. Given the tighter schedule, Obergruppenführer Richter and Herr Brandt have last minute work to complete at the Black Hole and requested that Petra and I come to pick up Gruppenführer Baur."

"Well if that's the case, then you two are welcome to wait here in the guard house with us until the plane arrives," Sigurd offered.

Despite Emma's courage and poise, she could feel herself beginning to mentally unravel. Sensing the danger of the moment, Petra jumped in, "That is so kind of you, Sigurd, but Emma and I have to rehearse what Obergruppenführer Richter and Herr Brandt instructed us to discuss with Gruppenführer Baur upon his arrival and on the drive to take him back to the Black Hole. We are going to park out by the hanger at the end of the runway and wait there while we rehearse together."

Bear closed the trunk and came around to join Sigurd alongside Emma's car door. "You are all clear and I didn't find any Bauernfrühstück, or my favorite Apfelkuchen during my search," Bear joked, referring to a farmer's breakfast and apple custard cake.

Emma was beginning to recover, but Petra answered, "Aw, poor Bear! Next time we come so early, we'll bring you and Sigurd a hearty breakfast. That's a promise!"

"I'm holding you to it," Bear responded. Looking over his shoulder, he opened the gate, allowing them entrance to the landing field. The landing field was simple, consisting of a single 2,300-foot-long concrete runway running southeast to northwest. A bright red and white weather sock rippled at the end of the field. A medium-sized protective hanger to temporarily shelter incoming aircraft had been built, and an outdoor fuel depot with an above ground fuel storage tank sat next to the hanger.

Emma smiled and waved at Bear and Sigurd as she drove through the gate and headed out toward the hanger at the end of the runway. She looked at Petra and gave a big sigh of relief. "Oh my god, thank you, Petra!" she exclaimed. "I was getting too flustered and starting to panic."

Petra nodded. "I could tell you were struggling, and I knew that I had to come up with something. That rescue plane better be on time, or we're going to have to come up with even more crazy excuses!"

Wednesday, March 7, 1945, at 6:30 AM local time, the Black Hole Project secret landing field, southwest of Salzburg, Austria and in the air over southeast Austria

Back inside the guard house, Sigurd wasn't totally buying the women's explanation for the change in plans. "Bear, Obergruppenführer Richter specifically spelled out the description of Gruppenführer Hans Baur's airplane and the details of his arrival today, telling us how important his visit was and that he would personally be here."

Bear responded, "My young corporal, everyone knows that Obergruppenführer Richter and Emma, along with Herr Brandt and Petra, are all friends and lovers. But if you want to question those women, then you have my permission to call Obergruppenführer Richter and/ or Herr Brandt, using our direct phone lines to Richter's Berchtesgaden office or to the Black Hole. But just know, you might piss somebody off." Sigurd, now sitting at the work desk with his hand on the phone to the Berchtesgaden office, pondered Bear's comments for a few minutes.

In the air over southeast Austria, twenty minutes out, were three British SOE operatives flying an exact replica of Hitler's personal Junkers Ju 52/3m airplane named Immelmann II, bearing the flight numbers D-2600. Pilot Addison "Ed" Ratliff, co-pilot Philip "Phil" Dawson, and commando Lawrence "Larry" Baker had flown covert missions together before and were handpicked for this bold and risky rescue operation, which had been very hastily devised and code-named "Fräulein Freedom." They had deliberately minimized the necessary crew and kept the weight of the plane to a minimum so as to maximize their speed and efficiency getting in and out of the secret landing field; they were not expecting major interference, given the mission intel provided. The three men were not heavily armed, but they were carrying British Lanchester submachine guns manufactured by the Sterling Armaments Company, using 50-round detachable box magazines containing 9×19mm Parabellum cartridges.

The German commercial airline Deutsche Lufthansa had begun flying the Junkers Ju-52/3m aircraft on heavily traveled commercial routes, such as Berlin to London and Berlin to Rome, in late 1932. Twenty-five countries throughout Europe, North and South America purchased the aircraft for commercial use during the 1930s, which made finding one for this mission relatively easy. The iconic prop-driven tri-motor airplane had three BMW 132T radial piston engines, developing 715 horsepower each. It had a wingspan of 97 feet and measured 62 feet long from nose to tail. The Ju-52/3m was a rugged, reliable aircraft with good handling. It could land as slow as 60 mph and take off at 62-75 mph, giving it good short-field landing capabilities. The all-metal plane was easily recognized, due not only to its three-engine configuration but also to a box-like, corrugated fuselage that gave it an almost unfinished appearance. The SOE had done a superb job of making this plane look like Hitler's own.

Sigurd overcame his momentary reluctance and tried calling the phone line connecting them to the Berchtesgaden office. No one answered. Then he tried the line connecting them directly to the Black Hole. Someone always answered at the Black Hole: usually Gunther Brandt, because he virtually lived there. In the Black Hole Project vault, the phone was ringing. Klaus Richter thought he was dreaming that a phone was ringing, but he couldn't drag himself there fast enough to answer it. He tripped and fell as he answered the phone, and the impact of the fall helped him to somewhat regain consciousness. Klaus, feeling very disoriented and confused, also noticed that he was butt naked as he held the phone receiver in his hand and stared at it. Sigurd heard the commotion and was startled by how loud Obergruppenführer Richter's voice was as he shouted, "Richter here! Who the hell is this, and what do you want?! What time is it?!"

Oh, no! I should have never made this call, Sigurd thought. "Sir, it's Corporal Seigfried Haagan at the Black Hole landing field. It's 6:30 AM, and Frau Hoffman and Frau Vogel are here to pick up Gruppenführer Hans Baur. They say that his plane is arriving at sunrise. I am so sorry to bother you, but you told us that Baur would arrive mid-morning and that you would personally pick him up. I thought I would just double check with you that everything is okay."

Klaus was still not fully connected to reality, but he sensed that he drank too much the night before and something had changed. "I will be there in thirty minutes, give or take. Don't do anything; wait for me to get there."

Sigurd enquired, "Shall I let Frau Hoffman and Frau Vogel know that you are on the way?"

"No, I will speak with them when I get there. That is all, Corporal." Klaus hung up the phone and walked naked into the Black Hole Project vault. Seeing his clothing scattered about the floor of the machine's racetrack, along with Gunther's clothes, he hurriedly got dressed and took a quick look in the kitchen. Emma's and Petra's empty coffee cups were on the counter and there was still some lukewarm coffee in the pot. Klaus took the lid off the pot and guzzled down the bitter brew. His emotions were not altogether clear yet; he wasn't quite sure if he was angry, afraid, or embarrassed.

Klaus went to Gunther's bedroom and found him sound asleep, snoring loudly. He shook Gunther hard, noting he was also naked, and only half-covered with the sheets. Gunther was slow to wake up and Klaus yelled, "Get the hell out of bed, Gunther! It's Wednesday morning, and the women are at the landing strip to pick up Baur. Something is wrong! My brain feels like it is about to explode, and I am headed over to the landing field in a hurry!"

Gunther groggily responded, "Shit, my head feels like it is on fire! What the hell did we drink last night? You go ahead, and I'll get myself and this place ready for Gruppenführer Baur's arrival."

Klaus turned and headed out of the Black Hole in a rush, shouting at Gunther as he was leaving, "If you're wondering, your clothes are all flung around the racetrack!" Klaus had driven his personal car for this day to pick up the VIP, Hans Baur. Using his high-level Nazi connections to make the acquisition, Klaus was driving a 1936 silver and black Mercedes-Benz 500K Cabriolet A. The K designation stood for Kompressor (German for supercharger), which was only fitted to these performance cars. Slamming the throttle pedal to the floor engaged the Roots-type supercharger, prompting the five-liter, straight-eight engine to produce 160 horsepower, making the car capable of over

100 mph. The 500K used a world's first independent suspension with a double wishbone front axle, double-joint swing axle in the rear, and separate damping coil springs at every wheel location. Klaus's model had the optional five-speed transmission, of course. He was shifting gears and driving like a madman, trying to set a speed record to the secret landing field while simultaneously trying to clear his head with the window down and the cold wind blowing in his face.

At 6:50 AM, ten minutes after sunrise, British SOE pilot Ed Ratliff and co-pilot Phil Dawson arrived at the coordinates they had been given and spotted the lone airstrip below. Dawson looked over his shoulder and shouted to commando Larry Baker, "Get ready, Larry! We are going in hot and fast, and as soon as we circle at the end of the runway, you get that door wide open. Be ready to provide cover for those two women and pull them on board ASAP. Phil will cover your back once we're on the ground." Ed flew past the runway from the south and steeply banked to come in and land from the northwest. He could see the hanger at the other end of the landing field, and Emma's parked four-door sedan.

It was a quiet morning and everyone at the field heard Ed and his team fly over and turn to make his landing approach. Emma and Petra hugged each other with excitement and relief. Staring out the front windshield of their car, the two women saw the plane turn and line up with the runway. Both Bear and Sigurd grabbed binoculars and promptly confirmed it was a Junker's Ju-52/3m, fitting the description and bearing the flight numbers D-2600. Sigurd commented, "Well, damn; those women knew what they were talking about. And that Gruppenführer Baur is not wasting any time getting that plane down on the ground."

Just as the plane touched down on the runway, Klaus arrived, barreling in at high speed and skidding to a screeching stop at the guard house. Emma and Petra were getting out of their car, and Emma was the first to see Klaus's car in the distance. She shouted at Petra, "Klaus just pulled up to the guard gate! We have to run for it!" The plane came to the end of the runway near the hanger and turned sixty yards away from Emma and Petra's position. Commando Larry Baker threw the port side door open and scanned the field of view with his Lanchester submachine gun. Emma and Petra started to run for the plane.

When Klaus came to a stop and looked out onto the field, he saw what he first thought was Baur landing in the Führer's airplane, with Emma and Petra parked in Emma's office car waiting by the hanger. He started to address Bear and Sigurd as they came out of the guardhouse and walked toward his car. Bear, glancing out at the runway, stopped cold in his tracks and said, "What the hell?!" Klaus looked back at the runway and could not believe his eyes. Both Emma and Petra were sprinting toward the plane, which had turned to face northwest back down the runway and had kept its engines running. Klaus had perfect vision and could see the outline of a man with a gun standing at the open port side door, waving Emma and Petra on.

It dawned on Klaus what was happening, and it hit him like a ton of bricks. He was carrying his Luger P08 pistol, but knew he needed more firepower. He ordered Sigurd to give him his MP 40 submachine gun and told Bear to shoot the fuel depot next to the hanger until it exploded. Sigurd opened the gate while Bear ran toward the fuel depot storage tank and opened fire, emptying his machine gun's entire clip into the above ground fuel storage tank. As soon as the gate was open, Klaus floored his Mercedes-Benz 500K, making the Junkers Ju-52/3m in the distance his target.

Emma was running ahead of Petra and twenty yards from the plane when the fuel storage tank near the hanger exploded with a giant fireball. The forceful shock wave of the blast knocked Petra off her feet and sent her crashing to the ground. She yelled for Emma who stopped, turned, and went back to help her friend get up. Emma put her arm around Petra and helped her hobble to the plane. Ed Ratliff could see Klaus coming through the gate in his Mercedes and he fired up all three of the BMW 715 horsepower radial piston engines and stood hard on the brakes. Ed yelled back to the cabin, with his usual British wit, "I'm not being funny, but I haven't got all day." Larry Baker pulled Petra on board first and then Emma. The moment they were on board, Baker yelled, "GO, GO, GO!" He and Phil Dawson fired their guns at Klaus through the open door. Seeing the flashing guns, Klaus immediately swerved, which slowed him down, but he evaded the bullets. The moment that Ed released the brakes and pushed his three radial engines to full power, it became a race between the Junker's Ju-52 getting off the ground and Klaus coming at them from an angle to the left and behind them on a collision course.

Klaus, still a tiny bit foggy but now adrenaline charged, muttered to himself, "This has all got to be a bad dream, goddammit!" He had to accelerate, shift through his gears, and steer at the same time, making him unable to shoot at the escaping Junker's Ju-52 with the Nazi MP 40 submachine gun sitting in his lap. He was determined to ram the plane with his car and prevent it from taking off. By this time, Bear and Sigurd were watching this "death race" from the entrance gate and silently cheering for Klaus to win.

In the pilot's seat of the plane, Ed Ratliff knew beyond a doubt that he was in the race for his life. The moment that Larry Baker had yelled "GO," Ed pushed the aircraft and its engines for all they were worth. When he had released the brakes, they surged forward with such force as to throw Larry, Petra, and Emma toward the back of the plane's cabin, while Phil Dawson had managed to hang on for dear life. As they accelerated down the runway, Dawson clawed his way back into the co-pilot's seat. Dawson yelled at Ed above the roar of the engines at full power, "If we make it, it's only because we thought ahead to keep our weight down!"

Ed, glancing back over his left shoulder at the oncoming Klaus in the 500K Mercedes-Benz, yelled back, "Call out our speed, Phil; the moment we hit seventy-five miles per hour, I am pulling up *hard*! And *hell yes*, we are going to make it!"

Phil complied, loudly shouting the speed increases every few miles per hour. "Sixty-three...sixty-seven...seventy-two...*seventy-seven!*" Ed pulled back hard on the wheel to make the plane defy gravity. In the back of the plane, Larry Baker was trying to help get both Emma and Petra off the floor and seated, then get to a window to check on Klaus's status.

Klaus had already shifted into fourth gear and was approaching at an oblique angle, trying to judge if he could or would make contact with the aircraft before it got too far off the ground. As he hit 75 mph, he decided it was now or never. Grabbing the MP 40 submachine gun with his left hand, Klaus kept his foot glued to the accelerator pedal. The front end of his Mercedes-Benz 500K missed the undersurface of the ascending Junker's Ju-52 by inches, but his roof scraped across the belly of the plane. He managed to fire a burst with his machine gun into the underbelly of the plane. The friction of the roof of his car grinding against the plane's underside violently shook the barely airborne and ascending aircraft, and also caused Klaus to temporarily lose control of his Mercedes-Benz. He dropped the submachine gun on the runway, grabbed the steering wheel with both hands, and braked hard as he emerged from underneath the plane. The rear end of his Mercedes swung counterclockwise and when he hit the grass on the other side of the runway, the car was drifting sideways almost parallel to the plane. Emma was sitting on the starboard side looking out her window, and as Klaus's car swung around, their eyes met. His eyes were burning like the fires of hell, and hers showed no emotion whatsoever. She was on her way to London.

CHAPTER TWELVE:

BAD LOVE MOSQUITOES OVER LONDON

"Flying has torn apart the relationship of space and time:
it uses our old clock but with new yardsticks."
—Charles A. Lindbergh

*Saturday, April 14, 1945, at 8:00 AM local time, Royal Air Force
105 Squadron, No. 8 Group, Pathfinders landing field,
village of Bourn, in South Cambridgeshire, England*

Following our Bad Love Gang group meeting at the White Hole Project on the evening of Sunday, December 21, 1975, Bowmar, Bucky, Pumpkin, Waldo, and I planned the details of the group's time-travel operation to go find Hannah Lieb in early 1945 and get the vial of gene therapy medicine to her. We had identified a few certain things about this undertaking, based on the cues and tips that Blue Nova One had doled out to me and Bowmar. She had only shared a few clues, and knowing how intelligent she was, Bowmar and I concluded that she had told us exactly what we were required to know. We understood that we needed to use our connections to arrange a meeting with Winston Churchill in London on Sunday, April 22, 1945. That meeting seemed like the cornerstone of making this mission a success.

It was clear that Churchill had valuable information to share with us that somehow involved the new-found destiny of the Denver Project and our White Hole Project time travels. During our time in London, the group would stay at the renowned Goring Hotel.

We also knew that we needed to learn how to fly the famous British-built de Havilland Mosquito, also called the "Wooden Wonder," or "Mossie." The legendary Mosquito had gained glory in several bold bombing operations, the most famous being Operation Jericho in February 1944. Nine Mosquito bombers, flying out of a British Royal Air Force (RAF) base in Hertfordshire, England, attacked the Amiens Prison in German-occupied France on the edge of the Somme River Valley. The plan was to try and free French Resistance prisoners held by the Nazis. The Mosquitos came in at a very low altitude, accurately delivering low-level waves of bombs that effectively destroyed the prison buildings' outer and inner walls, as well as the Nazi guards' barracks. A total of 255 allied prisoners escaped through the breaches in the buildings and walls; however, 182 were soon recaptured. The Resistance prisoners who did successfully escape to freedom were later able to expose over sixty Nazi Gestapo agents and informers, significantly impacting the German counter-intelligence force.

On January 30, 1943, dodging in and out of clouds at 400 mph, Royal Air Force Mosquito bombers from the 105 Squadron howled across Berlin in their first daylight bombing attack on Germany's capital. Nazi Reichsmarschall Hermann Göring, the Commander of the German Luftwaffe, was giving a speech at the time of the attack, extolling and commemorating the 10th anniversary of the Nazis seizing political power in Germany. The bombers banked and streaked towards their intended target: Berlin's Haus des Rundfunks, the headquarters building of the German State Broadcasting Company. As Göring's microphone went live and he began to speak, the unmistakable roar of the incoming British Mosquitoes became audible over the radio. The broadcast engineers faced an impossible choice; they could relay the embarrassing sounds of the British air raid, unfolding live, or they could shut down the transmission. In Reichsmarschall Göring's moment of glory, they cut the live feed and dove for cover, taking his speech off the air. Years prior, Göring had promised the people of Germany that no enemy aircraft would ever cross the country's borders. He was beside himself with anger that he had been made to look like a fool.

In preparation for this mission to 1945 Europe, Bucky and I used the White Hole Project to travel back to the Read House Hotel in Chattanooga, Tennessee on Friday, April 13, 1945. We had been there on this same day, the day after President Roosevelt's untimely death, during our prior mission as the Bad Love Tigers to secure the White Hole Project and Area 51. On that mission, we had left the hotel at 8:15 AM. This time, we clocked it to reenter the hotel at 8:30 AM and told the front desk that Bucky had forgotten something in his room. Bucky then used his direct line and contacted Vannevar Bush with his orders as required by the Denver Project.

Bucky proceeded to detail specific instructions for Vannevar to get us access to train to fly de Havilland Mosquitoes at the Royal Air Force 105 Squadron, No.8 Group, the Pathfinders in the village of Bourn, in South Cambridgeshire, England. We were scheduled to arrive early the following day. Bucky also explained to Vannevar that he needed to call President Truman on or after Tuesday, April 17th and have him arrange for a meeting between us and Winston Churchill in London on Sunday, April 22, 1945. Churchill should place the details of his preferred meeting time and place in a confidential envelope and send it to the front desk at the Goring Hotel. Finally, Vannevar needed to make reservations for the Bad Love Gang to stay at the Goring Hotel in London from Saturday, April 21, 1945, until Saturday, April 28, 1945. Of all the people involved in the White Hole Project, Vannevar Bush was the best equipped to understand without hesitation the strange demands and curious scheduling needs of the Bad Love Gang time travelers, as requested by Bucky and the Denver Project.

Bucky, Pumpkin, Willy, and I were the first of the Bad Love Gang to depart from the White Hole Project in Oak Ridge, Tennessee on Saturday, December 27, 1975. Bowmar was teaching Spaghetti Head, the Runt, and Mary how to run the controls of the White Hole Project, and Waldo was there as well to see us leave. The four of us who were experienced pilots were going early to train to fly de Havilland Mosquitoes. The rest of the group would meet us one week later at the Goring Hotel in London. We were zapped by the White Hole to the Royal Air Force 105 Squadron, No. 8 Group Pathfinders landing field in South Cambridgeshire, England, landing there on Saturday, April 14, 1945, at 8:00 AM local time. Bourn has existed as a settlement for over a thousand years. Landing there put us about sixty miles north of the Goring Hotel in London.

Throughout growing up in the 1960s, I had loved watching movies about World War II, especially anything that pertained to WWII Allied aircraft and airpower supremacy. One of my all-time favorite movies was *633 Squadron*, a 1964 British war film directed by Walter Grauman and starring Cliff Robertson and George Chakiris. It was the first WWII aviation movie to be shot in color and Panavision widescreen. The plot got underway when Royal Norwegian Navy Lieutenant Erik Bergman, a Norwegian Resistance leader (played by George Chakiris) traveled to Great Britain to report the secret location of a German V-2 rocket fuel plant. The movie's fictitious Royal Air Force No. 633 Squadron was subsequently assigned to destroy it. The squadron was led by Wing Commander Roy Grant (played by Cliff Robertson), a former Eagle

Squadron pilot who was an American serving in the RAF before the US entered the war.

The Nazi rocket fuel plant was strategically located in a seemingly impenetrable location beneath an overhanging cliff at the end of a long, narrow fjord lined with rows of defensive German anti-aircraft guns. The only way to destroy the plant was to fly the 633 Squadron's fast and highly maneuverable de Havilland Mosquito fighter-bombers through the defended fjord, bombing the crap out of that cliff until it collapsed and buried the facility for good. The squadron trained in Scotland, where there were narrow glens mimicking the fjord.

The Norwegian Resistance was tasked with destroying the anti-aircraft defenses lining the fjord immediately before the scheduled attack. However, the Resistance fighters were ambushed and killed, leaving the rows of Nazi defensive anti-aircraft guns intact. Upon learning of the failed attempt to silence the defensive guns, the British RAF vice-marshal radioed and gave Wing Commander Grant the option to abort the mission. Grant courageously decided to press on, even with the odds of victory stacked against him and his daring Mosquito squadron. The action scenes were incredible for the 1960s era of movies as the Mosquitoes flew through a hail of Nazi anti-aircraft fire to reach their target. The factory was destroyed, but at the cost of the entire squadron.

I loved the background music during the movie, especially the **"Theme to 633 Squadron,"** played by The New Zealand Symphony Orchestra. As the four of us traveled through the White Hole time tunnel to our 1945 destination of the RAF 105 Squadron, No. 8 Group Pathfinders landing field in the village of Bourn, England, the **"Theme to 633 Squadron"** was pounding loudly in my music brain. While the music was playing, I had a dream or vision of flying a de Havilland Mosquito fighter-bomber on a night mission right past London's Big Ben at low altitude. I was rudely awakened or shaken out of my vision when we landed in a field next to the Pathfinders' runway. We gathered ourselves up and headed to the commander's office.

The Pathfinders were assigned as target-marking squadrons in RAF Bomber Command during World War II. No. 8 Group operated at night, using the British-designed Oboe radar system to guide the main bomber squadrons to their targets. The Mosquitoes led the way and would locate and mark strategic bombing targets with flares so that the main bomber force could properly aim at their night targets and increase the accuracy of their bombing. They flew the B Mk XVI Mosquitoes, the most impressive of the war-time bomber Mosquitoes with a pressurized cabin that gave it an operational ceiling of 35,000 feet and powerful twin Merlin 72 engines, each with 1,710 combat horsepower. These Mosquitoes had the bulging bomb bay needed to carry a 4,000-pound cookie, or blockbuster bomb: the largest conventional bombs used in World War II by the Royal Air Force. The term *blockbuster* was originally a name coined by the press and referred to a single bomb that had enough explosive power to destroy an entire city block or large building. Alternatively, with the help of an Avro bomb carrier, the same Mosquito bomb bay could carry six 500-pound bombs.

Vannevar Bush had immediately used his high-level military connections to get the word of our impending arrival to Air Chief Marshal Sir Arthur Travers Harris of the Royal Air Force Bomber Command. Known as "Bomber" Harris by the British press, he then contacted Air Vice-Marshal Donald Bennett, who had led the Pathfinder Force (No. 8 Group RAF) since July 1942. Bennett was an Australian aviation pioneer and bomber pilot who rose to be the youngest air vice-marshal in the Royal Air Force. He was an outstanding pilot, a superb navigator, and reportedly was also capable of getting down and dirty while overhauling an aircraft engine. In July 1942, British Bomber Command had started making nighttime raids deep into Germany, but these early bombing missions were largely ineffective because only about a quarter of the bomb loads were delivered on target, which at that time was defined as coming within three miles of the aim point. Bennet worked uncompromisingly and relentlessly to improve night-time bombing accuracy standards, and he was in command of a Path-finder Force of nineteen air squadrons when we arrived. Bennett was not a popular leader; known to be personally difficult and somewhat aloof, he had earned respect from his crews but little affection.

Bennet was there to meet us as we walked into the commander's office. Two RAF pilots who had been sitting and talking with Bennett stood at attention when we entered the room. Bucky was dressed as USAAF Captain Jack Smith, Pumpkin (Darby Nelson) and Willy (Billy Blanchert) were dressed as USAAF lieutenants, and I (Bubble Butt) kept my wartime persona as USAAF Colonel Kevin Schafer. Being the "ranking" officer of our group, I introduced the four of us using our proper names but had initially planned to let Bucky and Pumpkin do most of the talking. Bennet started the discussion with an Aussie accent and a stern glare at me. The first words out of his mouth were, "You look too young to be a Colonel there, Schafer. What's your story?"

I thinly smiled and replied, "I get that comment a lot, Air Marshal Bennet." Before I could go further, Bucky spoke up. He had a serious expression, staring at Bennet as he spoke.

"I have worked in USAAF Special Ops since 1942, and Colonel Schafer saved my life during a top-secret mission into Nazi-occupied Poland this past November. He was promoted based on his heroic actions during that operation. Don't underestimate him, Air Marshal."

Bennet's posture eased somewhat, and he calmly replied, "Oh, hell; I'm twenty years younger than all the other RAF group commanders and find myself at odds with the RAF 'gentlemen's club' on a regular basis. They all think that I'm too young and brash, not to mention Australian, but I get the job done. That pleases Air Chief Marshal Harris and makes him look good. I understand that you men are here on another top-secret mission and are scheduled to meet with the Bulldog himself, Winston Churchill, a week from tomorrow. These two men work for the British 'Ministry of Ungentlemanly Warfare,' AKA Special Operations Executive." He then introduced RAF Captain Addison "Ed" Ratliff, and RAF Lieutenant Philip "Phil" Dawson, and we all shook hands.

I commented, "The 'Ministry of Ungentlemanly Warfare' has a nice ring to it. We work for the Denver Project, but all of us are members of the Bad Love Gang and tend to answer to our nicknames. I'm Bubble Butt, or BB, Captain Smith is Bucky, Lieutenant Nelson is Pumpkin, and Lieutenant Blanchert is Willy. We're all pilots, here at Bourn for a week of intensive training to fly the Mosquitoes—although Pumpkin does already have some experience flying the Mossie."

Ed Ratliff spoke next. "The SOE keeps their cards close to their vests, but we started training for a special ops mission ten days ago, flying Mossies through deep canyons and dropping dummy four thousand-pound cookies at altitudes as low as fifteen hundred feet against hillsides. We were told late yesterday that you four blokes were coming to train with us. Both Phil and I were specifically chosen for this assignment, but we don't know what the target is or where it is located. We're all going to find out next Sunday; we will be meeting Churchill with you and your group. In the meantime, Phil and I are assigned to work hand in hand with you nonstop, practicing with the Mosquito Wooden Wonders for the next week. We've got a lot of work to do; are you chaps ready to fly?"

Pumpkin replied, "Gentlemen, we were all born to fly. How about we take some Bad Love Mosquitoes over London on our way out of here to make this mission training bloody well blinding!"

Bennet put his hands on his hips and finished the discussion. "Welcome to the Pathfinders, men. Whatever the hell you are asked to do, make us proud."

CHAPTER THIRTEEN:

THE GORING

"My tastes are simple: I am easily satisfied with the best."
—Winston Churchill

Saturday, April 21, 1945, at 10:00 AM local time,
The Goring Hotel, 15 Beeston Place, Central London

The Goring Hotel was founded by Otto Richard Goring, AKA O.R. Goring. Born in 1869 in Saxony, Germany, he moved from Germany to London in 1893 and become a banquet waiter at the Hotel Metropole. A brilliant visionary, Otto Goring saw great promise in a plot of land situated at the Buckingham Palace end of what is known as Beeston Place. He obtained the land on a 99-year lease from the Duke of Westminster. After clearing the land for construction by removing a public house and several cottages, the path was laid clear for the last grand hotel to be built during the reign of King Emperor Edward VII, or the Edwardian era. Otto Richard Goring opened the Goring Hotel on March 2, 1910, and it was declared to be the first hotel in the world in which every guest room had a private, en suite bathroom and central heating. When it opened in 1910, there were 50 guest bedrooms on four floors.

With the outbreak of World War I, the Goring Hotel interestingly became the command center in 1914 for the chief of the Allied Forces. The WWI Allied War effort was being run from the Goring kitchen, and a direct telephone link was established between General John "Black Jack" Pershing and American President Woodrow Wilson. After WWI ended, O.R. Goring purchased the freehold of the property for 19,000 pounds sterling and subsequently made plans to extend the building further to the side and add a fifth floor, which would ultimately result in 96 guest rooms. In 1921, O.R. Goring introduced air-conditioning to the Goring Hotel by installing an enormous fan on the roof that could pipe air into every room. Vacuum cleaners were attached via outlets in the skirting boards and reportedly, some guests' underwear embarrassingly got sucked out into the air and blown across London! O.R.'s son, Otto Gustav (O.G.) Goring, was appointed hotel manager in 1924, becoming managing director of the hotel in 1926. That same year, the new hotel wing and restaurant envisioned by his father were opened.

During the coronation of George VI and his wife Elizabeth as king and queen of the United Kingdom at Westminster Abbey in May 1937, the Norwegian crown prince stayed at the Goring Hotel. He rather notably shared his fondness for the Goring and was quoted as saying, "At Buckingham Palace, I have to share a bath with five people! Here, I have one to myself." In 1944, a Fox film crew stayed at the Goring Hotel on their way to board landing craft for the Normandy D-Day Invasion. That crew famously made the first ever color footage of WWII action. On Saturday, April 21, 1945, at 10:00 AM local time, the Bad Love Gang checked into the historic Goring Hotel. We were met at the front desk by Otto Gustav Goring bearing an envelope marked *Confidential* in his hand, addressed to us from none other than British Prime Minister Winston Churchill. The clandestine purpose and top-secret nature of our 1945 London visit required that our group's stay there would never be recorded in the annals of the Goring Hotel history books.

Bucky, Pumpkin, Willy, and I had finished our week of intensive flight training with the Mosquitoes in conjunction with RAF Captain Addison (Ed) Ratliff, and RAF Lieutenant Philip (Phil) Dawson on Friday and told them that we looked forward to seeing them again at Sunday's meeting with Churchill. The four of us took an army Jeep from the airbase at Bourn and drove to the Goring Hotel on Saturday morning. Spaghetti Head, Mary, and the Runt had used the White Hole Project to send Bowmar, Waldo, Meatball, Ben, Crazy Ike, Goondoggy, the Pud, Crisco, Cleopatra, Tater, and the Black Box to landing coordinates in the southwest corner of St. James's Park. That location was only a short walk to Goring Hotel. Everyone was dressed in the same WWII military attire that we used on our epic April 1945, road trip across America to safeguard the security and integrity of the White Hole Project and Area 51. It was perfect timing for all of us as we met in the Goring Hotel lobby, high fived and group hugged. Bucky, as head of the Denver Project, and our USAAF two-star major general, Waldo, approached Otto Gustav Goring at the front desk.

Bucky announced, "I'm Captain Jack Smith, and there are fourteen of us here to check in for a one week stay."

"I am Otto G. Goring, son of our hotel founder, Otto R. Goring, and I have received word regarding your stay here," Otto replied. "I have a letter to give to you from Prime Minister Churchill's office." He handed the envelope marked *Confidential* to Bucky and continued, "Churchill told us if we could manage to take care of his mother and the queen, we should be able to take care of your Bad Love group." He paused, smiled, then said, "I also received a very brief call directly from the new American President Harry Truman, imploring me to look after you, Captain Smith, and your group. I have to say, we haven't had that kind of a request from an American president since we opened our doors in 1910." He handed out fourteen room keys and stated, "Whatever you need, let me or the staff know, and we will be here to assist you."

Waldo faced Otto and enquired, "What can you tell me about Churchill?"

Otto replied, "Well, sir, it is not a secret that we actually did take good care of his mother. Back in 1919, Lady Randolph Churchill took up residence here at the Goring for a while; that was when we made his acquaintance and got to know him. He is fond of the Goring and continues to hold important meetings with allied leaders here in our Silver Room from time to time. He has courage, perseverance, and a tremendous sense of history and destiny. When all of Europe thought that Adolph Hitler could be appeased to keep the peace, Churchill maintained that 'An appeaser is one who feeds a crocodile, hoping it will eat him last.' One thing that we all have observed is his keen wit and quick sense of humor. For example, earlier this year when Field Marshall Viscount Montgomery said to him, 'I neither drink nor smoke and am a hundred percent fit', Churchill's reply was: 'I drink and smoke and I am *two* hundred percent fit!' Matching his wit is a tall order; if you are to meet with him, you certainly will never forget the encounter."

"I want to take a gift for him from our group that he will enjoy. Since he likes to dine here, Otto, what is his favorite cigar? And specialty drink?" Waldo asked.

"He loves Cuban cigars, namely Romeo y Julieta and La Aroma de Cuba, but Romeo y Julieta is his favorite. He has recently gained affection for the Armenian Ararat Cognac, which was offered to him by Stalin during the Yalta Conference this past February. I will prepare a gift for you to give to him consisting of a box of Cuban Romeo y Julieta cigars and a bottle of Ararat Cognac. I will have it delivered to your room later today."

Crazy Ike overheard Waldo's exchange with Otto and blurted out, "I hope my key works in your door, Waldo, because that sounds like a gift that I'd like to sample first to see if it would meet with Winnie's approval!"

Waldo turned and adroitly replied, "Listen, Lieutenant Eichenmuller, if you so much as touch that gift, I'm going to re-circumcise you with my combat knife and sterilize my surgical bed with that Cognac."

The Bad Love males grabbed their crotches, making faces and feigning to be in terrible pain while the group at large cackled at Waldo's comeback. Pumpkin clutched Crazy Ike's shoulder and using a deeper voice (sounding a bit like Sean Connery as James Bond) in his heaviest British accent cried, "No rumpy pumpy for *you* on this trip, my shagless girlfriend!" Pumpkin's face turned bright orange and Crazy Ike's face turned beet red while we all tried to contain a fit of laughter.

Bucky then announced, "Everyone go find your rooms, drop off your stuff, and meet in my suite in fifteen minutes." We all did as directed and reconvened in Bucky's suite to discuss our next steps. Bucky, Pumpkin, Willy, and I brought the group up to speed about our week of training to fly the Wooden Wonder de Haviland Mosquitoes. We opened the Black Box, and I snatched my Marantz boom box and shoebox of cassette tapes while Crisco grabbed her camera. Then Bucky opened the confidential envelope from Churchill and read its contents out loud to the group. *"Dear Captain Smith; I shall be most interested to meet with you and your Denver Project colleagues tomorrow, Sunday, at two thirty PM. We will convene in my Cabinet War Room, located beneath the Treasury Building at the Clive Steps, King Charles Street, across from the east side of St. James Park. I have invited a few additional guests. After speaking with your President Truman, I trust you can find your way to the meeting. Enjoy the benefits of the Goring Hotel and get some rest before our meeting. We will have much to discuss. Sincerely, Winston Churchill.'"*

I wondered out loud, "Doesn't two thirty seem late in the day to have a meeting?"

Reminding us of his southern heritage, Tater bellowed, "That man Churchill is probably busier than a one-legged cat in a sandbox!"

We all busted out laughing at Tater. Bowmar gave us a dose of history and reality. "I studied Churchill's rather unorthodox routine, which was paradoxically effective and allowed him to accomplish an awe-inspiring amount during his lifetime. He would wake up at about seven thirty or eight AM, remaining in bed to eat his breakfast and read the newspapers. Then he would get up to shave and take a bath, after which he would get back into bed. Churchill continued working from his bed, reading essential letters and dictating memos and correspondence to his private secretary that would be mailed or delivered directly to government officials and private citizens. By eleven AM, he was dictating his upcoming speeches faster than his secretary could keep up, while sipping on a whiskey and soda.

"Lunch was predictably served at one to one fifteen PM. Churchill loved delicious food, various alcoholic beverages, and enjoyable company. He would typically have lunch with his guests while relishing some champagne. After the midday meal, he would take a relaxing stroll to the goldfish pond and feed the ducks and swans. Nearly all his official meetings and visits were scheduled in the afternoon, and he rarely went to the War Room (where we are scheduled to meet with him tomorrow) before noon.

"At or after three PM, he would change into a comfy silk vest, climb back into bed and take his afternoon nap. He was quite fond of his naps and attributed much of his immense productivity to them, claiming that humans were not meant to work straight through from morning to midnight. After waking from his nap at about five PM, he spent time with his family; Churchill loved to play cards with them. Around seven PM, he would have another bath and get ready for dinner.

"Dinner with invited guests was served at eight PM, an enchanting and scrumptious meal accompanied with plenty of drinks and his favorite Cuban cigars. Churchill was frequently the center of the conversation, and he and his guests would stay up sharing stories until ten PM or later. Following dinner, Churchill would return to his study to begin working again. He would frequently continue to toil, dictating three to four thousand words to his aides, well past midnight—sometimes not stopping until two or three AM. He would subsequently retire and sleep until about eight AM, then start again."

Cleopatra cut in, "Maybe you should learn a lesson from Churchill and take an afternoon siesta now and then, my little sleepless Bowmar brainiac. Perhaps your feet would start to touch the ground from time to time."

Waldo added, "Don't tell anybody at the Oak Ridge National Laboratory, but pretty much every day, I find myself a quiet corner somewhere and take a little nappy-poo. It's the best thing ever!"

Laughing at Waldo, I interposed, "Bowmar's history lesson does explain why we are meeting Churchill at two thirty tomorrow: We are catching him between lunch and his afternoon nap. What do you say we all take a walk and check out Buckingham Palace, St. James Park, and Downing Street, then take a practice walk to the War Room entrance for tomorrow's meeting? We can also check out Big Ben and the Westminster Bridge. All of that is within easy walking distance from here."

There was general agreement to proceed with that plan of action, but Crisco had a special request. "I want to go to the Abbey Road crossing where the Beatles photographed their *Abbey Road* album cover, too." Holding up her camera she continued, "I brought my Canon and I want to get a picture of our gang crossing the road there. That would be so cool!"

My music brain kicked into high gear, remembering that the Beatles' album *Abbey Road* was recorded in 1969; it came after *Yellow Submarine* and before *Hey Jude,* at least in North America. I started rifling through my box of cassettes while Goondoggy and Crisco eyeballed what I was doing. I knew full well that Goondoggy's favorite Beatles' song was *"Hey Jude."*

Crisco asked, "Are you going to play *"Something,"* from the *Abbey Road* album? It's such a beautiful, mellow love song."

"Don't do that," the Pud protested. "You'll put me to sleep, or into a music induced coma. Regarding love, I do want to find someone who will look at me the same way that I look at a chocolate cake."

"I'd slap you silly right now, but shit splatters and this is a nice room!" Cleopatra snapped.

Crisco, annoyed, punched him and exclaimed, "Do y'all ever feel the urge to tell someone to shut up even when they aren't talking? Just shut up, Pud!"

"Hey, BB, play 'Hey Jude:' you know I can't get enough of that action," Goondoggy said.

Crazy Ike, whose rock and roll music tastes were more closely aligned with mine, cynically added, "Shit, that song lasts forever! We'll miss our meeting with the Bulldog tomorrow, listening to that tome."

I found what I was looking for in the music collection and looked over my shoulder at Goondoggy, saying, "This is the B-side of 'Hey Jude,' as I plugged in a cassette and hit the play button. In 1968, there were three versions of the Beatles' song **"Revolution"** recorded and released, all during sessions for the Beatles' self-titled double album, also known as the White Album. There was a slow, bluesy composition entitled *"Revolution 1"* that made the final cut for the White Album. There was an abstract sound collage entitled *"Revolution 9"* and a faster, hard rock version of *"Revolution 1,"* released on the B-side of the *"Hey Jude"* single and simply called **"Revolution."** That version was included on the *Hey Jude* album. The single song peaked at number twelve on the Billboard Hot 100 in the US but topped the singles charts in Australia and New Zealand. The song opened with Lennon's guitar blasting like a machine gun, followed by Paul McCartney letting out one of rock and roll's great screams, then lead vocals by Lennon with strong guitars throughout from Harrison and Lennon. The song was so hot, they nearly burned up the mixing console in the recording studio.

The music got the Bad Love Gang's blood moving as we rocked out to the Beatles' **"Revolution"**. We all knew that we had come a long way with our time-travel adventures and were out to change the world in some small but positive way. We definitely were planning to save the future for Hannah Lieb. As the music faded, I responded to Crisco's special request. "We probably won't get to Abbey Road today; it's about ten miles northwest of here, and really the opposite direction of where we are headed to check out the meeting location."

Meatball added, "Let's not forget that we are primarily here to find Hannah and get the gene therapy medicine to her." Ben gave Meatball a hug.

I reassured him, saying, "I was just pondering that, Meatball, and it is really *the* reason we are all here in 1945 London. We are going to stick to our plan and ask for Churchill's help to locate Hannah. Based on all that we know so far, and four of us having been trained to fly de Havilland Mosquitoes, I suspect that some of us are going on a mission related to Blue Nova One's clues, and some of us are going to be on the hunt to locate Hannah. You can bet that you'll be part of that group."

Meatball responded, "I'm good with that. How about we all take a walk and check out Buckingham Palace and Big Ben?" We all high-fived, gave Meatball hugs and slaps on the back, and made our way out of the Goring Hotel, turning right as we left through the front door.

CHAPTER FOURTEEN:

HORSES, KNIGHTS, AND THE MONARCHY

"It is not the walls that make the city, but the people who
live within them. The walls of London may be battered,
but the spirit of the Londoner stands resolute and undismayed."
—King George VI

Saturday, April 21, 1945, at 11:30 AM local time,
Buckingham Palace, London

Leaving the Goring, we turned right, made another immediate right
past the side of the hotel, then turned left onto Buckingham Palace
Road. As we started walking down Buckingham Palace Road, Bowmar
began telling us about how in the 18th century, this road was known
as Chelsea Road and was often frequented by highwaymen. These
highway thieves were raiders who usually journeyed and robbed travelers by horse as compared to a footpad, who traveled and robbed
people on foot. Highwaymen and highwaywomen (often dressing as
men), mounted on horseback, were widely considered to be socially
superior criminals compared to footpads and operated until the late
19th century. There was a long traditional history of treating highway
robbers as heroes, starting with the medieval outlaw, Robin Hood,

who was regarded as an English folk hero. As he was telling us about all this history, we soon came upon the Royal Mews on the left side of the road, a collection of equestrian stables built for the British royal family. This gave Bowmar even more fodder to continue his horse stories.

Of course, all this talk about horses got my music brain daydreaming about various horse-themed songs, one of which started blaring loudly in my head. It was **"Crazy Horses,"** by The Osmonds. When the song came out in late 1972, I couldn't believe my ears. I was astounded that it was by the wholesome, goodie-two-shoe, bubblegum pop music group, the Osmonds! They had used a heavy rock riff and lyrics that led the song to be initially banned in South Africa. The band experimented to create an organ sound that mimicked the sound of a neighing stallion in the chorus. It was none other than Donny Osmond playing the electric organ; his voice was changing too much with puberty at the time, and his singing was temporarily on the sidelines. **"Crazy Horses"** was the only hit record from the Osmonds to feature Jay Osmond as lead vocalist. The single version reached number one in France, the Netherlands and Belgium, number two on the UK Singles Chart and number fourteen on the US Billboard Hot 100. This was a surprisingly badass Osmonds' rock song, with amazing energy! I was temporarily rocking out in my head and oblivious to our progress.

Crisco and Cleopatra were walking next to me, excited to see the front of Buckingham Palace. Cleopatra punched me in the right shoulder to bring me out of my hypnotic music-mind trance. "Hey, Buckingham Butt, don't we make a turn soon to see the palace? My little genius brother can't quit talking about horses, for some reason."

The shoulder punch brought me back to reality. I shifted into my John Wayne persona and sauntered over to Bowmar, who was apparently just about finished with his horse stories. Doing my absolute best John Wayne impersonation, I interrupted Bowmar with a soft shove and said, "Well, neigh and whinny there, pardner! I'm gonna get up on my saddle, and tomorrow I'll buy me a horse. There are a couple of purdy little ladies here itching to see a queen's palace. You know of any palaces around these here parts, pilgrim?" Bowmar looked at me, smiling but a bit confused.

The whole group burst out laughing at what was one of my better renditions of the Duke. Pumpkin turned, looking back at Crisco and Cleopatra, and announced, "That's a smashing idea, my ladies; Buckingham Palace is the bee's knees! Follow me, and we'll check out the Victoria Memorial and the palace."

We followed Pumpkin, turning left on Spur Road, then continued walking to the Victoria Memorial in front of Buckingham Palace. Bowmar, undeterred by my "cowboy Kev" John Wayne interruption, enthusiastically resumed his 1945 London tour guide role. "Victoria was queen of the United Kingdom of Great Britain and Ireland from mid-1837 until her death in 1901. Her queenly sovereignty lasted sixty-three years and seven months, was famously known as the Victorian era, and was longer than any of her predecessors. Her reign ushered in a historical period of industrial, scientific, political, and military transformation within the United Kingdom, and was marked by a great expansion of the British Empire. In 1876, the British Parliament voted to give her the additional title of empress of India.

"We are standing at the end of a road called The Mall, and this Victoria Memorial is a monument to Queen Victoria. It was King Edward VII who suggested that plans be made to develop a memorial to Queen Victoria following her death. The memorial was designed in 1901 by the sculptor Sir Thomas Brock and was unveiled in May 1911, but not completed until 1924. The statue of Queen Victoria in front of us is over eighteen feet high and made of Italian Carrara marble, although the bulk of the memorial was made from Pentelic marble from Greece. The entire memorial, weighing over five million pounds, is eighty-two feet high and one hundred four feet wide. As well as Queen Victoria, the other statues you see represent courage, constancy, victory, charity, truth, and motherhood."

Listening carefully to Bowmar at this point, I picked up a stray stick on the ground and used it as a scepter to have a little fun with the gang. I first approached Crazy Ike and asked the whole group to circle around us as I bade Ike to take one knee before me. As would be expected, he at first resisted my request, knowing abuse was on the way, but gave in to the peer pressure of the rest of the Bad Love Gang. I then tapped both his shoulders with the stick and loudly announced, "Just as Her Majesty Queen Victoria would bestow knighthood on her loyal subjects, I hereby appoint and declare Crazy Ike as the Knight of Motherhood!"

Everyone burst out laughing and Crazy Ike, who could lie, cheat and steal his way out of any trouble he ever created or encountered, asserted with an ear-to-ear, rascally grin on his freckled face, "You got this wrong, Bubble Pants, hands-down I would be the Knight of Truth!" We all laughed even more, trying to visualize that radical concept as Ike gamely said, "Help me understand how I fit into the motherhood role."

I smiled and responded, "Well, none of the other ones fit you very well, and every time we're out here time-traveling you're sniffing around like a freckled horny toad looking for a one-night stand. One of these days you are going to make someone a mother, and god help us all if there is ever another Crazy Ike on the lose!" Nearly everyone chimed in and said, "Amen to that, Bubble Butt!"

Then I asked the Pud to take a knee. He subtly rolled his eyes and replied, "Oh, shit; why not?" as everyone else giggled. I then continued as I tapped both his shoulders with my makeshift scepter, "Despite recently receiving genuine knighthood on planet Azur, I hereby appoint and declare the Pud as the Knight of Constancy, for always doing an average job on your typical, run-of-the-mill, time-and-space-travel missions, with the standard and expected mediocre outcome." The Pud, looking around the circle, gave everyone a big, toothy grin. He stood up and bowed as the gang bellowed, "Way to go, Pud!"

Next up was Goondoggy, who gladly took a knee while everyone hollered "GOONDOGGY"! so boisterously that I'm sure people around us were wondering what the hell Goondoggy meant. I resumed my role, tapping both Goondoggy's shoulders and then grabbing his left forearm, raising it up as I pointed to his Azurian reconstructed left hand while trying to show it to everyone. "This is the hand of truth and I declare it, and the attached human body known as Goondoggy, as the Knight of Truth."

Goondoggy got off his knee and went around the circle high-fiving everyone with his new left hand and avowed, "With your help and with this hand of truth, we shall find Hannah. And if called to active duty by Sir Winnie, we shall bring the Nazi scum to their knees!"

We all cheered, and Pumpkin proclaimed, "That sounded like a Churchill speech."

"That brings me to you, Pumpkin, so take a knee," I stated. Pumpkin's face was already starting to turn bright orange.

Pumpkin took his obligatory knee and cried out, "Don't be taking the piss at me, Bubble Bloke." Half the group were laughing and half scratching their heads, not knowing that British slang meant to mock or make fun.

Tapping his shoulders with my faux scepter, I dubbed Pumpkin. "You are now and forever known as the Knight of Charity, for adopting Ben as your son as we flew the B-17 Phantom Fortress named Bad Love out of Nazi-controlled Poland and to freedom in Belgium. However, looking at that glow on your face, you are not the White Knight, but the *Orange* Knight of Charity!"

As we all chortled at Pumpkin's orange blush, Ben hugged Pumpkin and looked at me with a boyish scowl, stating, "The adoption was great, but you and Crisco need to learn how to numb up the area better when you put those GCPDs in people's butts, BB butt doctor!" Ben had complained loudly when his global cosmic positioning device was placed.

Bucky, trying to keep a straight face, chimed in, "I'll second that sentiment, Ben. BB and Crisco dug one of those things out of my butt and then put a new one in its place. When the left side of my head stopped hurting from being grazed by that Nazi bullet, then I realized how much my ass hurt."

Tater interjected, "I remember that moment, Bucky. You didn't know whether to rub your watch or wind your butt! Probably didn't know your butt from your elbow, you were so damn confused. We were all shakin' like a dog shittin' peach seeds, but somehow Bubble Guts and Willie flew us the hell out of there while Cleopatra put that Nazi on the motorcycle into a full body cast."

Tater's southern outburst sent everyone into peals of laughter, and then Willie threw in his two cents. "It's a shame this memorial doesn't have a shit your pants statue! I would be in line for that turdy knighthood after BB and I flew head-on in our P-40 War-hawks at that group of four Japanese Lily bombers, with a closure rate exceeding 500 mph and all guns blazing. Now I'm flying the de Havilland Mosquito Wooden Wonder and *wondering* if I'm coming out of this one alive. We flew model airplanes made of balsa wood as kids. Now we're flying actual wooden airplanes going 415 mph and carrying a single 4,000-pound bomb that can blow up a city block—or if something goes wrong, turn me and that plane into a gazillion tooth picks! What the hell am I doing here? I don't want to become a toothpick!"

Goondoggy reacted to that one. "Hey, I'm proud of you, bro. If you get turned into toothpicks, I'll gather them up and put them in that machine on Azur that rebuilt my left hand. Maybe you'd come out of there as the next Björn Borg," he teased, referring to the famous Swedish tennis player who won the French Open in 1974 and 1975, on his way to become the world's number one tennis player. "I'd like to see you up your tennis game a little bit."

Willy responded, "Very funny, Goondoggy, I'll take my racket and stick it up your ass when that happens!"

"Bring it on, Bud, bring it on!" Goondoggy shot back as we all cackled at their brotherly banter.

After the laughter died down, I asked Cleopatra, Crisco, and Waldo to all three take a knee. Waldo might have protested, but Crisco and Cleo quickly put their arms around his shoulders and pulled him down on one knee. He hardly resisted as he muttered, "What's an old fart like me gonna do when two strong women gang up on him? I got no choice, so you better make this good, Queen Bubble Butt."

"Relax, there, General Baldo, before you lose the few remaining hairs on your shiny head," I teased. "So, to you who charges baldly—oops, I meant boldly—into harm's way whenever danger threatens—and to Crisco and Cleo, who have shown their mettle bombing errant volcanoes—I proclaim you three the Knights of Courage." I tapped them all on their shoulders with the stick scepter. "Although Cleo nearly lost this honor with her blood-curdling scream when looking into the eyes and jaws of Meggy the megalodon."

Cleopatra, smirking at me, cynically shot back, "Oh, well; I guess I should have just calmly and nonchalantly said, 'Hey everyone, take a look at that big, seventy-five-foot-long fish with razor sharp teeth that is about to swallow us whole. Oh, and by the way, have a nice day.'"

Everyone chuckled at Cleo's comeback. Crisco added, "I may have gained some courage on these time travel missions, but that doesn't mean I won't still hold you responsible if you ever get us killed. I want more of the 'have fun' part of our motto; you, Bucky, and Goondoggy can continue to flirt with the 'don't die' element."

I winked at Crisco, then faced Meatball and said that I had one more knightly honor to bestow. Everyone gathered around Meatball, who took a knee. "I saved the best for last, Meatball. You have been carrying quite a burden since learning of Hannah's fate with breast cancer and knowing that you have a son with her named Elijah, who is thirteen years older than you." I tapped his shoulders with my scepter and decreed, "Meatball you are the Knight of Victory. This time-travel mission will be a victory for you, Hannah, and Elijah, and a defeat of Hannah's breast cancer!"

Looking at Meatball, Crazy Ike added, "I saw your eyes meet Hannah's when you stepped in front of that Nazi soldier's rifle pointed at her father's chest. I thought, Oh, crap, I better stop that guy from pulling that trigger, Meatball has a rendezvous with romantic destiny! Sure as shittin', I was right."

Meatball eyeballed Ike and asked, "Are you saying that you ordered that Nazi guard to stand down because you were worried about my future romance, and not about saving my life?"

Crazy Ike, with his most mischievous grin, answered, "Well, Meatball, I never really thought of it that way, but I do put a very high priority on romance." Crisco and Cleopatra punched Ike's shoulders at the same instant as the rest of us laughed some more, and I proclaimed that the Victorian knighting ceremony was over.

As a group, we made the short walk to the front gates of Buckingham Palace, the 1945 London home of the monarch King George VI and Queen Consort Elizabeth. The king and queen had remained at Buckingham Palace throughout World War II, but they did send their two daughters, Princesses Elizabeth (who later became queen) and Margaret, to Windsor Castle for safety. King George VI was born in December 1895 in the reign of his great-grandmother Queen Victoria (whose statue we had just admired) and was named Prince Albert of York. Known as "Bertie" among his family and close friends, he was the second son of King George V. As such, he was not expected to inherit the British throne and spent his early life in the shadow of his older brother, Edward. When their father King George V died in 1936, Albert's older brother Edward VIII ascended to the throne for a short time. With a reign of only 326 days, the shortest of the United Kingdom's monarchy, Edward abdicated the throne to marry the twice-divorced American socialite Wallis Simpson in what amounted to a constitutional crisis. Edward VIII was replaced by his younger brother Prince Albert, who became King George VI and rose to the throne. Originally known as Buckingham House, built for the Duke of Buckingham in 1703 and enlarged during the 19th century, Buckingham Palace became the London residence of the British monarchy on the accession of Queen Victoria in 1837.

Of course, we were all schooled on these intriguing historical facts by Bowmar as we viewed the building through the gates, admiring Buckingham Palace and the guards standing duty while Crisco took pictures. When she was done, we made an about-face, headed down The Mall, and then veered to the right onto a path in St. James's Park on our way to 10 Downing Street and to locate the entrance to the Churchill War Room. Our next encounter took us all totally by surprise.

CHAPTER FIFTEEN:

A BLAST FROM THE PAST

"A gypsy told me I was going to do great things.
I was going to make all kinds of money."
—Dolly Parton

Saturday, April 21, 1945, at 12:30 PM local time,
St. James's Park, London

T he most direct route to 10 Downing Street was to veer to the right off The Mall and take a shortcut through St. James's Park, walking along the north side of St. James's Park Lake. It was a beautiful London spring day, and the park was picturesque with abundant foliage and flowers. As we approached the lake, we were admiring the variety of ducks and swans enjoying the lake when I noticed Ben running away. He was advancing up ahead of us along the north shore of the lake in a sprint, dashing away from our group. I looked for Pumpkin, who was behind me. Talking to Crisco, he was oblivious to the situation, so I started to run after Ben.

Ben had a good head start, but he was not going to get away from my Bubble Butt sprinter's legs. I yelled, "*Ben! Stop!* Wait up! Why are you running?" He ignored me as if he were laser focused on something ahead of him. I was closing the gap to about thirty yards between us when I saw Ben stop beside a young boy feeding the park birds, then witnessed the two of them hugging each other and jumping up and down, shrieking for joy! I was at a loss; who on Earth could Ben be rejoicing with?

A few seconds later, I caught up to Ben and recognized that he was celebrating with Barsali Loveridge, now age six, whom we had rescued from certain death in the Holocaust at Chelmno, Poland, during our first time-travel mission. Ben had aged a full year, but Barsali had only aged five months. Despite their age difference of nine and six, their friendship had been forged by fire in their escape from the Holocaust and Nazi-controlled Poland. They were overjoyed to see each other again. I hugged Barsali, then turned and looked at Ben. "Holy shit, Ben! You are starting to run pretty fast for a nine-year-old! And you must have the eyes of an eagle, to recognize Barsali from that distance."

Barsali looked puzzled. "I thought you were eight years old, Ben, but you do look a lot bigger than the last time I saw you."

At that moment, I was grabbed in a firm hug from behind and kissed on the right cheek. All I could see at first was straight, jet black hair. Then I heard a rich, feminine voice with a mysterious accent speaking softly into my right ear. "Welcome back, future boy! Did you come looking for me?" I knew that voice; I turned and looked directly into the piercing eyes of Vadoma Loveridge, Barsali's mother, the beautiful Roma/Gypsy lady in her mid-thirties whom we had rescued in Chelmno. I swear, for a moment, looking at Vadoma's jet black hair and staring into her eyes, I felt like I was face-to-face with Cher. Even though I knew Cher was Armenian/American, my visual optics connected with my outrageous music brain, and it started playing **"Gypsys, Tramps, and Thieves,"** by Cher.

In my mind's eye, I could see Cher singing this song on the TV stage of the *Sonny and Cher Comedy Hour* from the back of a Gypsy wagon with her big black hair, dangling, oversized earrings, and a loose, flowing, Gypsy dress. The song described the life of a girl born on the road in a wagon of a traveling show. It contained themes of racism, teenage pregnancy, and prostitution, but was met with critical acclaim and earned Cher her first Grammy Award nomination in the Best Female Pop Vocal Performance category. When it was released, **"Gypsys, Tramps, and Thieves"** became the biggest-selling single in the history of MCA Records, hitting number one on the Billboard Hot 100 and on the Canadian Singles Chart at the same time. It reached number two in Malaysia, Singapore, and New Zealand, number three in Ireland, and number four in the UK and Australia. All of us in the Bad Love Gang knew the words to this song, and my mind showed us dancing and singing the song as we circled around the Gypsy wagon. For some reason, Vadoma allowed me to stay in my trance; perhaps she had me in a Vulcan mind meld and was enjoying the music of the future.

I snapped out of it eventually. She simply smiled at me, sending a little chill down my spine as the rest of the group arrived. Cleopatra and Crisco were the first to give Barsali and Vadoma big hugs, and the rest of the group quickly followed suit. After all the hugs and kisses, Vadoma looked around and enquired, "Where is Spaghetti Head, the tail gunner who fired the first shots when we escaped Poland? And where is the Runt, who made that B-17 ball turret into such a lethal weapon?"

I was shocked that Vadoma remembered them and saw that they were missing from our group. I answered her question with a question. "Vadoma, how on earth could you remember their names, much less their positions on that B-17 Flying Fortress?"

She answered, "My young Bubble Buttress future boy," I blushed just a bit at this, and the rest of the group giggled, "how could I possibly forget the people who rescued my son and I from the hands of the Nazis? Like a famous photograph or motion picture of history, I can see every one of you in slow motion as you did your parts to save Barsali and me and deliver us to freedom. We owe you all a debt that is unmeasurable to be repaid."

I responded, "You and the group we rescued are all privy to the fact that we came here from the future. Spaghetti Head and the Runt are back in the future, running the machine that transported us to Poland last November and then again here for our present mission." I introduced Bowmar to Vadoma as Cleo's brother, and the guy who ran the time machine when we rescued her and Barsali. She took both of Bowmar's hands, holding them firmly and piercing his eyes with hers.

Staring into Bowmar's eyes, she continued almost without pause, "Yes, I could sense that there was someone brilliant in the background watching over all of you. I am pleased to meet you, Bowmar, and I cannot help but feel that you have been sent here by someone far, far away."

Bowmar, locked onto Vadoma's eyes, replied unflinchingly and without hesitation, "Yeah, you might say that; her name is Blue Nova One, and 11.5 billion light years away from here definitely qualifies as 'far away.'" He smiled at her and let her hands go.

Meatball nudged Bowmar to the side and grabbed Vadoma's hands, anxious to talk with her. "Vadoma, it's great to see you and Barsali again...and I am hoping that you can help us. By the way, I remember that you were the first one of group we saved to really believe I was from the future, that first night in Chelmno that we all spent in the church together."

Vadoma gave Meatball a big hug and said, "I knew you were telling the truth, Meatball; you have such a caring and positive energy about you. You told us that you were from Oak Ridge, Tennessee in the United States in the year 1974 and had used a time travel machine called the White Hole Project to come and save us." I was marveling at Vadoma's recollections. She continued, "You fell head over heels in love with that beautiful Jewish girl, Hannah Lieb. Based on General Waldo's orders to take good care of us," Waldo bobbled and bowed his bald head to our crowd, making us chuckle, "we all traveled here to England and safety together by transport plane from Belgium. After reaching England, and before we all parted ways, Hannah shared with me that she was pregnant with your child."

Meatball's eyes started to well up with tears and he asked, "How long ago did you part ways with Hannah and her family? Can you help us find her? It is so important to her future!"

Vadoma suggested that we all sit down in the grass together and we did so, forming a tight circle to relax and talk. She then began her story starting when we had all parted ways in Belgium in November 1944. "I can tell you what happened, which should help to give you all perspective and some clues...but I do not know exactly where Hannah and her family are located at this very moment. After you dropped the twelve of us off at Chièvres Air Base in Belgium in late November and took Ben with you, they kept the remaining twelve of us together at the airbase, which was being run by the US Army Air Force. It was a busy place, with war planes flying missions around the clock. They also used it as a transportation station for US soldiers returning home, and there was a German POW camp there as well. They kept telling the twelve of us that they did not 'have a protocol' to process Holocaust survivors rescued on a special secret mission by an American Airforce general and his crew, with orders from the highest Allied command levels. From our point of view, we were all just grateful and relieved to be alive and out of Nazi-controlled Poland.

"If you will all recall, our group of twelve was me and Barsali; Daniel, Mazal, Zelda and Rhoda Roth, as well as Rhoda's mother,

Rachel Soros; Avigail and Asher Goldberg; and David, Sarah, and Hannah Lieb."

Ben interjected, "I was running from the Nazis who took my parents, and Asher was the man who helped me get away."

Crisco added, "I loved his wife, Avigail. She was my kind of woman: always bluntly telling you exactly how things stood, but making you laugh in the process."

Meatball was feeling better and commented, "Avigail *was* a hoot. She could see that Hannah and I were attracted to each other. She was in her mid-seventies and offered to distract the guards at the church with her 'exotic charm' so Hannah and I could sneak by and go on a date. Of course, that didn't happen that night, but it was comic relief when we were all stressed out to the max. I was really taken by the Roths' story. David, his wife, two daughters, and mother-in-law were getting ready for their Friday evening Sabbath dinner at their family farm when German SS soldiers burst in, let them pack a single suitcase, and took them away at gunpoint. How wicked was that?" Everyone shook their heads in anger and disgust.

I remarked, "Avigail was one of a kind, for sure. We were trying to rush and get everyone on board the B-17 'Bad Love' Phantom Fortress to get the hell out of Poland, and bullets were starting to fly. In the craziness of the moment, I pushed Avigail on her rump to help her get through the side hatch faster. Rather than slap my hand, she looked back at me as she popped through the hatch and declared, 'BB, you bad boy! I haven't been touched like that since Asher and I first met!'" Everyone burst out laughing. Since I hadn't previously shared that story with the group, it offered up quite a visual, coming from a seventy-five-year-old woman in the midst of crisis, calamity, and an evolving shoot-out with the oncoming Nazis.

Cleopatra nodded. "Yeah, it was at that very moment that Meatball was in a virtual lip-lock with Hannah, seeing stars and thinking the noise around us was fireworks rather than oncoming Nazi gunfire. I had to yell at those two to come out of their romance trance and get on board the plane!"

Meatball, blushing just a bit, responded, "Well, as you wisecracked when you screamed at us, *'Me and Mrs. Jones'* had a thing going on! And you know, we were a bit oblivious to the fact that death was descending upon us."

My unstoppable music brain started playing **"Love Is Like an Itching in My Heart"** by The Supremes while Crazy Ike jumped in. "Exactly, Meatball. Being horny is my natural state, and now you know what it feels like. I rest my case, you hopeless, lovestruck basket case!"

The song **"Love Is Like an Itching in My Heart"** was from the album "Supremes A'Go-Go" and was the first album by an all-female group to reach number one on the Billboard 200 album charts in the United States. The single version hit number nine on the US Billboard Hot 100 and number three in Canada. In my mind's eye, I could see the Supremes in their bright-yellow, sequined gowns rocking out and performing this song on the Ed Sullivan Show. The lyrics described being bitten by the love bug and no matter how hard you tried, you couldn't scratch the itch it created. It was the perfect description of what had happened to Meatball and Hannah. Now we just had to find her.

Bowmar got us back on point. "OK, boys and girls. Let's refocus and get back to Vadoma's story and see where it might lead us."

A little relieved, Meatball remarked, "Thanks, Bowmar. I owe you one."

Vadoma continued, "After spending a little more than two weeks at Chièvres Air Base in Belgium, they flew the twelve of us by transport plane to the largest US airbase in England, Burtonwood airfield, in early December. It was located a couple of miles northwest of the city of Warrington, in Cheshire. We were told that it was the largest airfield in all of Europe, and home to about seventeen or eighteen thousand American soldiers servicing the United States Eighth, Ninth, Twelfth, and Fifteenth Air Forces aircraft. That place was enormous! Some of the soldiers we met there said it was the largest US air base outside of the United States! They provided accommodations for us there, but again we were repeatedly told that there was no protocol or procedure to assimilate us, as Jewish and Gypsy refugees from Nazi-controlled Poland."

Bowmar spoke up. "Your story is not unexpected. After Adolf Hitler came into power in 1933, he and the controlling Nazi party legislated policies that would culminate in the Holocaust. Jews began to flee Germany, Austria, and German-occupied Europe. For example, more than three hundred thousand left Germany, and there were more than one hundred fifteen thousand Jews who left Austria by the end of 1939. Most of those who got out early were young and trained in a field, or college educated. Initially, Germany encouraged Jews to leave; but then they started to tighten a noose around the necks of Jews, restricting the amount of money they could take from their own German bank accounts and imposing high emigration taxes. Hitler's Nazi government totally forbade any Jewish emigration after October 1941. The German Jews who remained in Germany, and those from annexed Austria at that time, were mostly elderly and were taken to ghettos and murdered, or taken to Nazi concentration camps, where most of them died or were killed. As we all know, a total of six million European Jews and a quarter million Romani Gypsies died at the hands of the Nazis before World War II was over.

"Although Jews could get away from the antisemitic onslaught initially, it became difficult to find countries where they could live—particularly after the initial wave of Jewish immigrants were accepted in

Europe, Britain, and the United States. Some came here to Great Britain on transit visas, which meant that they stayed in Britain temporarily, while waiting to be accepted by another country. Others found specific employment or a guarantor. And then there was the famous Kindertransport which included thousands of Jewish children from Nazi Germany and Nazi-occupied territories who were given homes in the United Kingdom just before the war started. The children were placed in British foster homes, schools, farms, and hostels. All said, there were about seventy thousand Jewish refugees who were received into Britain by the start of World War II on September 1, 1939. An additional ten thousand made it into Britain during the war. That would include you, Vadoma, along with Barsali and the rest of the group we rescued. You guys got here through military bases controlled by the USAAF. I'm guessing that created some bureaucratic headaches for someone."

Waldo confirmed it, winking at and trying to tease Bowmar a bit in the process. "Not that Bowmar really knows what the hell he is talking about," Bowmar puckered his brow at Waldo, "but he is right about the military needing an approved procedure to do just about anything, especially the US military on soil outside of the USA."

Bucky added, "You got that right, General Baldo."

Bowmar, totally ignoring Waldo's harassment, kept his attention on Vadoma. "You and Barsali are here with us now. How did you and the others manage to leave the USAAF base at Burtonwood?"

Pumpkin was sitting next to Vadoma. She grabbed the sides his head with both her hands, looked into his eyes, and ran her right hand gently through his hair. Exaggerating her accent, she said, "I had made 'special' friends with an American soldier named Jason Roberts whom they called JR; he was about your age. I asked him to take me and our group off the base for New Year's Eve celebration." Pumpkin's face lit up a brighter shade of orange than we had ever seen, making us all roll with laughter.

Vadoma carried on, "This is where it gets interesting, and will hopefully help you find your way to the Lieb family and Hannah. During the month of December 1944, while we were held at the base at Burtonwood, we got to know many of the soldiers. They all were confident that the war would end soon, sometime in 1945, and that the Allies would decisively win. We regularly talked about getting our lives back. Daniel, Mazal, Zelda, and Rhoda Roth, as well as Rhoda's mother, Rachel Soros, all planned to return to their family farm in Poland. Avigail and Asher Goldberg were also determined to try and return to their home in Lodz, Poland. My husband and Barsali's father, Manfri, was shot and killed by a Nazi guard the day that we arrived by train in Lodz, Poland to be transferred to the ghetto there. It was Asher Goldberg who rescued me and Barsali that day Manfri was murdered, and then Asher and Avigail hid us in their home from the Nazis. Being a widow, I told the group that my plan was to stay here in England with Barsali and make our future here. After what I tell you next, Barsali and I found a great community of Romani Gypsies living in the London Borough of Ealing. We live about nine miles west of here, and I brought Barsali here today to see Buckingham Palace and enjoy the park.

"It was David, Sarah, and Hannah Lieb who really came up with a plan to get us all moving again toward the future. David was a well-to-do, highly trained, and respected construction engineer at the largest salt mine in Poland, located in Klodawa. David knew that he had extended family living somewhere in Great Britain and France, along with his strong family and business connections in Poland. Sarah had family in Poland, and extended family living in Palestine. David came up with a plan to leave the air base at Burtonwood with his family, the Roth family, Avigail, and Asher and go to Liverpool, England, which was only about seventeen miles west of Burtonwood, where he knew there was a well-heeled, strong Jewish community. He suspected he had family ties there as well. David promised to help the Roth family, Asher, and Avigail get back to Poland when the war ended and told his family they were going home to Palestine after the war. He wanted to help me and Barsali as well, but I told him that we would be fine on our own.

"I told JR that we all wanted to make merry on New Year's Eve in Liverpool, and JR made it happen. He 'borrowed' a base truck and we all drove together to Liverpool for a fabulous, memorable New Year's celebration, which all of us desperately needed! That night, Hannah told me she was sure that she was pregnant with Meatball's baby, but she was afraid to tell her parents. I told her, 'Honey, this is World War II, and we are living in historic times. The twelve of us would be dead if it were not for Meatball and his gang from the future. That baby you are carrying is a miracle child. Accept it, cherish it, and who knows? Maybe Meatball will come back!' Now look, we are all here together again! Who could have ever imagined?"

Meatball gave Vadoma a big hug and said, "Vadoma, you are amazing. I am getting all jittery inside with the feeling that we can find Hannah! What happened in Liverpool?"

Pumpkin was staring at Vadoma and enquired in his British way, "Why is that puckish grin on your face?"

Vadoma finished her story, "Well, somehow, JR drank too much on New Year's Eve and passed out at the party we attended. I told the rest of group that Barsali and I were going to find our way to London. They pleaded for us to stay with them, but it was time to say goodbye. We all hugged and cried like babies, for all we had been through together! David reassured me that he and the rest of the group would find safe haven in Liverpool until the war ended. We parted ways in the early morning of January 1, 1945. You need to go to Liverpool in your search to find Hannah."

Crisco blurted out, "Heck yeah, I want to go to Liverpool! That is the home of the Beatles!"

Bowmar commented, "No offense, but there is a lot more history to Liverpool than just the Beatles."

As we all got back on our feet and stretched, I exclaimed, "Holy shit! What an amazing turn of events! Vadoma, how about you and Barsali come with us on a little walk over to Downing Street and the Churchill War Room entrance, and then join us for dinner at our hotel? I think we will be splitting our group in two. Some of us are headed to Liverpool, and some of us to destinations yet unknown... but we're going to find out tomorrow."

CHAPTER SIXTEEN:
THE BULLDOG'S WAR ROOM

"Men occasionally stumble over the truth, but most of them pick
themselves up and hurry off as if nothing ever happened."
—Winston Churchill

Sunday, April 22, 1945, at 1:00 PM local time,
the Goring Hotel, Central London

During a marvelous and sumptuous dinner at the Goring Hotel
Dining Room the night before, we had discussed our plans and
decided to split into two groups. Group one included Meatball,
Cleopatra, Crisco, Waldo, the Pud, Ben, Vadoma and Barsali, who
would all travel to Liverpool, England in the hunt to find Hannah
Lieb. Group two was comprised of Bowmar, Bucky, Pumpkin, Willie,
Crazy Ike, Goondoggy, Tater, and me; we would meet with Churchill.
We also knew that RAF Captain Addison "Ed" Ratliff and RAF Lieutenant Philip "Phil" Dawson, whom we had trained with for flying
the de Havilland "Wooden Wonder" Mosquitoes, would be attending
the meeting with Churchill. Blue Nova One had told Bowmar to have
Bucky use his presidential connection to Harry Truman to arrange
the meeting with Winston Churchill in London on Sunday, April 22,

1945, and that day was upon us. We did not know exactly why we were going, or what Churchill had in mind that would include us and the Denver Project, but we trusted there was a solid reason behind Blue Nova One's guidance.

After a leisurely Sunday brunch together, we all met in Bucky's suite before parting ways. Waldo, Bowmar, Bucky, and I had discussed how to communicate between the two separated groups. We told Waldo to call us on Sunday night at the hotel with their progress, and we would share what Churchill had planned for us. The Black Box Protocol was also in effect, and it had been reliably recalled back to the future earlier that morning. Bowmar had sent a note inside the Black Box to Mary, Spaghetti Head, and the Runt, letting them know that half our gang was leaving for Liverpool in the more focused search for Hannah Lieb, and the other half would meet with Winston Churchill that afternoon. He told them to send the box back at 9:00 PM London time, with the precise coordinates to the beautiful and private Goring Hotel Garden. He told them to send a couple of extra GCPDs (global cosmic positioning devices) with a plan to recall the Black Box again the following morning. Bowmar, as always, was thinking ahead about how the White Hole Project time machine might be needed to help us accomplish this mission.

As we were about to break up into our two groups and head out, I picked a song to play on the Marantz boombox to get everyone motivated for the quest out in front of us. I told the gang that the tune was relatively new for us; it had been released in August 1975. We all loved hot cars and riding motorcycles; I hinted to the group that the song was about hitting the road for high adventure. Everyone was trying to guess out loud, but it was Crazy Ike who yelled out, "Springsteen!" I pointed at him nodding my head in affirmation and yelled back, "Bingo!" as I hit the play button on the Marantz. Bruce Springsteen's early anthem **"Born to Run"** blasted out and got us all rocking and singing together.

The tune captured the spirit of restless teenagers like us, yearning to hit the road and live life to its fullest. **"Born to Run"** was Springsteen's first worldwide single release and the single version was his first top 40 hit, reaching number 23 on the Billboard Hot 100 and number 17 on the US Cash Box Top 100. I told everyone to replace Wendy's name with Hannah as we belted out the lyrics together.

Meatball was genuinely happy to know he was getting closer to finding Hannah. Over the loud music he shouted out, "Yeah, baby! Let's launch this rocket!" When the music faded away, we all hugged, wished each other good luck, and headed out of the hotel.

As we were walking toward the exit, Crisco tapped my shoulder from behind and softly said, "Listen, Colonel Bubble Butt; I'm really glad to be going to Liverpool, but wherever you guys are going, don't die."

I smiled at her and answered, "We'll see you in a few days, Sergeant Nurse O'Sullivan. Get your first syringe ready to give Hannah the shot to beat breast cancer, and maybe a second shot to beat Father Time." She looked at me, puzzled. I winked at her and shrugged.

Sunday, April 22, 1945, at 2:30 PM local time,
Churchill's Cabinet War Room, London

Bowmar, Bucky, Pumpkin, Willie, Crazy Ike, Goondoggy, Tater, and I, all dressed in our military attire, presented to the War Room entrance and introduced our group as the Denver Project, scheduled to meet with Prime Minister Churchill. They were expecting us, and we were escorted by a guard, Sergeant Griffiths, to Churchill's fortified underground Cabinet War Room. I was the ranking USAAF officer as Colonel Schafer, and Bucky was himself as Captain Jack Smith, the officer in charge of the Denver Project. Bowmar kept his role as Tuskegee Airman First Lieutenant Nathan Williams. Pumpkin, Willie,

Crazy Ike, and Goondoggy were all dressed as USAAF lieutenants. On the other hand, Tater had insisted on keeping his persona as a US Marine Corps officer, First Lieutenant Danny Ford. We had been teasing him a bit on the walk over and he smartly told us, using his typical southern flair, that we had our noses so high in the air we could drown in a rainstorm. We had a nice laugh of relief to ease our tensions before going into our top-secret meeting.

We had met US Presidents Franklin D. Roosevelt and Gerald Ford in person and spoken to Harry Truman by phone in our time travels, but meeting Winston Churchill in person had all our hearts pounding with anticipation as we entered his Cabinet War Room. We all knew that he was regarded as one of the greatest wartime leaders of the 20th century. While Churchill did not yet know this in 1945, Bowmar had reminded us that he won a Nobel Prize in Literature in 1953 for his speechmaking. Not that we would dare try, but Bowmar also warned us that we would never outwit "Winnie." He gave us the example of play-wright George Bernard Shaw, the famous Irish comic-dramatist, literary critic, and socialist propagandist who had also won a Nobel Prize for Literature back in 1925: Shaw had once sent Churchill a note with an invitation to see his opening night performance of the play *Saint Joan*. The playwright enclosed two tickets for Winston and joked, "One for yourself and one for a friend...if you have one." Expressing sorrow at not being able to attend the opening night, Churchill wrote back and asked for tickets for the second night, "if there is one." He had an amazing sense of humor and sense of history. We would not be disappointed.

Inside the Cabinet War Room, meeting tables were arranged in a tight rectangle and Churchill was seated in the middle of the head table by himself, with his back to a large map of the world draped on the wall directly behind him. The room was reasonably well-lit by World War II standards, with bright lights hanging over the meeting tables from the ceiling above. We recognized and acknowledged RAF Captain

Addison "Ed" Ratliff and RAF Lieutenant Philip "Phil" Dawson, who were both seated at the table to Churchill's right. There was a third soldier seated next to Phil, dressed in combat or commando fatigues. There were two sharply dressed and attractive women seated at the table to Churchill's left. Everyone stood when we entered the room, and I quickly studied the two women we did not yet know. One was five feet six inches tall with a medium build, wearing a black dress suit, and had long, straight, blonde hair and blue-green eyes. The other woman was tall at five foot nine or ten, and slender but shapely, with luminous, pale skin and thick, curly red hair; she was wearing a gray dress suit. Both were wearing low-heeled black pumps, so I may have slightly overestimated their heights.

Churchill smoked as many as ten cigars a day. His ever-present cigars were trademark accessories of his public persona. He embraced the conviction that smoking cigars helped invigorate him to face the formidable charges of his challenging political destiny. His cigar habit dated back to 1895, when after graduating from the Royal Military Academy Sandhurst, he and a fellow officer had traveled to Cuba, which was fighting for its independence from Spain. During his short time spent in Cuba, he was smitten by one of its most celebrated and admired products: Cuban cigars. The Cuban cigar brands Romeo y Julieta and La Aroma de Cuba became his two most-preferred cigars. For the remainder of his life, certain Havana cigar dealers, friends, and people in the know would send him shipments of his prized Cuban cigars. In a 1932 collection of essays entitled *Thoughts and Adventures*, he mused, "How can I tell that my temper would have been as sweet or my companionship as agreeable if I had abjured from my youth the goddess Nicotine?" As he stood from his chair to greet us, I noticed him holding an unlit cigar in his left hand.

The guard who had led us into the Cabinet War Room, Sergeant Griffiths, was the first to speak as he saluted Churchill. "Mr. Prime

Minister, these officers are the representatives of the Denver Project here to meet with you."

Prime Minister Churchill responded, "Thank you, Griffiths; that'll be all." Griffiths stepped away while Churchill waved his arm to the right and greeted us. "Welcome, gentlemen. Some of you are already acquainted with Captain Ed Ratliff and Lieutenant Phil Dawson." They both saluted us, and we returned salutes. "Joining them today is SOE commando, Lawrence 'Larry' Baker." We exchanged salutes with him as well. Turning to his left and extending his left hand, which was holding the cigar, he said, "I'd like to introduce you to two of our distinguished and accomplished SOE spies, Emma Hoffman and Petra Vogel." Both Emma and Petra bowed their heads to us in acknowledgement, and we nodded in return.

Churchill then continued, "We certainly have some ground to cover here today. I had a rather intriguing conversation with your new American president, Harry Truman, about your group and the Denver Project. If it weren't for Emma's and Petra's story, which you shall shortly hear, I would have thought Truman drank more than me with his fantastical story about you being time travelers. Then he told me that you call yourselves the Bad Love Gang. Harry seemed a little discomfited by that name, but I, on the other hand, might be convinced to join you!" We all chuckled and started to relax a bit. "I believe it is fully prudent to look ahead, but problematical to look further than you can see. So I look forward to our discussion here. Please introduce yourselves, and we'll get started."

Bucky, as the official head of the Denver Project appointed by FDR and the oldest member of our present group standing before Churchill, got us started. Bucky introduced himself as Captain Jack "Bucky" Smith, and promptly presented the gift to Churchill that Otto G. Goring had prepared for us at Waldo's request: a box of Cuban Romeo y Julieta cigars and a bottle of Ararat Cognac. Churchill looked at the gift, smiled and said, "You're off to a good start, Captain! Let's see how persistent you can be."

Bucky smiled and responded, "It was our mutual good friend President Roosevelt who personally appointed me head of the Denver Project, but I doubt I'd be alive and standing here before you now if it weren't for the Bad Love Gang. Half our gang is headed to Liverpool, and half are here. As Ratliff and Dawson already know, we all have nicknames. So I am going to have everyone introduce themselves and share their nicknames as well."

Churchill declared, "Franklin was my friend and our nation's friend, and I miss him. I recently wrote that I thought it was cruel that he will not see the victory that he did so much to achieve. Since you were personally acquainted with him, what you are about to learn at this meeting will take on more meaning. I used to sign telegrams to him using my nickname, 'Former Naval Person.' Please proceed with the introductions, taking your seats at the table as you go." We all introduced ourselves by name and nickname, then sat down. Announcing our nicknames drew smiles throughout the room.

There was a moment of silence as Winston lit his cigar and gazed around the room taking his first puff. He said, "Despite the fact that the war against Germany is all but over, we have a potential lingering problem with that bloodthirsty guttersnipe Adolf Hitler. It seems that Hitler's deepest, darkest secret is a grandiose scheme to take his Nazi ideology to the future. We have reason to believe that he will try to execute that plan very soon; we are here today to make certain that not only he be foiled, but to perhaps learn something in the process." He looked around with a smirk and carried on, "God knows that I love to learn, although I can't say the same about being taught." That brought some chortles around the room.

"I somehow evaded many flying bullets and shrapnel in my early and mid-twenties as a member of the Cavalry, and later as an officer in the Infantry. It taught me to believe more in destiny than in luck. Emma and Petra are here with us at this moment because they are both women of destiny. Luck alone could not possibly account for the paths that they took to work together as spies for the SOE. Whereas the Denver Project is assigned to protect a top-secret time-travel machine called the White Hole Project, Emma and Petra are going to tell you the depraved story of Hitler's Black Hole Project, and why we must stop it. Emma, let's start with you."

Emma politely smiled at the Prime Minister, thanked him and began, "My real name is Ela Hellberg, and I and my Jewish family are from Strasbourg, France in the Alsace region. After the Fall of France to Nazi Germany in June of 1940, when anti-Semitic laws came into force, my father, Adam Hellberg, became a leader in the French Resistance. His brother, my Uncle Seth, works for the SOE. Despite my father's opposition, I convinced him and my uncle to give me a role in helping the Allies to fight Nazi Germany. Uncle Seth assigned me to the SOE, and my law firm changed my identity from the obviously Jewish Ela Hellberg to the apparently German Emma Hoffman.

"I got my big break in the spring of 1941 when I landed a job working for Robert Heinrich Wagner, a Hitler confidant and the Nazi chief of civil administration for Alsace. Wagner was on a mission to rid Alsace of Jews, earning himself the nickname the Butcher of Alsace. Even though I was working for such a wicked man, Wagner was the one who opened the door for me at the Black Hole Project. Key to my story is a Nazi soldier, SS Obergruppenführer Klaus Richter, who had a distinguished military record serving under Wagner." At that moment, a frigid chill ran up and down my spine. I had heard the name Klaus Richter from Blue Nova One. He was the Nazi lieutenant general who had murdered Nova's husband, Blue Rhett One, by putting a bullet in his head.

"Emma, the Nazi soldier you refer to, Klaus Richter, killed Blue Rhett One, the husband of our dear friend, Blue Nova One after discovering Blue Nova One's alien drilling expedition and blue exotic matter in the German Black Forest in late November 1941," I explained.

Both Emma and Petra looked shocked, and Churchill spoke, "How could you know this, and what exactly do you mean by 'alien drilling expedition?'"

"I am not talking about 'alien' from another country, I am talking 'alien' from another *planet*. Azur is a sister planet to Earth, and we have been there. Blue exotic matter is required to make time and deep space travel possible, and it is considered an essential element on Azur. They had been running low on blue exotic matter and were searching the universe for a new source. Blue Nova One first discovered blue exotic matter here on Earth in the German Black Forest in 1941. She, her husband, Rhett, and their crew were nearly done with their blue exotic matter drilling expedition in November 1941 in the Black Forest when they were ambushed by Klaus Richter's Waffen-SS Nazi squad. Richter fired a fatal shot into Rhett's head before the aliens escaped.

"We met Blue Nova One in June 1942 in a forest of southern China while on an assignment from President Roosevelt. We found a way to get to Blue Nova One's planet, and just recently went there to get the cure for breast cancer for one of the Holocaust victims we rescued on our first time-travel mission. Her name is Hannah Lieb, and we have tracked her trail back here to England. We are here now with half our group searching for Hannah to give her the breast cancer medicine. The rest of us are here with you at this moment because Blue Nova One told us to meet with you. She was concerned that the Nazis got their hands on the blue exotic matter that was left behind, and what they might do with it."

Petra gazed at Churchill and softly said, "Bubble Butt is correct. The Black Hole time-travel machine depends on blue exotic matter to function. I know that it came from a mysterious Nazi operation in the Black Forest."

Churchill then eyed me and our group as he puffed on his cigar. "I may need to open this bottle of Cognac sooner rather than later. If I accept what you are saying as the truth, then it sounds like the Nazis tried to get war started on two planets. Leave it to Hitler to find another front to fight on! After he and Nazi Germany invaded the Soviet Union in 1941, I said if Hitler had invaded hell, I would make at least a favorable reference to the devil in the House of Commons. I am no less inclined now to stop that fiend from invading the future. I will accept your truth; let us stay on task."

CHAPTER SEVENTEEN:
OPERATION NO TIME

"I like things to happen, and if they don't happen,
I like to make them happen."
—Winston Churchill

Sunday, April 22, 1945, at 3:00 PM local time,
Churchill's Cabinet War Room, London

C hurchill snuffed out the remnant of his first cigar and reached to his inner coat pocket for its replacement, which he initially held unlit. He then bade Emma to continue with her story.

"Klaus Richter rose in the Nazi military ranks after discovering the blue exotic matter in the Black Forest. Hitler personally promoted Richter to the rank of SS Obergruppenführer and made him the head of security for the top-secret Black Hole Project in March of 1942. Wagner recommended to Richter that I be among his first new hires to his office in Berchtesgaden. Given this elite Nazi recommendation, I found myself embedded as the lead administrative assistant working at the secretive planning office for the Black Hole Construction Command Center in the town of Berchtesgaden when it opened in August 1942. The Black Hole was Adolf Hitler's pet personal project and was purposely constructed close to his home and southern head-quarters, the Berghof, built on the Obersalzberg above the town of Berchtesgaden. It has become the most shadowy project in the history of Nazi Germany." Emma looked at Petra and said, "Your turn, Petra."

"I am also Jewish, from a German Jewish family in Göttingen, a university city in Lower Saxony, Germany," said Petra. "Both my parents taught mathematics at the University of Göttingen, and my older brother Karl became a mathematician and physicist. He took a position at Cambridge University here in Britain in 1930, and subsequently joined the faculty at the University of Edinburgh in 1940, working with Max Born. Karl was recruited by the SOE; that is how I subsequently became connected to the SOE."

Bowmar enthusiastically interjected, "Max Born was a famous German physicist and mathematician and played a central role in the development of quantum mechanics. He also made contributions to solid-state physics and optics, winning the 1954 Nobel Prize in Physics for his research in quantum mechanics and the interpretation of wave function. He is one of my physics heroes!"

I held my hands over my face and muttered, "Bowmar, it is 1945 and you just gave away the future of 1954."

Bowmar humbly replied, "Oh! Yeah, oops... Did I just say that? I'm sorry, I got so excited."

Tater had to comment, in his southern twang, "Well, bless your pea-pickin' little heart there, brainiac; you made a boo-boo! Maybe that there time machine is numbing some of your neurons!" The whole room laughed as Bowmar scowled, then laughed at Tater.

Churchill, who knew more about the atomic bomb than Truman when he took office, mused, "Well, at least now we know that we haven't blown up the world by 1954. Who knows? Maybe I'll be prime minister in 1954!" He looked at all of us, and I noticed that Bowmar betrayed a slight smile.

Petra continued, "As a matter of fact, like the rest of my family, I was also drawn to the science of physics. I personally trained under Max Born at the University of Göttingen. He is Jewish and was suspended from his professorship at the University of Göttingen after the Nazis came to power, and that is why he left Germany and emigrated to the United Kingdom. My family and I were very deliberate and careful to conceal our Jewish heritage from the Nazi Party. Another German physicist, Werner Heisenberg, was awarded the 1932 Nobel Prize in Physics for the creation of quantum mechanics. I had become interested in quantum mechanics and after Max Born left Göttingen, I went to work as a research associate under Heisenberg at the University of Leipzig. Heisenberg was also a principal scientist in the German nuclear weapons program, and I became one of his close, trusted associates.

"Other than Klaus Richter, whom we mentioned previously, the other key person in this tale is Gunther Brandt, a protégé and respected colleague of Werner Heisenberg. I knew that he regularly communicated with Heisenberg regarding quantum mechanics theory. Following a March 1942 meeting at the Berghof, Hitler assigned Brandt and Richter to a top-secret, high-priority project, which I later learned was the Black Hole Project, using the blue exotic matter discovered in the Black Forest. Heisenberg, not knowing the specifics of Brandt's top-secret project but trusting me and my growing grasp of quantum mechanics theory, recommended my physics services to Brandt in August 1942. I joined Brandt's small team of physicists at the Black Hole Project in September 1942, and that is when I first met Emma at the office in Berchtesgaden.

"After getting to know Emma a bit, I asked her if she had ever been to Baker Street. She answered, 'That is a bit of an *irregular* question.' The SOE are known as the Baker Street Irregulars, of course. We literally hugged each other nearly breathless and went for a long walk together that day, comparing notes. Emma told me that her father was a leader in the French Resistance, and she knew how to contact him if and when she ever needed to flee Germany. We knew that we were part of possibly the most secretive project in Nazi Germany. Together, we determined that day to learn as much as we could, then escape when the time was right.

"Over the course of the next year, Emma started sleeping with and virtually living with Klaus Richter and had convinced him that her love for him was strong and real. I did the same with Gunther Brandt. Richter was in command of all security for the Black Hole Project, and Brandt was tasked to build the Black Hole Project time machine. Both were personally appointed by the Führer; they both reported their progress directly to Hitler. None of Hitler's inner circle knew about the existence of the Black Hole Project, even though they all regularly gathered for meetings with Hitler at the nearby Berghof. Since Brandt and Richter were so close and depended on each other to keep everything running smoothly, the four of us became best friends and eventually an inseparable team to complete the Black Hole Project on time for the Führer's upcoming departure to the future."

Bucky immediately enquired, "What do you mean by 'the Führer's upcoming departure to the future?'"

Petra responded, "According to my pillow talk with Gunther Brandt, the Führer has planned to escape to the New World of South America in the future. Gunther has been instructed to send Hitler exactly thirty years into the future, to the Pontifical Catholic University of Chile in Santiago. He plans to make that happen very soon, possibly just days from now."

Willy, who was Catholic by faith, chimed in with an impassioned question. "Why would Hitler want to land at a Catholic University in Chile? That bastard *has* no religion!"

Churchill added, "Touché, Willie! I always say, 'If you are going through hell, keep going,' and leave Hitler there, where he belongs!" We all laughed.

Crazy Ike observed, "Thirty years from now puts him in our time era of the mid-1970s. I think we should go find him, stick a GCPD up his ass, and then put him in the White Hole with coordinates to Stalin's back yard here in 1945. Stalin and the Ruskies would give him a real nice homecoming!"

The Prime Minister was enjoying himself. "I'd pay a hefty price to see Stalin in the ring with Hitler with no holds barred. I have a feeling that quirky, mustached Nazi would find himself strangled on the ropes! Comrade Stalin and his country have had an inexorable and inflexible resolve to fight Hitlerism to the end, until it is finally beaten down. That day is upon us, and the Soviets are knocking at the eastern gates of Berlin as we speak."

"According to Richter," Emma said, "Hitler thought he could manipulate Catholicism and religion in general to his advantage. He believed the University would be safe and fertile ground to connect with the German community in Chile and begin to execute his plans for the future. He is planning to take Gunther, Klaus, and his private pilot Hans Baur along with him, as well as enough blue exotic matter and gold for the future. I took a classified call from Hans Baur to Klaus Richter in late February, requesting the coordinates to the Black Hole Project's secret landing field. Bauer had arranged for a test flight from Berlin to deliver Hitler's gold and personal clothing the morning of Wednesday, March 7, 1945, using Hitler's private Junkers' airplane, Immelmann II. I saw this as our best opportunity to get away and to deliver the details of Hitler's escape plan into the hands of the British SOE."

Captain Ed Ratliff continued, "That was the day that Phil, Larry, and I swooped into those coordinates to pick these two women up in a

Junkers Ju-52/3m fitting the description of Hitler's plane, bearing the flight numbers D-2600. It seems we had a bit of a race to get away from that Richter chap, who wanted to spoil our fun and love of flying. The roof of his Mercedes-Benz 500K scraped the underbelly of our plane and gave us a good ride as we took to the air."

"More like a rollercoaster ride!" Petra complained.

SOE Commando Larry Baker remarked, "Well, that Richter chap, as you call him, managed to put a burst of machine gun bullets into the underbelly of that plane, a couple of which nearly ruined my day."

Churchill interposed, "You are a fortunate man, Larry; nothing in life is so exhilarating as to be shot at without result." That comment brought some more chuckles from the room.

Emma commented, "In all seriousness, when Klaus Richter fires bullets, he rarely misses; he is a cold-blooded killer when it comes to serving the Führer and the Third Reich. Many people have lost their lives at the hands of Richter, if even only under the suspicion of spying on the Black Hole Project. He grew up idolizing—no, *worshipping*—the Führer as a deity in the Hitler Youth Program. It is ingrained in him. Do not get caught in the crosshairs of his brainwashed aim. And one more thing: Hitler ordered Gunther and Klaus to wire the Black Hole Project time-travel machinery to self-destruct after they are all transported out of there. Hitler did not want anyone trying to follow them into the future."

Winston lit his second cigar, took his first puff, and pondered for a moment before he spoke. "Well, on that sober note, I must say that it was Harry Truman who called and urged me to involve the Denver Project in dealing with Hitler's Black Hole time-travel machine and diabolical plan to escape to the future. He told me about Roosevelt's last known letter, hand-written to Truman in the morning before Franklin died of his stroke. In that letter, FDR put his full support behind Captain Jack 'Bucky' Smith and the Denver Project to protect the future. That certainly is enough of a recommendation for me to hang my bowler hat on. So, what say you, Bucky and the Bad Love Gang?"

Goondoggy, eager to speak, was the first to respond. "How about we just do this the old-fashioned way, and bomb the living shit out of that Black Hole place tomorrow morning?!" He looked at me and Bucky and asked, 'Haven't you guys been practicing dropping those 4,000-pound cookie bombs against hillsides all last week, using those Wooden Wonder Mosquitoes? It's time to bomb that mother back to the stone age! You know, like Barney Rubble's time."

The rest of us in the Bad Love Gang couldn't help but giggle at Goondoggy. He was always so basic and candid. But there was something more about this operation that was tugging at me, and Bowmar got to the heart of it.

"Blue Nova One wanted us to run this operation," Bowmar stated. "She knew what she was doing when she gave us all the clues we needed to be sitting here with the prime minister on this day in history, with this company of people. She did not try to tell us exactly what to do or when to precisely do it, she just trusted that we would figure it out from here. From where I sit, having the de Haviland Mosquitoes bomb the Black Hole location into oblivion is definitely part of the plan." Goondoggy pooched his lips out and nodded, looking proudly first at Bowmar and then around the room, creating more amusement.

Bowmar resumed explaining his thought process. "But bombing that place is the second step. Bubble Butt and I discovered the White Hole Project, and we know that machine inside and out. I have been obsessively studying the physics of blue exotic matter and time-travel for the past eighteen months. Petra, Gunther Brandt, and their small team of physicists are brilliant to have created a similar time-travel machine in the same time frame as Albert Einstein and his team. There is something to be learned here." Petra softly smiled at Bowmar, and I could have sworn I saw a hint of affection. *All these incredibly cerebral and intelligent women like Blue Nova One and Petra are attracted to Bowmar; this could spell trouble some day!* I thought.

Petra commented, "I am German by birth, and Jewish by heritage and faith. This I know for certain: The Germans are richly gifted in the sciences of math, physics, and engineering. They are industrious, work hard, and know how to build things. Gunther Brandt's talents have been unfortunately misdirected for malevolent purposes in building the Black Hole. I am confident that the Black Hole will work; we were beginning to test it before Emma and I escaped. Bowmar's premise of learning something is very sound. It would be fascinating for you to know how the Black Hole Project was constructed and be able to compare it to the White Hole Project built independently in America. Maybe there is a better time machine to be built using the best technologies from both projects."

Churchill interposed, "Well, first I'd like to say that there is no limit to the ingenuity of man, if it is properly and vigorously applied under conditions of peace and justice. That Black Hole Project was built under the conditions of Hitler's oppressive tyranny, terror, and fear." He smiled as he looked around the room. "Secondly, the Germans do not have a monopoly on building things. We Brits also build things that dependably work!"

Listening to Bowmar, I knew what he was thinking. A plan started to materialize in my mind. As Petra and then Winston both spoke, my capricious music brain connected with my evolving strategy and started to play **"No Time"** by The Guess Who as was I visualizing a mission. I loved the song. The single version came out in September 1969 and went to number one in Canada, hitting number five on the US Billboard Hot 100. It also ranked in the top 20 in New Zealand and the UK. I remembered it best from 1971, when my sister Denise bought the *The Best of the Guess Who* album, which reached number 12 on the Billboard top LPs chart in the United States. The album cover looked like the band members were standing in a flooded barn with the sun at their backs. The songwriting team of guitarist-singer Randy Bachman and lead singer-keyboardist Burton Cummings wrote **"No Time"** as a twist on or reverse of a Dear John letter. The Guess Who was the most successful Canadian rock group of the late 1960s and early 1970s, and Canada's first rock superstars.

I came out of my music brain daydream just as the prime minister finished speaking and loudly blurted out, "I've got it!" Everyone looked at me a bit cross-eyed except for Bowmar and Bucky, who both probably half-expected me to come up with something.

Pumpkin, scratching his shoulders, teased, "Yeah, my bloke BB! I think I got it too."

Churchill half-chuckled and surprisingly joined in, scratching his chest with his right hand. "By George, I think it's spreading; I think I have it too!" By then everyone was laughing, and I could feel my face blushing warm red.

As the laughter subsided, I said, "We'll call this *Operation No Time*, and it will be synchronized to take place in two segments. But first, Petra, please tell me that you have the exact geographic coordinates for the Black Hole time-travel launch stage."

Petra answered, "Absolutely; we could not connect and send from point A to point B without having the precise coordinates of point A. However, the machine is designed to send time-travelers out, not to recall them back."

"Perfect, Petra," I replied. "For phase one, we will use the White Hole Project to send a group of us directly to the Black Hole Project launch stage. We'll spend no more than an hour there, taking pictures, gathering data and examining the way it is built and engineered. If there is any unused blue exotic matter on site, we'll try to take it with us. After that hour expires, we will be recalled back to the White Hole.

Phase two will be synchronized to start as we are zapped away, and that will be the Bad Love Mosquitoes bombing the Black Hole back to the stone ages." I winked at Goondoggy, who smiled back. Then I asked, "Emma and Petra, since you two are completely familiar with the Black Hole, would you consider going with us on this mission?"

Emma admitted, "I am terrified about seeing Klaus Richter again and him taking revenge on me. He does not hesitate to kill. On the other hand, if and when he sees me, it may at least temporarily cloud his judgement and give us an advantage. You can count me in, but we must be prepared to deal with Richter's violent side without hesitation."

Petra responded, "Gunther Brandt is not a violent man. He is hyper-intelligent, a bit eccentric, and a workaholic insomniac. He is also unexplainably loyal to Hitler. I would expect that he may try to run if he senses peril or danger. With my background in quantum mechanics and the work I have done on the Black Hole, I welcome the chance to go with you to experience time travel and to see the White Hole Project." She smiled again at Bowmar.

Prime Minister Churchill finished the meeting: "Based on all the intelligence we have gathered on the Allied Forces advancing on Berlin from the west and the Soviet Forces advancing from the east, we believe that Hitler will attempt to leave his Berlin Führerbunker and make his move to escape to the future late this week, or the weekend at the latest. We do not have inside eyes on him. Therefore, your *Operation No Time* has the green light from me, but you must launch early Wednesday morning—that is, on April 25, 1945—at the latest. I can see why my dear departed friend Franklin was fond and my new friend Harry is fond of the Denver Project and the Bad Love Gang. So, here are my parting words to you all: never give in. Never, never give in...and KBO!"

Bucky asked, "What is KBO, sir?"

"Keep buggering on; keep buggering on, Bucky."

CHAPTER EIGHTEEN:

DARK DAYS

"Dictators ride to and fro on tigers from which they dare
not dismount. And the tigers are getting hungry."
—Winston Churchill

Sunday, April 22, 1945, at 3:00 PM local time,
Adolf Hitler's Führerbunker in Berlin, Germany

B*litzkrieg*, which means "lightning war" in German, was the term that
described the successful tactics used by Nazi Germany in the early
years of World War II. German forces swept through Poland, Norway,
Belgium, Holland, and France with astonishing speed, victories that
justifiably put the rest of the world on edge. During the Fall of France
in the span of only 46 days in May–June 1940, the conquering German
soldiers seemed nearly superhuman as they pressed forward day after
day without seeming to need sleep or rest. The regular German army
(Wehrmacht) soldiers and Nazi Storm Troopers (including Klaus Richter's squad) were using a secret weapon: Pervitin, a drug that had been
widely dispensed to the troops. Using Pervitin, the soldiers of the
Wehrmacht could stay awake for days at a time and march many more
miles without resting.

Pervitin, patented in 1937 and developed by the Temmler pharmaceutical company based in Berlin, contained methamphetamine in its purest form. It was introduced in 1938 and marketed as a wonder drug for alertness and as an anti-depressive. It was briefly even available over the counter to the general German population. Known in more modern times as crystal meth—or ice, in its purest form—the drug also had many euphemistic names in the Third Reich, such as Hiter's Speed, Stuka-Pills, Goering-Pills, or Panzerschokolade (tank chocolate). Temmler produced Pervitin on an industrial scale for the German war effort. Thirty-five million Pervitin tablets were manufactured as an initial supply for the Wehrmacht in preparation for the attack on France. Based on a total invasion force of about 3.4 million troops, that would calculate to an average of ten pills per man. In reality, front-line combat units and Nazi Storm Trooper units probably received considerably more Pervitin.

The problem with Pervitin was that what goes up, must come down. The German population and army that became drug dependent experienced symptoms such as nausea, hallucinations, diminution of cognitive capacities, anxiety, depression, and physical exhaustion with drug shortages and subsequent withdrawal. Nazi SS-Gruppenführer Leonardo Conti, the Third Reich's health top official, reclassified Pervitin in 1941. The general public could no longer purchase it without a prescription, but its use for military purposes continued unabated; the prohibition was totally ignored among the ranks of the military. Despite this attempted legislation, the hook was set. Consumption did not decline much, even among civilians.

While Adolf Hitler may not have used Pervitin, his history of mind and body altering drug use and addiction was astonishing and was sparked by Dr. Theodore Morell. Morell had become a famous gynecologist and venereal disease specialist in Berlin who treated politicians and celebrities. He joined the Nazi Party when Hitler came to power in 1933. In 1935, Dr. Morell got a call from the Nazi SS office to come immediately to their headquarters to treat Henrich Hoffman, who was Hitler's inner circle personal photographer. Morell treated Hoffman with some solution in the form of an injection (his hallmark way of administering medicines), and he promptly felt better. After that exaggerated "life-saving" medical encounter, Morell became Henrich Hoffman's personal physician.

In 1936, Hoffman introduced Morell to Hitler when the Führer complained of severe stomach cramps after a heavy meal. Morell suggested an injection of glucose and vitamins to treat the problem, and Hitler consented. Morell gave him an injection that contained glucose, vitamins, and a trace amount of methamphetamine and/or an opioid, which subdued the pain and "cured" Hitler instantly. Morell subsequently began treating Hitler with various commercial preparations, including a combination of vitamins and Mutaflor, a hydrolyzed E. coli bacteria-based medication, which successfully treated Hitler's intestinal problems. Hitler became convinced of Morell's medical genius, and Dr. Morell quickly became part of the Führer's inner circle.

Morell's early success in suppressing Hitler's stomach cramps seemed to make Hitler unusually reliant on Morell's subsequent diagnoses and prescriptions. Thus began a devoted, mutually dependent relationship that lasted to the end of Hitler's reign. Thanks to his incredibly close association with Hitler, Morell billed himself as the Führer's personal physician, building a list of high-status clients in Nazi Germany; Morell amassed a small fortune, and even acquired a previously Jewish-owned Czech company to mass-produce vitamins and animal hormone remedies.

During his time as Hitler's personal physician, Morell kept detailed notes and private medical records. His notes later revealed that the doctor injected Hitler almost daily with various drugs and drug cocktails, including animal hormones and steroids, amphetamines for energy, barbiturate sleeping pills, and opiates. No one knew at the time exactly what Morell was injecting into Hitler—but as far as Hitler was concerned, it worked. The particulars were a secret kept between the two men. Morell's personal notes indicated that he gave Hitler some 800 injections over the years of their relationship. Morell was always next to Hitler and boasted that he was the only person who saw Hitler every day.

Morell reportedly gave Hitler his first dose of a drug called Eukodal before an important meeting with the Italian leader Benito Mussolini in July 1943. Eukodal was the German brand name for the potent synthetic opiate oxycodone, a pharmaceutical cousin of heroin. Hitler loved Eukodal. In late 1944, when the military situation was steadily deteriorating, Eukodal made him euphoric even when reality was cause for despair. Despite his top generals carefully trying to warn him that they were going to lose the war, the drugs made him feel invulnerable and on top of the situation, ensuring an ongoing continuum of grandiose and disastrous military decisions.

Herman Göring, who himself was known to have been addicted to morphine, coined a nickname for Dr. Theodore Morell that stuck: "Der Reichsspritzenmeister." Although this peculiar term does not have an exact English translation, it could be variously interpreted as "Injection Master of the German Reich," or "The Master of the Imperial Needle." Basically it implied that Morell overused injections and drugs when faced with assorted medical problems. Despite Morell's unpopularity with the Führer's inner circle of confidants, Hitler stayed faithful to his creepy, quacky personal doctor until the very end, and Morell was with him in the Führerbunker on this day in April 1945. Hitler's faithful friend and personal pilot, Hans Baur, was also present in the Führerbunker.

Berlin was bombarded by Soviet artillery for the first time on April 20, 1945, which also happened to be Hitler's fifty-sixth birthday. By the evening of April 21, 1945, Soviet Red Army tanks had reached the northern outskirts of the city. Felix Steiner was a decorated Waffen-SS commander who had led several SS divisions and German corps during World War II. He was the prestigious recipient of the Knight's Cross of the Iron Cross with Oak Leaves and Swords. On January 28, 1945, Steiner was placed in command of the 11th SS Panzer Army, assigned to defend Berlin from the Soviet armies advancing from west. On April 21, 1945, during the Battle for Berlin, Steiner was placed in command of what Hitler called "Army Detachment Steiner." Hitler ordered Steiner to envelope the advancing Russian front through a pincer movement, from the north of Berlin. Steiner, a seasoned combat veteran, knew his unit was outnumbered by ten to one. He recognized that his units were made up of some soldiers, Hitler Youth teens, and emergency Air Force and Navy troops that were inadequately trained and understrength. He refused to attack and made it clear on April 22, 1945, that he did not have sufficient capacity for a counterattack during his call to the daily situation conference in the Führerbunker.

Hitler walked into his afternoon staff conference meeting in the Führerbunker after everyone was already there and waiting to discuss the evolving military situation in the Battle for Berlin. When he was informed that the Steiner counterattack had never happened and that the Soviets were now entering the northern suburbs of Berlin, Hitler flew into a mad rage, pacing around the floor and screaming at everyone present in the Führerbunker conference room. "Steiner has deserted and failed me, the Wehrmacht and SS are all incompetent traitors! Will not anyone stand and defend Berlin and the Fatherland?! Our disloyal and deceitful commanders are insolent and have become cowards in the face of our enemies! We are losing and we deserve to lose with such demonstration of weakness! The war is lost, but I will stay here to the end!" He left the conference room visibly angry and shaken.

Hitler walked down the hallway directly to the doorway of the Führerbunker telephone switchboard. The switchboard operator, SS Sergeant Rochus Misch, looked up in surprise, "Yes, Mein Führer, how can I help?"

The Führer impatiently responded, "Get Obergruppenführer Klaus Richter and Herr Gunther Brandt on my private line immediately! Put the call through to my desk phone in my office. Schnell, Sergeant!"

Five minutes later, seated at the desk in his private study, the phone rang. "Do I have Obergruppenführer Richter and Herr Gunther Brandt on the line?"

On the phone line, Sergeant Misch replied, "Yes, Mein Führer. I will hang up, and they are both ready to speak with you." Hitler heard the click of Misch hanging up.

"Herr Brandt, it has been three months since we spoke in January about my time-table. Is the Black Hole fully operational and ready for my departure?" Hitler asked.

Gunther Brandt replied affirmatively. "Yes, Mein Führer, the Black Hole time-travel machine is now fully operational, and I have it programed and ready to send you, Hans Baur, Klaus Richter, and me exactly thirty years into the future to the Pontifical Catholic University of Chile in Santiago. We will take our clothing, the gold that you sent last month, and the remaining blue exotic matter. Klaus and I have wired the Black Hole Project time-travel machinery to self-destruct after we are all transported to the future. When exactly can we expect your arrival here?"

Hitler relaxed a bit and more calmly answered, "That is an admirable report, Gunther, on a day filled with wicked and corrupt news of our army's unending failures. Stalin's tanks have breached northern Berlin, and the battle for Berlin is reaching its final days. Today I will assign Gruppenführer Baur to make preparations to fly the two of us to the Black Hole landing strip, arriving at dawn on Thursday morning. Obergruppenführer Richter, I will expect you to be there waiting to take us to the Black Hole."

Richter replied, "Yes, Mein Führer, I will be there with a covert SS security detail so as not to raise any local suspicions of your presence. So far, our nearby and well-hidden SS and Wehrmacht mountain troop units have not yet engaged any enemy incursions."

"When Baur and I arrive, I will be dressed in civilian clothes for the time-travel trip to South America. Let the security detail know ahead of time, Klaus."

"Understood, Mein Führer. Is there anything else we should know?" Richter enquired.

"There is one more element to mention; Gunther, is there any weight limitation to the time-travel transport unit?" Hitler asked.

Gunther replied, "None that I am specifically aware of, to transport out. Of course, I am not sure about the landing process on the other side of the time-travel trip, having never done it before. Why do you ask?"

"I am sending my personal physician, Dr. Morell, to Berchtesgaden," Hitler disclosed. "He will leave tomorrow morning. He is a large, portly person, and there is no room for anyone else but me and Baur to fly out of here on Thursday. If he makes it to the Berchtesgaden office on or by Wednesday, he will call you, Klaus. You will then get him to the Black Hole to go with us. If he does not make it by Wednesday, then we leave him behind."

Klaus replied, "I will be on standby if he arrives on time, Mein Führer."

"Very well, gentlemen. The time has nearly arrived to take *Mein Kampf* to the future. I shall see you at dawn on Thursday—or contact you immediately if there are any changes of plans." He hung up the phone and silently breathed a sigh of relief.

Next, he summoned Dr. Morell and told him that he needed to leave the following morning, April 23rd, and get to Berchtesgaden by

Wednesday to contact Richter. Finally, he sent for Hans Baur. Baur had already carefully devised a plan to allow Hitler to escape from the Battle of Berlin. He had a Fieseler Fi 156 Storch, a small German liaison aircraft built by the Fieseler aircraft company, held on standby. The small plane could take off from an improvised airstrip in the Tiergarten, Berlin's most popular inner-city park, near the Brandenburg Gate. Hitler told Baur, "Hans, you must be prepared to fly us to the Black Hole landing strip early Thursday morning, arriving there at sunrise."

Baur was one of the few people who was truly close to Hitler. As his private pilot and personal friend, he was in Hitler's presence practically every day from 1933 to 1945. Baur did have a concern as he sat down to speak with Hitler. He had made the earlier test flight from Berlin to the secret Black Hole landing strip in March, delivering Hitler's gold and personal clothing, and had clocked the flight distance at 340 miles. The Fiesler Storch had a range of 240 miles. He did not want to risk having to stop anywhere to refuel at this late point in the war with Hitler on board the plane.

"I spoke to Hanna Reitsch," he informed the Führer, referring to the famous World War II female German aviator and test pilot, "and we agreed that the Arado Ar 96 trainer will make a better escape plane from the improvised airstrip in the Tiergarten. It has a range of six hundred sixty miles and will get us to the Black Hole twice as fast." The Arado Ar 96 was the Luftwaffe's standard advanced trainer plane during World War II. "I will have one on standby, fueled and ready for us on Wednesday—just in case we have to leave a day early for any reason."

"When we leave the Führerbunker at three thirty AM on Thursday morning, I will be dressed in civilian clothes, Hans. Clear the way for us to leave unnoticed. When we walk out of here, we are going to the future. No one can know what happened to us, understood?" Hitler demanded.

"Yes, Mein Führer, understood."

CHAPTER NINETEEN:
BLACK IS BLACK

"I think we all wish we could erase some dark times in our lives.
But all of life's experiences, bad and good, make you who you are.
Erasing any of life's experiences would be a great mistake."
—Luis Miguel

*Wednesday, January 7, 1976, 12:00 AM Midnight local time,
the White Hole Project in Oak Ridge, Tennessee*

*Wednesday, April 25, 1945, at 6:00 AM local time, the Black Hole
Project near the shoreline of the picturesque Lake Königssee in
the Malerwinkel forest of Bavaria, Germany*

After leaving Churchill's Cabinet War Room late Sunday afternoon, the entire group present—minus the prime minister—had retreated to the Goring Hotel to flesh out the details of *Operation No Time*. Otto G. Goring kindly provided us with a small private conference room at the hotel, and we made our plans there. Afterwards, in the early evening, Bowmar and I took Emma and Petra to Bucky's suite, explained the White Hole time travel process to them, and then implanted global cosmic positioning devices (GCPDs) into their buttocks. Emma declared, "What I do for God and country!" Petra wanted to examine and disassemble the GCPD; she kept asking

Bowmar questions about its contents and quantum physics properties. Thanks to Bowmar's foresight, the Black Box came back to us on Sunday night, April 22, 1945, at 9:00 PM London time, landing in the private Goring Hotel Garden. When the Black Box was zapped back on Monday morning, we sent it with instructions to recall Bowmar, Crazy Ike, Goondoggy, Tater, me, Emma, and Petra to the White Hole on Tuesday.

We agreed to conduct the mission in two parts. For phase one, Emma Hoffman, Petra Vogel, Bowmar, Crazy Ike, Goondoggy, Tater, and I would use the White Hole Project to send us directly into the Black Hole Project at 6:00 AM on Wednesday, April 25, 1945, using the precise coordinates provided to us by Petra. Bowmar and I had been best friends since childhood, and I had rarely seen him so totally pumped and excited to go on an adventure. He seemed oblivious to the dangers involved. I supposed he was fixated on learning the physics secrets of the Black Hole Project, especially that it was designed to take time-travelers to the future. The White Hole Project, with its current configuration, had limitations; it could only send us back to and recall us from points throughout 1942–1945, during the World War II time era.

Crazy Ike, Goondoggy, Tater, and I were all armed to the teeth with Thompson machine guns, Colt .45 M1911 pistols, and Mk grenades to provide protection. Emma would show us the lay of the land inside the Black Hole Project and where to seal the access points, while Petra would work with Bowmar to take pictures, gather data, and review the techniques of how the Black Hole was built and engineered. One hour was not much time, but we did not want to take any unnecessary chances. Our primary motivation was to destroy the Black Hole before Hitler could use it to escape to the future. We took the Black Box with us in case there was any loose blue exotic matter or other items of interest to take back. I personally made certain to take the Reach Out device that Blue Nova One had given to me. For some reason, I was having foreboding feelings about this mission.

Emma did not expect any armed resistance inside the Black Hole other than the possibility of an encounter with Klaus Richter, whom we all viewed as an accomplished deadly assassin. Emma pointed out that there were always SS guards posted around the clock outside the Black Hole to prevent any unauthorized entry to the highly secretive project. Without Klaus Richter's express approval, those guards were not allowed to enter the Black Hole because its contents and purpose were so highly secretive.

Mary, the Runt, and Spaghetti Head continued to operate the White Hole Project controls. They would give us exactly one hour at the Black Hole Project, then zap us back to Oak Ridge at 7:00 AM before returning Emma and Petra to London. They would then send the rest of us back to Liverpool, England to join the other half of the Bad Love Gang in the search for Hannah Lieb.

For phase two, Bucky, Pumpkin, Willie, RAF Captain Ed Ratliff, and RAF Lieutenant Phil Dawson (along with assigned navigators) would be flying five de Havilland Mosquitoes, each carrying 4,000-pound cookies, or blockbuster bombs. Their job was to bomb the site, destroying and burying the Black Hole Project, which was located about four miles south of Berchtesgaden and built into a steep hill-side near the shoreline of Lake Königsee. The lake, surrounded by the steeply rising flanks of mountains like a fjord, stretched five miles in a south-north direction; the Black Hole Project had been con-structed near the northern end at a bend in the lake. The Bad Love Mosquitoes would start their run at the south end of the lake and bomb the entrance location of Black Hole as they banked hard to the left, with the plan to make it and the hill it was built into to collapse. I was disappointed not to be flying the sixth Mosquito with them, after training for the bombing run and imagining the destruction wrought by dropping one of those blockbuster bombs. The Bad Love Mosquito Squadron was scheduled to drop their bombs starting at 7:30 AM sharp, thirty minutes after we had departed from the inside of the Black Hole Project.

Of significant interest, we learned from Ratliff and Dawson that the head of British Bomber Command, Air Chief Marshal Sir Arthur Harris, had made the decision to conduct a large air raid on Obersalzberg later the same day. Hitler's Berghof and the Eagle's Nest pavilion were the raid's primary targets, while secondary targets included the houses of other senior Nazi officials and the barracks used by the Waffen-SS units assigned to defend Obersalzberg. The town of Berchtesgaden was not a target. A total of 359 British Avro Lancaster heavy bombers drawn from 22 squadrons were to be escorted by British fighter squadrons and North American P-51 Mustang fighters from the Eighth Air Force. They were scheduled to begin bombing Obersalzberg at 9:30 AM. Sixteen Pathfinder de Havilland Mosquito bombers from our same No. 8 Group were assigned to guide the bombers to Obersalzberg using their Oboe navigation systems. April 25, 1945, looked to be a bad day for the Führer, with his beloved Berghof, Eagle's Nest, and the top-secret Black Hole Project all targets for Allied destruction.

Emma, Petra, Bowmar, Crazy Ike, Goondoggy, Tater, and I were zapped from the White Hole Project directly onto the Black Hole Project launch stage, arriving at precisely 6:00 AM on Wednesday, April 25, 1945. The seven of us stood together in a tightly held group hug, with the guys surrounding the two women in the middle, when we launched from the White Hole. Petra had informed us that the Black Hole launch stage was only six feet in diameter. We landed off-balance on the Black Hole launch stage; Crazy Ike, Goondoggy, and I all fell backwards and sideways from the stage onto the surrounding floor, bumping up against the lower racetrack and making a lot of noise with our gear and all. Except for a few bangs and bruises, no one was injured badly. As we had rehearsed, we all assumed firing positions with our weapons drawn as we tried to quickly recover and clear our heads from the time-travel journey.

The Black Hole Project room lights were all on, but the room was initially vacant and eerily quiet. The room—or vault, as we liked to call it—was enormous. Some of the walls visible were composed of raw, exposed cut stone; others were covered in poured concrete. I looked up and around us and sure enough, there was an upper cyclotron racetrack above us with an inverted funnel shaped connector designed to telescope down and connect to a lower racetrack surrounding the launch stage. I could see the glow of blue exotic matter inside the inverted funnel connector. There were nearly wall-to-wall computers softly whirring, and multicolor lights on the computer wall boards were intermittently flashing. One sight especially caught my attention and sent a cold shiver down my spine, with the reality of our present time and location in history. On the wall not fully lined with computers behind the master control desk panel, and hanging from above, there was a massive red flag with a black swastika on a white disc, the official flag of the German Third Reich—the flag of Nazi Germany.

The control desk panel faced the launch stage and a sizeable, framed portrait of Adolf Hitler hung on the wall directly behind the desk and below the Nazi flag. I already felt uncomfortable with the surroundings, and we had just landed. Looking up again, I noticed that the upper cyclotron racetrack was fixed in its place and did not move up and down like its counterpart at the White Hole Project; only the inverted funnel connector containing blue exotic matter telescoped down from the upper racetrack. Although the whole Black Hole Project was much bigger and bulkier, its overall configuration reminded me more of the time-and-space-travel machine we had used at the Queen's Island Space Center on planet Azur than our own White Hole Project in Oak Ridge, Tennessee.

Detecting no immediate threats in the room, I lowered my Thompson machine gun and shared my initial observations with Bowmar, who was also already mentally busy looking around the inside of the Black Hole Project vault. "Bowmar, if nothing else, figure out how these computers talk to the racetracks about connecting the present time to a specific time and place in the future without the upper racetrack having to mechanically move."

Bowmar replied, "I've already noticed the same thing, BB. This place looks more like the machine on planet Azur than the White Hole. I guess the German physicists think like the Azurians."

Petra took that as her cue. "I have worked with Max Born, Werner Heisenberg, and here at the Black Hole with Gunther Brandt. We German physicists think in terms of quantum mechanics: that light and matter exhibit properties of both particles and waves. A fundamental feature of the theory is that it usually cannot predict with certainty what will happen, but only give probabilities. In 1925, Max Born and Werner Heisenberg formulated the matrix mechanics representation of quantum mechanics. Born's rule in 1926 gave the probability that a measurement of a quantum system would yield a given result. But there is a tradeoff in predictability between different measurable quantities in quantum mechanics. Heisenberg's uncertainty principle in 1927 stated that the more precisely the position of some particle is determined, the less precisely its momentum can be predicted from initial conditions, and vice versa."

"In 1925, Albert Einstein told a young physics student named Esther Salaman that he wanted to know how God created this world. He said, 'I'm not interested in this or that phenomenon, in the spectrum of this or that element. I want to know His thoughts; the rest are just details,'" Bowmar added.

Petra smiled at Bowmar, then continued, "I love that quote! Even people like me, who love quantum mechanics, yearn for a unifying physics theory. In the world of quantum mechanics, we think a particle can act like it's spinning in two opposite directions at the same time or existing in two or more locations simultaneously. What if a particle can pulsate, oscillate, or exist in ten dimensions or locations at the same time? And what about the concept of negative mass? I have been studying blue exotic matter with Brandt. It is clearly multidimensional, and it has undeniable negative mass characteristics or anti-gravity properties that violate certain energy conditions and show strange attributes. I think that even Brandt would agree with me that a lifetime could be spent studying the complex physics of blue exotic matter."

From the shadowy corner across the vault, we heard a voice say, "You're right about that, Petra. Blue exotic matter holds the secrets to the universe, and I do plan to spend my life unlocking its secrets. It's a shame that I'll be doing that without you by my side." Goondoggy and Crazy Ike trained their guns in the direction of the voice, and I told Tater to cover the rest of the room with me. Gunther Brandt, a six-foot tall, slender man with dark brown hair, wearing a worn and wrinkled khaki jumpsuit, emerged from the corner with his hands held up. Crazy Ike immediately went over and frisked him, then told us the man had no weapons.

As Brandt came closer and into the light, he appeared a bit haggard, with his unkempt, dark-brown hair, a three-day beard, and slightly sunken, bloodshot eyes. He and Petra stared at each other for a moment. He continued, "I don't know how you got in here, Petra, but you should not have come back. This place is crawling with security, and you will never get out of here alive. Unless all of you are suicide commandoes, you will all die if you try to damage this machine in any way." Then he glanced at Emma. "Hi, Emma. You especially should not be here. You left Klaus in a bad way."

Tater quickly studied Brandt, then looked at me and drawled, "He looks like ten miles of bad road. You want me to jerk a knot in his tail and put him in the corner?"

Despite being on high alert, I couldn't help but smile at Tater while Goondoggy and Crazy Ike chuckled a bit. Petra commented, "Everyone, this is Gunther Brandt. Gunther, I can see that you haven't changed your ways and probably have not slept for days. Is this machine ready to send the Führer to the future as planned?"

"Yes, it is ready, programmed, and fully operational."

"When is he coming?" Petra demanded.

"Very soon," Gunther replied.

"Why are you answering me so readily, Gunther?" Petra asked.

"Because you will never leave here." Gunther somberly stated. "Who are these intruders with you who are soon to perish?"

Goondoggy stepped forward, grabbing Brandt by the collar with his new left hand, holding his machine gun in his right hand. "We're the Bad Love Gang, Butt Face Brandt; remember that name when this is over. Can you remember that fact in your quantum brain?" Goondoggy looked at me and questioned, "Have you had enough, BB? I sure have."

I agreed, "Yeah, sit him down somewhere and keep an eye on him. He seems harmless enough, and maybe we'll have some questions for him later." I looked at my watch as I turned to Bowmar, Petra, and Emma, "Bowmar, we've got fifty minutes and counting. Do your thing with Petra and learn as much as you can while Emma shows us around. We'll get all the exits secured and seal this place off from the guards and outside world."

Wednesday, April 25, 1945, at 6:45 AM local time, the Black Hole Project

Emma led Crazy Ike, me, and Tater around the premises while Goondoggy kept an eye on Gunther Brandt. We locked and barred every doorway and hatch leading into the Black Hole vault. What we did not know was that after Emma and Petra had escaped to London on March 7, 1945, Klaus Richter and Gunther Brandt had made a security safeguard addition to the Black Hole: a passive alert or intrusion button that sounded an alarm in Richter's office in Berchtesgaden. Gunther had pressed the alarm before emerging from the shadows to confront us.

When Richter was notified of the silent distress signal at 6:12 AM, he speedily and methodically contacted all the Black Hole sentry stations manned by his most loyal Waffen-SS guards. None of his trusted guard corps had seen or heard anything unusual—and everyone had been placed on a higher state of alert by Richter, with the Führer scheduled to arrive on Thursday morning. He called Brandt's home but got no answer; however, it was not atypical for Brandt to spend the night working at the Black Hole. By protocol, he did not try calling the inside of the Black Hole; in case there had been an intrusion, he did not want to give any warning. He then had the guards discreetly and quietly try the entrances, and they soon called back to say everything was locked down. Richter could not make sense of this and decided he needed to attend to it personally. He had secretly devised an access hatch to the Black Hole vault that only he was privy to. He suspected that the silent intrusion alarm had somehow been accidently activated, but with the Führer arriving in twenty-four hours, he could take no chances.

At 6:45 AM, Nazi SS Obergruppenführer Klaus Richter, with his Luger P08 pistol drawn and ready, quietly and covertly entered through the back wall of a closed supply closet from a restricted access tunnel that had been created for this very purpose. The closet door looked ordinary, identical to all the other closet doors in the Black Hole Project vault. However, this specific closet door was locked and unlocked from the inside. Ventilation slits in the closet door made it easy to both watch and listen. Its strategic location along the wall to the left and behind the master control panel gave it a bird's eye, panoramic view of the main vault interior. Klaus immediately heard unfamiliar voices and could not believe his eyes when he gazed through the ventilation slits.

Directly in front of him, on hands and knees and looking up inside the master control panel cabinet with a flashlight, was a Black officer wearing an American uniform. He was being assisted by none other than Petra Vogel, and the two of them were taking notes and chattering away. Straight across the room, another American officer was standing guard over Gunther Brandt, who was sitting on the floor with his back against the wall and his head down. Klaus could hear other voices approaching from down the hallway that intersected with the wall were Gunther was located. Klaus was compelled to act swiftly, knowing that he was solely responsible for keeping the Black Hole secure and undamaged.

The moment that Goondoggy looked toward the hallway of the oncoming voices, Klaus stealthily slipped out of the closet door and was immediately upon Petra, who was behind Bowmar, kneeling and looking up inside the master control panel cabinet. He cold-cocked Petra on the back of her head with his pistol handle, sending her spinning to the floor semi-unconscious. Goondoggy thought he heard something and looked across the room. Seeing no one, he thought Petra was kneeling behind the control panel helping Bowmar. Goondoggy looked back toward the hallway opening and loudly queried, "Is everything okay, BB?"

Bowmar heard a soft thud on the floor behind him and asked, "Petra, are you okay?"

Klaus Richter, a six-foot tall, chiseled German athlete, age 28, with his adrenalin surging, grabbed Bowmar around the waist from behind, yanking him clear out of the control panel cabinet. He then strong-armed Bowmar, straightening him up still from behind, using his left arm. He simultaneously jammed the barrel of his Luger P08 pistol hard into Bowmar's right temple. He spoke into Bowmar's left ear. "I will kill you in a heartbeat. Don't say a word, nod your head if you understand." Bowmar, grimacing in pain from having the gun barrel shoved in his head, silently nodded.

Concurrent with gaining control of Bowmar, Richter observed three more American officers emerging from the hallway across the room: Crazy Ike, Tater, and me, along with Emma Hoffman. On seeing Emma, his blood boiled; his emotions roiled in an undefined kaleidoscopic cesspool. Bowmar felt Richter's grip tense and tighten to the extent that it became hard to breathe while Richter walked him out from behind the control panel and into the open. "Everyone drop your weapons now!" Richter demanded. "Show me your hands above your heads, or this man dies! You have to the count of ten to comply!"

All five of us gaped at Richter holding Bowmar at gunpoint. We were shocked that he had somehow made it into the vault and had the upper hand. Emma rapidly informed us, "That is Klaus Richter, and he will not hesitate to pull the trigger!"

I looked at my watch and softly said, "We are all out of here and back home in twelve minutes; we just have to talk and delay." Then more loudly I commanded, "Drop your weapons!" Everyone complied and the Thompson machine guns clattered to the floor.

Goondoggy was standing off to our right next to Gunther; the other four of us were grouped more closely together, with Emma standing in front and slightly to my left, while Tater stood in front of Crazy Ike, who was on my right. Klaus then shoved Bowmar from behind, sending him in our direction. For a split second, I was glad that Bowmar was joining us. But as he shoved Bowmar away in the direction of Goondoggy, Klaus snarled, "Join your friends in hell." At that instant, my heart started racing and I thought about the Reach Out button to call for Blue Nova One. The device was in my right pants pocket, and my hands were above my head. I thought, *surely if I lower my right hand, he will start shooting.*

What happened next was not how the movie in my head of us talking our way out of this was supposed to play. Emma tried to get Klaus to talk by saying, "Klaus, we came from the future. You can come to the future with us, but your beloved Führer will never make it here alive. His days are over."

Klaus icily replied, "When you left, the Führer became my only love. For your betrayal, you get two bullets, Emma." Klaus, a renowned Waffen-SS pistol marksman, used his reliable Luger P08 pistol loaded with eight 9mm rounds to robotically assassinate our entire group with precision. He started shooting from left to right, calculating one bullet per person—and two for Emma. His first shot went through Bowmar's back and into his heart, dropping Bowmar face first to the floor. As Bowmar was falling forward, the second shot went right through the middle of Goondoggy's neck; he went down choking and grabbing his throat. I always thought that one would have time to think and dodge or run in a scenario like this, but Klaus was firing too fast and with deadly accuracy.

Tater and Crazy Ike both took head shots, but I was partially shielded by Emma, who was standing directly in front of me. I was reflexively reaching into my right pants pocket as Richter's shot punctured the right side of my chest, clipping my right pulmonary vein. The force of the shot blew me backwards and down, but I did feel the Reach Out device firmly clenched in my right hand. Klaus methodically shot Emma in the head and chest next. Gunther Brandt had edged himself toward a secondary exit to his right while watching the mayhem. As I lay on the ground gasping for air, I could see that Klaus had turned and was walking toward the back of the control panel to put his last bullet into Petra. I squeezed the Reach Out button in my right hand with my last ounce of strength, and my world went black and silent...

CHAPTER TWENTY:

BLUE IS BETTER

"A true friend never gets in your way
unless you happen to be going down."
—Arnold H. Glasgow

Wednesday, April 25, 1945, at 6:49 AM local time,
the Black Hole Project near the shoreline of Lake Königssee
in the Malerwinkel forest of Bavaria, Germany

We all tend to learn much more from our failures or mistakes than from our successes. Too many consecutive successes foster pride—and pride is no great virtue to cultivate anyway. When Blue Nova One's beloved husband Blue Rhett One was killed by Klaus Richter in the Black Forest of Germany, a lot was learned from that event. During the detailed failure analysis of that mission, the Blue Azurians conceived, envisioned, and developed the thirty-second flashback in time. The flashback would potentially change some time continuum outcomes (primarily on planet Azur) without disrupting time or history too broadly. They commercialized the flashback invention for use in their Azurian Flashback vehicles to save lives. It wasn't perfect, but it did work; it had worked to save the lives of the Bad Love Gang on planet Azur.

When I had met privately with Blue Nova One before departing planet Azur, she told me that they wanted to do something extra special to show their gratitude for our successful rescue mission to the Republic. Her engineers came up with the device I called the Reach Out. If the Bad Love Gang ever got into a major plight or predicament in our time travels, where there was no hope and no solution, then she told me to press the Reach Out button. It would contact her directly and she would be there, thirty seconds prior to the time I hit the button to help—possibly putting herself in danger in the process, but that is what she offered. I managed to push that button as I was falling onto death's doorstep inside Hitler's Black Hole Project.

The clock inside the Black Hole was reset back thirty seconds in time. I was again standing behind Emma, with Crazy Ike next to me on my right and Tater in front of him. Goondoggy was off to our right, next to Gunther Brandt. Klaus Richter, standing in front of us, shoved Bowmar from behind, sending him in our direction. As he jolted Bowmar toward Goondoggy, Klaus pointed his Luger P08 pistol at Bowmar's back and growled, "Join your friends in hell." Emma spoke, causing Klaus to pause for a moment. "Klaus, we came from the future. You can come to the future with us, but your beloved Führer will never make it here alive. His days are over."

Klaus looked away from targeting Bowmar's back for a second. Glaring straight at Emma, he icily replied, "When you left, the Führer became my only love. For your betrayal, you get two bullets, Emma." In the twinkling of that split second, as Klaus looked back to refocus his aim on Bowmar and start shooting, Blue Nova One wondrously appeared between Klaus and Bowmar, blocking his line of fire. She looked different; her Azurian suit with Luna hood and heads-up display was not shiny silvery-white, it was blue and glowing. It was like looking into a deep blue sky. Her Luna artificial intelligence hood covered her face and eyes, leaving no exposed skin. I surmised that blue exotic matter was somehow involved, and that she was dressed for battle. I was correct.

Klaus's expression went from angry to startled and he bellowed, "Not you again! Are you back for more, bitch?!"

Gunther Brandt began to edge himself toward a secondary exit to his right while watching the encounter between Klaus and Nova.

Blue Nova One, confident and not at all rattled by Klaus's obscene insult, replied, "I'll take those two bullets and any others you can manage to fire before you meet your maker at the hands of a woman."

Nova's blue Azurian battle suit and Luna hood were dialed to full engagement, the mode that used blue exotic matter technology to reject any ballistic projectiles. Her battle suit's protective shield was fully weaponized; any physical contact engagement with a hostile force would electrically shock the opponent to neutrality or death.

Klaus, clearly rattled, took the bait and fired his first shot at Nova's forehead. The bullet decelerated and stopped before Nova could even feel any contact pressure, and it innocuously fell to the floor. He then emptied the remainder of his 8-round magazine, aiming for her chest; all seven of those projectiles fell harmlessly to the floor as well. He then hauled off and tried to kick Blue Nova One. She caught his foot and forcefully pushed him back, her Azurian battle suit covering her hands. The combined push and repulsive electrical shock emitted by the suit literally sent him flying backwards across the room. Klaus crashed into the back wall next to the closet door from where he had snuck into the room.

We all grabbed our Thompson machine guns off the floor. Blue Nova One sensed that they were all immediately pointed at Klaus Richter and ready to fire. She calmly walked toward him and held both arms out with her palms turned back toward us. Without looking at us, she firmly stated, "That won't be necessary; this is my battle." We lowered our weapons and watched. Nova softly spoke to her Luna

AI as she approached Klaus, "Defensive shield to maximum battle power."

Luna replied, "You will have three seconds of maximum battle power and then I will need to recharge."

Nova answered, "That is all I will need, Luna. Do it."

As Nova reached Klaus, he pulled himself up against the wall to stand and face her. Defiantly he said, "It seems your electrical powers came up short again, blue woman."

Nova responded, "I see no reasonable alternative but to prove you wrong." She stepped forward, reached under his arms and lifted him up against the wall as a supercharged electrical shock shot through his entire body for three straight seconds. We watched as his body violently vibrated, quaked, and quivered. His brain, spinal cord, and heart all essentially shorted out and when Nova let go, Klaus Richter limply slumped dead to the floor.

It was 6:54 AM, and we all ran across the room to hug Blue Nova One for saving our lives. As we did that, Gunther Brandt slipped away unnoticed out one of the exits. Bowmar was the first to embrace Nova and gave her an awkward kiss on the cheek as she peeled back her Luna AI hood. She smiled and winked at Bowmar, and then I grabbed both her hands. Gazing into her eyes, I said, "Thank you for the Reach Out device, and for coming to save us. We were all dead; now we are alive because of you." Then I tried to tease her just a little. "You told us that you were not a warring civilization and consciously sought to maintain peace."

Nova perceptively smiled at me and replied, "I did say that we choose peace and avoid war, but I also said that we are not naïve. I chose not to be naïve here today, Bubble Butt."

"Touché, Nova, touché!" I declared. I quickly introduced Emma, Petra, Crazy Ike, and Tater to Blue Nova One, and everyone profusely and graciously thanked her for the rescue. We watched as she briefly grabbed and studied Goondoggy's left hand and then broadly smiled at him, saying, "Looking good there, Goondoggy, looking good!" We all laughed.

It was 6:59 AM as I told Crazy Ike, Tater, and Goondoggy to give Nova all their grenades as did I. I asked Nova, "We have to go now, but can you use these to blow up the control panel and stage before you leave? Bucky, Pumpkin, Willy, and two Brits are flying in to bomb this place to smithereens at seven thirty AM."

Nova coolly agreed. "I'll make certain it's disabled, BB. Have a good trip and get that medicine to Hannah like we discussed." The clock hit 7:00 AM and the seven of us were zapped away from the Black Hole and Blue Nova One, on our journey back to the future.

Wednesday, April 25, 1945, at 7:30 AM local time,
the Black Hole Project entrance and the sky above the waters
of Lake Königssee in Bavaria, Germany

Bucky, Pumpkin, Willy, Ed Ratliff, and Phil Dawson were piloting five incoming B Mk XVI de Havilland, Mosquitoes, proudly calling themselves the "Bad Love Mosquito Squadron." These Mosquitoes had bulging bomb bays and each one was carrying a 4,000-pound cookie, or blockbuster bomb: the largest conventional bombs used in World War II by the Royal Air Force. These bombs had especially thin cylindrical steel casings that allowed them to contain approximately three-quarters of their weight in high explosives, whereas most WWII bombs contained about 50% of their weight in explosives. Each 4,000-pound blockbuster bomb contained over 3,000 pounds of Amatol, a highly explosive material made from a mixture of TNT and ammonium nitrate. A single bomb could destroy an entire city block or bring down a large building; the Bad Love Mosquitoes were getting ready to sequentially drop five of these monsters on the Black Hole Project.

The 4,000-pound cookie was regarded as a particularly dangerous payload to drop at lower altitudes. The recommended height above ground for dropping the cookie was an altitude of 6,000 feet. Releasing the bomb at a lower altitude posed risk to the aircraft dropping the bomb, damage from the shock waves caused by the explosion. Lake Königssee stretched about five miles from south to north and was about one mile across at its widest point, surrounded by the steeply rising mountain edges up to 8,900 feet. Bucky and Pumpkin had designed the mission for each plane to start its bombing run at the southern edge of the lake, with the distance to target at a bend in the lake 4.3 miles to the north. The target was on the east side of the lake. Flying at approximately 258 mph, they would be at the target in 60 seconds from the time they crossed the southern edge. The pilots would come in at 3,000–4,000 feet altitude and pull up hard, banking away to the west and accelerating to full military power as they released their cookie bombs to the target.

It was a daring and perilous bombing run that they had all trained for. Pumpkin, with his superior navigational skills and knowledge of the exact coordinates, would go first; he would attempt to mark the site with his bomb for the others to follow, and radio the rest of the group with any additional details. The planes would be spaced three minutes apart, with a total of 20,000 pounds of cookie bombs to be dropped on the Black Hole Project. From the time Pumpkin's lead Mosquito crossed the southern edge of Lake Königssee, the bombing mission would be complete in fifteen minutes or less.

Pumpkin radioed the four planes trailing him, informing Bucky, Willy, Ed, and Phil of his progress. "Bad Love Mosquito One to Bad Love Squadron, I am crossing the mark now, and we are on the clock! Nothing exciting to report. Just your bog-standard bomb run, really." Pumpkin's navigator, Maclin "Mac" Jones, clicked his stopwatch and the 60 second countdown started.

Bucky radioed back, "Save the British bumptiousness for now and do your job, Bad Love Mosquito One."

Pumpkin retorted, "Just wind your neck in and follow me, Bad Love Mosquito Two."

Cackles were heard over the radios from the other three trailing Bad Love Mosquitoes. Pumpkin reported, "Bad Love Squadron, we do have some patchy clouds layered at around four to five thousand feet, and some misty fog hugging the water below. I am having to weave in and out just a bit to keep my eye on the ball, over."

Willy answered, "Roger that, Bad Love Mosquito One. Just get your English arse out of there once you lose your cookies."

Pumpkin radioed, "Way to step it up, Willy! You're getting good with your poppycock."

Mac reported, "Twenty-five seconds to target." The howl and roar of the V-12 Rolls-Royce Merlin engines filled the lake valley.

Pumpkin directed, "Start the countdown at fifteen seconds, Mac."

There was radio silence for a few seconds, and everyone was on pins and needles knowing Pumpkin was about to drop the first bomb. Mac started his countdown. "Fifteen, fourteen, thirteen..." At the count of ten, Pumpkin blurted, "I can see the target ahead and flashes of small arms fire! The lake does bend to the west at the target point. We are almost there. Tallyho!" They left their radio on transmit and the Bad Love Squadron heard, "Three, two, one... Bomb is away!" Pumpkin vigorously shoved his throttles to full power and pulled up hard to the northwest. The small arms fire had originated from machine gun nests and Waffen-SS soldiers stationed around the Black Hole Project perimeter. Pumpkin's bomb hit just in front of the Black Hole entrance. Its unleashed destructive power smashed the infrastructure of the entrance, knocking out the machine gun nests and several Waffen-SS guard posts. Pumpkin and Mac's plane shuddered intensely from the shockwave, but they had turned and accelerated up and away from the blast, which helped them maintain control. The blast shook the earth and was heard for miles.

Pumpkin spoke into the radio, "Bad Love Two and Bad Love Squadron, we marked the target location well but there needs to be a couple of cookies thrown against the hillside behind my blast site, over."

Bucky, about to start his bomb run, stated, "Affirmative, Bad Love Mosquito One. I'll slingshot my cookie into the side of that hill and make that sucker come tumbling down!"

Willy added, "And I'll double down on that maneuver, boys." Ed and Phil chimed in to say they would bomb the rubble pile remaining.

Over the next twelve minutes, four more blockbuster bombs fell on the Black Hole Project. It felt like a series of earthquakes accompanied by intense thunder in the surrounding areas. Gunther Brandt had used an auxiliary escape tunnel and was hiking away on a trail to a German guard station located at the northern end of the Königssee lake. From an elevated turn in the trail to the north, he stood and witnessed the overwhelming destruction of the Black Hole Project wrought by the Bad Love Mosquito Squadron and their blockbuster bombs.

Wednesday, April 25, 1945, 9:00 AM local time,
the top-secret Black Hole Project Command Center
in the town of Berchtesgaden in Bavaria, Germany
and the Führerbunker in Berlin, Germany

Gunther caught a ride at the guard station and was taken to the Black Hole Administrative Command Center in the town of Berchtesgaden. He washed his hands and face, drank some coffee, ate a biscuit, and sat down at what used to be Emma Hoffman's desk, making everyone leave the office. He then dialed his direct contact number to the Führer's switchboard operator, SS Sergeant Rochus Misch, who answered the call quickly. Gunther said, "This is Gunther Brandt, and I need to speak privately with the Führer."

"Yes, Herr Brandt, give me a minute and I will get the Führer on his private line for you."

Several minutes later, the Führer picked up his private line. "Yes, Herr Brandt, what is it?" The line was quiet. In a louder tone Hitler enquired, "Brandt are you there?"

Gunther Brandt swallowed hard; his next words would be the most challenging of his life. "Yes, Mein Führer, I am here. Earlier this morning, the Black Hole Project was attacked and demolished by Allied commandos. I was there when they arrived, but I was able to escape before it was destroyed."

The blood in Hitler's face drained out. He appeared ashen and gaunt, and his voice changed "Who were they?" he rasped. "Russian, British, French, American? How could they get in there? It is so heavily protected!"

Hard as it was, Brandt told the truth. "They called themselves the Bad Love Gang, and they came from the future. There were two Jewish women, a Black American soldier, four other American soldiers, and a blue woman from another planet. They killed Klaus Richter, then blew up the inside of the Black Hole. Thirty minutes later, a squadron of British Mosquitoes dropped blockbuster bombs directly on the Black Hole, crushing it completely. I am devastated, Mein Führer. We worked so hard! The machine worked; it was ready to take us to the future. All is lost."

Hitler fleetingly replied, "Yes, Brandt, all is lost," and he hung up. A moment later he picked up the phone and requested that SS physician Werner Haase (who had replaced Hitler's personal physician Theodor Morell after he departed the Führerbunker) be sent to attend to him. When Haase arrived, Hitler asked him about the most reliable method of suicide. He recommended the pistol-and-poison method, combining a dose of cyanide with a gunshot to the head. When Haase departed the Führer's private study, Hitler agonizingly put his face in his hands and muttered, "Who the hell is the Bad Love Gang?"

CHAPTER TWENTY-ONE:

THE FIFTH BEATLE

"Of course I'm ambitious. What's wrong with that?
Otherwise, you sleep all day."
—Ringo Starr

*Wednesday, April 25, 1945, at 9:30 PM local time,
the Adelfi Hotel, Liverpool, United Kingdom*

W aldo, Bowmar, Bucky, and I had discussed how to communicate between the Bad Love Gang group going to Liverpool and our half of the group meeting with Winston Churchill. As planned, Waldo had called us Sunday night at the Goring Hotel with their progress report, and we had shared with him what Churchill had planned for us. Waldo, in his persona as USAAF Two Star Major General Paul Thompson, had "snagged" two British Army Jeeps for their group to use to get to Liverpool. It was a little more than a 200-mile drive from London to Liverpool. "Thank God the Brits kept the Jeep steering wheel on the left side; my brain might have gotten twisted like a pretzel if I had to drive from the right side," Waldo commented during our call. Vadoma had recommended, money permitting, that their group stay at the Adelfi Hotel in Liverpool. That is where her "special friend," the American soldier named Jason Roberts (whom they called JR), had taken her and the Holocaust refugees we rescued for their 1945 New

Year's Eve celebration. Waldo had taken plenty of WWII-era British pounds sterling from the safe in the White Hole Project's wardrobe warehouse to pay for hotels and mission expenses, so Vadoma's wish was granted.

Waldo, Meatball, Cleopatra, Crisco, the Pud, Ben, Vadoma, and Barsali had all checked into the Adelfi Hotel in Liverpool on Sunday evening, April 22, 1945. We gave Waldo the details of our mission to take out the Black Hole Project as directed by Churchill and scheduled for early Wednesday morning, April 25, 1945. We decided that Bowmar, Crazy Ike, Goondoggy, Tater, and I—along with the Black Box—would be zapped by the White Hole to St. John's Gardens, an open space in Liverpool to the west of St George's Hall, after sunset on Wednesday. From there, we would walk to the hotel. Bucky, Pumpkin, and Willie, after returning to the Royal Air Force Pathfinders landing field in South Cambridgeshire, England from their bombing mission on Wednesday, would procure a Jeep and drive the 180 miles to Liverpool. At 9:30 PM, despite our brush with death at the Black Hole Project earlier that day, we had all successfully reunited, gathering at the French cuisine restaurant inside the Adelphi hotel.

The Adelphi Hotel had quite a storied history. In 1826, hotelier James Radley opened the original hotel located on the first public recreation space in the city center, which was called Ranelagh Gardens. Fifty years later, the first Adelphi was torn down and the second Adelphi opened in 1876, having no similarity to its predecessor. Hotel number two provided a more luxurious experience, with over 300 rooms run by about 140 attentive staff. The second Adelphi was the most striking hotel in Liverpool's city center. In the late 1800s, the Adelphi was world-renowned not only for its service, but also for its famous turtle soup. In the basement of the hotel, they built a set of heated tanks to keep live turtles for the soup, which was not only served at the hotel, but was also dispensed around the country for various banqueting events. One of the most notable guests of the hotel during the 1800s was Charles Dickens, who listed the Adelphi as one of his favorite hotels.

In 1892, the Adelphi changed hands from James Radley to hotelier William Towle. Eighteen years later, to keep up with the changing times, the building was again demolished, and the third Adelphi Hotel was built in its place. It was rumored that a 23-year-old Adolf Hitler worked a short stint at the third iteration of the hotel during its construction in 1912; however, this dubious anecdote was never confirmed. The third Adelphi, designed by Frank Atkinson, opened in 1914 and the building once more surpassed the hotel that came before. Adelphi number three marvelously enclosed a heated indoor swimming pool, tennis and squash courts, Turkish baths, shooting galleries, and two restaurants specializing in both French and English cuisine. Each room of this Adelphi was fitted with a new, amazing, state-of-the-art technological marvel: a telephone.

Situated close to the waterfront and the famous Albert Dock, the Adelphi became the most preferred hotel in Liverpool for wealthy passengers traveling on ocean liners, including the Titanic. The Adelphi became a common Liverpool stop-over connection, making it a leading hotel and a popular location for noteworthy actors and celebrities (including Frank Sinatra and Judy Garland, among others), foreign dignitaries, and various politicians. Prime Minister Winston Churchill, known to be fond of the hotel, hosted strategy meetings at the Adelphi. The Adelphi narrowly missed being bombed in the Liverpool May Blitz of 1941, which saw many parts of the city center ruined. In December 1942, the British baronet and aristocrat Sir "Jock" Delves Broughton was found dead in one of the hotel's suites; he had committed suicide when he returned to England after being put on trial and acquitted for lack of evidence in the murder of his wife's lover in Kenya. In the midst of World War II, with death and deprivation strangling

Europe, the sensational trial and acquittal of Sir Broughton in Kenya had turned the spotlight on the decadent behaviors and extravagant lifestyles of the idle rich English aristocrats living in various African countries while trying to avoid the realities of the war in Europe. This was understandably not well-received by the public.

In late April 1945, the Adelphi was a signature hotel for celebrities and politicians, making it a renowned flagship for Liverpool. Somehow lost in the records of time, nearly the entire Bad Love Gang had checked into the Adelphi Hotel unnoticed in their quest to rescue Hannah Lieb from a future fate of breast cancer and to reunite her in some way with the father of her baby, our very own Meatball. As we sat down for dinner, we were all exhausted—but also exhilarated, to have come this far and to be back together again. We were seated at a long table, with Waldo and I at the ends and seven seated on each side across from one another. Our half of the group started by sharing our harrowing day to infiltrate and then to destroy the Black Hole Project. Adolf Hitler would not be going to the future, and that was cause for celebration! When we told the part of the story about Blue Nova One's role in the adventure, everyone was amazed and grateful that she had become part of our time-traveling destiny. My curiosity about the search for Hannah Lieb was consuming my thoughts so I enquired, "Can someone bring us up to speed on your efforts to find Hannah?"

As I half-expected, Meatball excitedly got the discussion rolling. "We've been here in Liverpool a full three days, and despite a little side-track tour from Crisco…" Crisco was grinning ear to ear and winked at me… "we are getting closer. I think Hannah is here in Liverpool; I can feel it in my soul. We started asking around on Monday about the Jewish community here in Liverpool. Everyone has been trying to help us, maybe because except for Vadoma, Barsali, and Ben, we are all US military. And General Waldo over there is very demanding when we don't get answers."

Waldo was beaming as he commented, "Well, I can't shoot anybody; we're in friendly territory! So, I just scare them a little bit with my authority, and they tell us what we need to know."

We all laughed, and Meatball continued, "Our first solid clue came at the Greenbank Drive Synagogue, located near the entrance to Sefton Park. For our current time in history, that place is pretty new; it opened in 1937. We met the rabbi there on Tuesday, and he directed us to go check at the Princes Road Synagogue."

Cleopatra added, "Yeah, that Greenbank place was classic Art Deco, and walking out of there, our group stumbled into a little destiny, you might say."

Crisco nudged Cleo and impatiently took over. "A *lot* of destiny, Cleo! As we were leaving through the front door, we ran into a well-to-do family of four who were meeting with the rabbi after us. The father and his two sons were all wearing pinstripe trousers and black jackets, and they had bowler hats on. The mother wore a full-length, pleated black dress with long sleeves and a pretty black hat. The older boy was ten years old, and his younger brother was eight. Ben and Barsali, trying to help us on our search, went running up to the two boys, introduced themselves, and asked them if they knew the Lieb, Roth, or Goldberg families."

Ben said, "I introduced myself as Benzion Kaplan, but told them to call me Ben. The mother liked me right away; she shook my hand and said her name was Malka Epstein. She said *Malka* meant 'queen' in Hebrew, and that her husband, Harry, and everyone else called her 'Queenie.' And they had just moved to Queens Drive! We shared our nicknames with them, and that made us all laugh together. The older brother was named Brian, and his younger brother was Clive. Brian said that he was born in Liverpool, but they had moved to Southport. He didn't like the schools there, so they were moving back to Liverpool."

Crisco, nearly hyperventilating, shrieked, *"We met the ten-year-old 'fifth Beatle,' Brian Epstein, and his family!"* Not everyone was tracking Crisco 100% about the "fifth Beatle"; some were thinking that meant Ringo Starr, who had replaced the original Beatles' drummer, Pete Best, in 1962. Our walking, talking, human encyclopedia Bowmar filled in some blanks. He told us the future story of the 27-year-old Brian, who was running the Epstein family record shop near the Cavern Club on Mathew Street in Liverpool. On November 9, 1961, he went to see John Lennon, Paul McCartney, George Harrison, and their drummer at the time, Pete Best, perform a lunchtime concert at the Cavern Club. Down in that darkened, dank, smoky, crypt in the middle of the day, there were crowds of admiring kids watching those four Liverpool lads play their brand of music. From the moment he first saw them perform, Epstein was struck by their rhythm and beat, their music, and their sense of humor on stage. When he met them afterwards, he was again taken by their personal charm and on that day, it all started...

Brian Epstein talked the band into signing him as their manager in early 1962. He immediately went to work raising their profile, both inside and outside of Liverpool. He cleaned up their image, having them get similar haircuts and nicer clothes (the identical Mohair suits were his idea). Epstein also taught them to take the low bows they made after performing. He negotiated their first big recording contracts, arranging for their debut on The Ed Sullivan Show and concert trips to the United States, the launch of Beatlemania, and movie deals. He was the one who had conveyed utter and total belief in them, and the certainty that just as he had, the entire world would fall irrepressibly in love with them.

Brian was the original guiding management light for The Beatles, and the man who kept them together by smoothing over the rough edges and always encouraging them to collaborate. He worked with the Fab Four until his sudden death, from an accidental overdose of sleeping pills in his home in London on August 27, 1967. From a professional standpoint, when Brian died, the band had lost the man who took them from nothing in Liverpool to incomparable heights in the entertainment industry. Later, John Lennon said he knew The Beatles were finished when Epstein died. "I knew that we were in trouble then," John said. "I didn't really have any misconceptions about our ability to do anything other than play music."

When Bowmar finished, I asked Crisco, "Since you were the one who realized that you all were talking to *the* Brian Epstein and his family, how did you part ways?"

Crisco smiled and replied, "I knew I wasn't supposed to say anything about the future, but before we walked away, I gave Brian a big hug and was softly humming **'Penny Lane'** by The Beatles while I hugged him." She smiled and started bobbling her head back and forth while humming **"Penny Lane."** Most of the table chimed in, humming the melody along with her—and of course, my music brain was playing along with the tune.

"Why did you pick that one, Crisco?" I enquired.

"That song makes me happy, and before we went to the Greenbank Drive Synagogue, I saw on the map that the street Penny Lane was close by. I wanted to see it and get some pictures, so I was already humming it on our way to meet the rabbi. Paul McCartney wrote it and made mention of the sights and characters that he recalled from his upbringing here in Liverpool in the lyrics. We walked to Penny Lane when we left the synagogue; that's what Meatball meant by me having us take a little sidetrack tour."

"Did you go to the Princes Road Synagogue?" I asked.

Meatball replied, "We went there today, among checking on some other leads. They told us to come back tomorrow at nine thirty AM sharp, so we are starting there tomorrow morning. It is really not that far from here, and they said someone would be there to help us tomorrow."

Vadoma added, "I sense that we are getting close. It would be perfect timing now that all of us are together again."

"Yeah!" the Pud exclaimed. "How about we make it better than an average day tomorrow!" We all laughed and called it a night.

CHAPTER TWENTY-TWO:

TWO SHOTS

"Love recognizes no barriers. It jumps hurdles, leaps fences, penetrates walls to arrive at its destination full of hope."
—Maya Angelou

Thursday, April 26, 1945, at 9:30 AM local time, the Princes Road Synagogue, Liverpool, United Kingdom

O ur entire gang got a great night's sleep, ate breakfast together at the English restaurant in the Adelphi Hotel, and then squeezed our group of sixteen (all but Vadoma, Ben, and Barsali dressed in military garb) into three Army Jeeps for the short ride to the Princes Road Synagogue. We thought we should take the Jeeps in case the subsequent search would take us beyond walking distances. Crisco brought her little medical bag containing the syringes and medical equipment, and I took the two vials of medicine for Hannah that Blue Nova One had given me. The first vial contained the gene therapy to repair Hannah's BRCA1 and/or BRCA2 mutations to prevent her future breast cancer; the second vial was an adult form of the Azurian vaccination formula, which I had not yet discussed with Meatball or the rest of the Bad Love Gang.

The Princes Road Synagogue congregation, known as the Liverpool Old Hebrew Congregation, outgrew their original Seel Street building in Liverpool in the late-1860s and decided to build a new, bigger, more impressive synagogue. A competition was held to engage an architect. The commission was awarded to William and George Audsley, a pair of architect Presbyterian brothers from Edinburgh, Scotland with no previous experience in building synagogues. They managed to design and construct one of the finest examples of Moorish Revival architecture in the landscape of British synagogues. Located on Princes Road in Toxteth at the edge of downtown Liverpool, the Princes Road Synagogue opened in September 1874. The new building seated more than 800 worshippers and was handed to the congregation by the building committee entirely free of debt.

As we pulled our three Jeeps up to the front, we were impressed by the design of the building we were about to enter. The towering, exotic red brick synagogue looked more like a medieval Middle Eastern or Spanish Moorish palace to us. The large arched entrance was set back in the center façade, and there was a beautiful Norman wheel stained-glass window above the double doors. The Victorian-style pediment roof was edged on each side by twin towers and large, circular turrets flanked both ends of the synagogue. A low brick wall with bushes above ran across the front of the property. Crisco had not gotten pictures the prior day, so she jumped out of the back of our Jeep and started shooting pictures with her Canon F-1 camera.

While Crisco was busy taking photographs and the rest of the gang were disembarking from the Jeeps and admiring the architecture, I noticed a woman with dark brown hair wearing a long sleeved, brown dress coming out of the front door to greet us. I took Meatball, Vadoma, and Bowmar with me to meet her. We all introduced ourselves and she told us her name was Eliana Adelman, but we could call her Ella. She explained, "After the war started, the boy choristers had to be evacuated. Most of the men went away on active-duty service, and a small group of us women were recruited to replace the males in the choir. So we have a mixed choir and I lead the women's group. I was asked to be here this morning to assist you. Why don't we all go inside? Hopefully, I can help you in some way."

Meatball, who introduced himself as Aaron Eisen, responded, "Thank you, Ella. We would like that very much."

As Ella turned to lead our group inside, Vadoma grabbed my right hand and whispered, "I like her already, future boy. I have a good feeling about this; she has positive energy."

I squeezed Vadoma's hand, looking into her deep eyes, and whispered, "Yeah, Vadoma, and she can sing too; that's good in my book."

As we walked inside, we were awestruck by the splendor of the place. The interior was stunning, with warm colors of ivory and green and the generous use of handsomely crafted woods and marbles. There were elaborate wooden arches, a barrel-vaulted ceiling embellished with lavish gilding and detailed hand painting; magnificent stained-glass windows adorned the walls. The extensive pews, which could seat 824 worshippers, faced the center and the Ark was in the rear. Ella pointed out the beautifully carved wooden bimah, the podium or platform from which the Torah was read, commenting that it had been donated by a local businessman named David Lewis. She also showed us that there were two stories of women's galleries running along the side walls, and one story of women's gallery running along the back of the sanctuary. Exquisitely carved, hand-painted, and gilded wood paneling separated the galleries from the sanctuary.

Ella encouraged us all to circle around her and we did so, leaving Meatball to face her while Bowmar, Vadoma, and I backed him up. Meatball began, "What I am about to tell you is actually a military secret, so I ask you not to share the details of this discussion with others."

Ella nodded. "I was told, and I see that you are American service-men and women on some type of information-gathering mission. Your secrets are good with me, and I will help you if I can."

Meatball continued, "Thank you, Ella. Our group here conducted a secret mission to rescue a small group of Holocaust victims from Chelmno, Poland in November 1944. We rescued thirteen, and three of them are standing here: Vadoma, Barsali, and Ben. Vadoma, Barsali, and the other ten people we rescued came here to Liverpool in January this year. They are the Lieb, Roth, and Goldberg families. On our mission, I fell in love with Hannah Lieb; she is pregnant with our child, and we are desperately searching to find her. Does this story or do any of these names sound familiar to you?"

Ella visibly froze for a minute before she warmly responded, "I have a question for you, Aaron."

"Sure, what is it?"

"Do you know the Hebrew meaning of my name, Eliana?"

I didn't know the answer, but I immediately stepped on Bowmar's left foot and sternly whispered, "Don't you say a word." He frowned at me and complied.

Meatball looked at Ella, puzzled, and said, "No, I do not know what it means. Please, tell me."

Ella answered, "It means, 'My God has answered me.' I know Hannah Lieb; she is certainly pregnant, and she sings in this choir with me and the other women. She has the most wonderful, beautiful, strong, amazing personality and soul. She is a special woman. We all adore her!"

Meatball's body started shaking, and he bawled uncontrollably. Cleo and Crisco both put their hands over their mouths and started to cry as well. They hugged each other and cried together, and I was fighting off tears while trying to embrace Meatball along with Vadoma, Ben, and Barsali. I looked around and to my amazement, nearly everyone was weeping for joy and relief, even Crazy Ike and Goondoggy. Waldo was standing there looking proud and shaking his head a bit. Pumpkin's face had turned orange and he was a blubbering Brit.

Through his snivels, the Pud declared, "I knew this was going to be better than an average day!" That helped us all to start laughing and giggling.

Waldo, maybe the only one not shedding tears, said, "All right, time to pull yourselves together boys and girls! We still have some work to do."

Ella, clearly touched by the emotions of the moment, grinned and enquired, "Does the American military always get this weepy?" No one answered, but we all laughed some more with relief.

Meatball, fighting through his sobbing and sniffles, asked Ella, "Do you know where we can find Hannah?"

Ella replied, "There is another coincidence here. You know how I told you all that a local businessman named David Lewis donated that beautifully carved wooden bimah? Well, he died in 1885, but he was famous, and he founded Lewis's Department Store in downtown Liverpool. The store was damaged early in the war by Nazi bombing, but is still operating in an adjacent building. Hannah is working there selling women's clothing. She works during the week; you should be able to find her there now."

The Pud marveled, "That place is right across the street from the Adelphi Hotel, where we have been staying! I've seen the bombed-out front of the store directly across the street from us. Hannah has been working across and a bit down the street, right under our noses since we started looking for her on Monday morning! I have an idea: Bubble Butt, you, me, Crazy Ike, Goondoggy, and Meatball need to ride together back to the hotel."

Ella, caught off-guard, questioned, "What kind of names are those?"

I answered, "Sorry, Ella, we call ourselves the Bad Love Gang, and we all have nicknames. Hannah can fill you in later, but we've got to go." We all gave Ella hearty hugs and thanks, then headed out the door on our way back to the hotel and then to Lewis's Department Store.

Thursday, April 26, 1945, at 11:45 AM local time, Lewis's Department Store, Watson Building on Renshaw Street, Liverpool, United Kingdom

Lewis's Department Store was established in 1856 by a young entrepreneur named David Lewis. He started with a men and boys tailoring shop, making ready-made clothing aimed at the working class. He believed in good customer relationships and his early slogan was "Lewis's are the friends of the people." In 1864, recognizing the significant clothing needs of the women population of Liverpool, he wisely expanded and opened a women's clothing department. In 1877, he visited Paris to see the world's first department store, Bon Marche, to take cues from their success back to his business in England. In 1879, he opened the world's first Christmas Grotto in Liverpool. He opened branches of Lewis's in Manchester and Birmingham as well as expanding into mail-order sales, tobacco, foods, coal, and many other departments. Liverpool's seaport gave him an advantage; he was able to cut out the middlemen wholesalers and buy straight from the shippers, making many luxury goods available to the working classes. For example, Lewis's sold tea cheaper than all other store chains, contributing to its status as the national drink. He was so keen on improving the life of Liverpool's working class that he launched his penny readings, which encouraged citizens to learn to read. After he died in 1885, the Cohen Family took the Lewis's stores forward, adding new departments and ideas. Lewis's grew and grew, and in the 1930s, additional stores were opened in Leeds, Hanley, Glasgow, and Leicester. Some stores had as many as 132 departments where everything could be purchased, from theatre tickets to exotic foods.

During the Nazi Luftwaffe Blitz of May 1941, Saturday, May 3, 1941, was the most fearsome and destructive of all the raids and was the most shattering night in Liverpool's history. Between sundown and dawn, wave after wave of Luftwaffe bombers roared overhead, dropping tons of high explosives and incendiaries onto the city. Liverpool's beloved landmark Lewis's Department store, and its roof menagerie, was gutted after taking a direct hit. The store was first hit by a small bomb that damaged the sprinkler system. The additional oil incendiary bombs that hit caused a massive fire, which resulted in three-fifths of the store being destroyed. In a remarkable effort, the surviving two-fifths of the store was transformed into an emergency shop using the adjacent structure, the Watson Building, and reopened the following month. It was amongst this background of history and location that the Bad Love Gang caught up with Hannah Lieb.

Despite all that we had gone through to acquire the cure for Hannah's breast cancer and then find her in her second trimester of pregnancy so that we could physically give her the medicine, the Bad Love Gang, as always, felt compelled to add some levity to a serious situation. The Pud had come up with a plan that he shared with us on the way back to the hotel and before we all walked over to Lewis's together. The Pud, Goondoggy, Crazy Ike, and Meatball were the four who had rescued the thirteen Holocaust victims from the Nazis at Chelmno, getting them safely aboard the B-17 Flying Fortress that we had named "Bad Love" to evacuate them from Nazi-controlled Poland. Other than Meatball, Hannah knew the Pud, Goondoggy, and Crazy Ike the best from the rescue at Chelmno. The three of them would take the lead in setting the stage for Meatball to surprise Hannah; the rest of us would watch from the perimeter.

We were all on the lookout for Hannah as we entered the store and found our way to the women's clothing department. Vadoma was the first to spot Hannah, who was focused on arranging women's dresses on a rack in the middle of the department. Vadoma signaled us and we all got dialed-in to watch from the perimeter while Crazy Ike, Goondoggy, and the Pud made their moves, with Meatball close behind. Crazy Ike was the first to make contact. He stealthily progressed, keeping his head down, to the opposite side of the dress rack that Hannah was arranging and to her right. He pulled a big dress off the rack, held it up to his body, and as Hannah raised her head, he asked, "Now, promise not to judge me, but do you think this color would look good on me?"

It didn't register with Hannah immediately; she looked a bit bewildered and started to laugh at about the time the Pud tapped her on the left shoulder. She turned toward him, and he queried, "Where is the department that has average-sized clothing that looks pretty average for an average sort of a guy at an average price?"

Her brain was starting to catch up with the sensory overload when Goondoggy popped up across the dress rack to her left and asked, "Is there a food department in this store? I'd like to buy some good old-fashioned spaghetti and..." He paused, acting like he couldn't find the next word.

Meatball then embraced her from behind and held her tightly, feeling her baby bump for the first time, and finished Goondoggy's line: "Meatballs. How about a Meatball to brighten up your day? By the way, ma'am, do they sell baby cradles in this store?"

Hannah shrieked with delight and squealed, "Crazy Ike, Pud, and Goondoggy, you guys are all zanier than ever!" She turned into Meatball's arms to face him, already crying tears of joy, and declared, "And you, Meatball, I love, love, *love* you, and yes, they sell baby cribs in this store!" They locked lips with tears streaming down their faces and the rest of us around the perimeter began to cheer and clap. Soon people who were standing all around the immediate area began cheering and clapping with us.

I thought Hannah and Meatball would never stop kissing! Of course, that got my music brain in motion, and it started playing **"Happy Together,"** by the Turtles. It was the perfect song to describe the moment, and even more interesting, it was the song that knocked the Beatles' *"Penny Lane"* out of the number one slot on the US Billboard Hot 100 in early 1967. The song stayed at the top of the US charts for three weeks during an incredibly competitive era. It went to number two in Canada and New Zealand, number three in South Africa, and peaked at number twelve in the UK in April 1967. I wished I had my boom box to blast it out right there in the middle of Liverpool's Lewis's Department Store.

Thursday, April 26, 1945, at 12:45 PM local time,
the Adelfi Hotel, Liverpool, United Kingdom

Hannah's manager agreed for her to take a long lunch hour and we walked across the street to the Adelphi for a wonderful celebratory lunch together. Hannah filled us in on the status of the whole group that we had rescued. She told us that her father, David, had met Rabbi Isser Yehuda Unterman, who would later become the chief rabbi of Israel and was teaching and giving lectures at a hostel on Princes Road, located across the street from the Princess Road Synagogue. She and her family were planning to move to Palestine as soon as the war was over. We all smiled because we knew that she would end up in Jerusalem, and that her dad would develop a successful road and building construction company there with two of his cousins. When we finished lunch, I told Hannah that we needed to go upstairs to meet with her and Meatball more privately.

We used Waldo's suite and it was just me, Bowmar, Crisco, Meatball, and Hannah. We all sat down together, and while Bowmar was just getting to know Hannah, he got the discussion started. "Hannah, I was running the time-travel machine when you, your family, and the other Holocaust refugees were rescued by Meatball and the Bad Love Gang. Bubble Butt and I undertook an effort to try and keep an eye on everyone we rescued in our time-travel missions. In November 1975, we discovered that you and your family were living in Jerusalem—and that you were dying of breast cancer that had spread throughout your body at age forty-nine. We sent Meatball to see you and your family in Jerusalem. He met with you, your parents, and your thirty-year-old child, the baby you are carrying now. When Meatball returned to us with the news of your fate, the Bad Love Gang vowed to try and get a cure for you, then find you and give you the medicine."

Meatball smiled and interjected, "I've been thinking a lot about this, Hannah, and have decided to call it the Bad Love Medicine."

Hannah playfully shoved Meatball's shoulder and replied, "I understand everything that you just said, Bowmar, but it seems to me that age forty-nine is a bit young to be dying of breast cancer."

"Smart observation, Hannah; that is correct," I agreed. "As it turns out, you are an Ashkenazi Jew and have an inherited condition that predisposes you to get breast cancer early. This will sound unbelievable, but we traveled to a distant planet called Azur in the quest to find a cure for you." I held up the first vial of clear solution and said, "This vial contains something called gene therapy, and it will prevent you from getting breast cancer."

Hannah replied, "Bubble Butt, I don't want to die of breast cancer at any age. I'm ready to take that Bad Love Medicine." She winked at Meatball.

I continued, "We really assumed that you would feel that way about shot number one. But there is a second vial of medicine that you might also want to take." Everyone looked surprised, especially Meatball. I held up the second vial containing the bluish-tinted liquid. "We can't leave Meatball with you here now; we are too afraid of what that might do to the time continuum." Hannah looked sad. "However, we have a solution that we think can work for you, Meatball, and your baby." Her expression lightened. "This second vial is a vaccine from the planet Azur. If we give this to you, it will vaccinate you and your baby and extend your natural longevity to one hundred twenty years.

"I would propose to you that this second vial is optional for you and Meatball. If you and Meatball agree that you want to reunite and stay together starting in 1976, then taking this vaccination would keep your lifespans roughly equal, starting in early 1976. Hannah, you would have to live and wait the next thirty years without Meatball. On the other hand, Meatball won't perceive the passing of that wait time; he'll go back to January 1976 with us, then come to Jerusalem to reunite with you, free of breast cancer—and looking young for your age, I might add."

Meatball, looking at Hannah, responded, "When I went to see you in Jerusalem in November 1975, I couldn't live with the thought of you dying of breast cancer, or dying period. My heart has ached for you ever since then. You never married; you stayed single and raised our child. I have been in the past, and in the future will always be, so wildly in love with you."

Crisco was getting teary-eyed again, listening to their exchange. Hannah asked Meatball, "What about our child that I am carrying?"

Meatball replied, "It's a boy; his name is Elijah, he is strong and handsome, and he is a soldier in special forces."

"I love that name!" Hannah professed.

"You should, you must have picked it," Meatball acknowledged.

Hannah smiled affectionately at Meatball and held his hands. "Knowing that you are coming in January 1976, and we can live long lives together, will make the next thirty plus years much easier to bear. I thought about you every single day and night since we parted ways in Belgium, and I watched you fly away in that plane called 'Bad Love.' I'm in this relationship for the long haul; we have an outrageous love story and I love you, Meatball, forever and ever!! Give me both shots, Crisco."

EPILOGUE

"History and experience tell us that moral progress
comes not in comfortable and complacent times,
but out of trial and confusion."
—Gerald R. Ford

*Saturday, January 17, 1976, 9:30 PM local time,
the State Dining Room on the State Floor of the Executive
Residence of the White House in Washington, D.C.*

Bucky, Bowmar, Waldo, Ding, and I had met with President Gerald Ford in the Oval Office six and a half months ago on July 1, 1975. He had warned us that our Russian KGB nemesis, Borya Krovopuskov, was still a threat and at large. He also gave us the green light to attempt intergalactic space travel using the White Hole Project in our quest to acquire a cure for Hannah Lieb's breast cancer. Much had happened since that meeting with President Ford. Exactly three weeks ago on Saturday, December 20, 1975, the Bad Love Gang had been knighted in a royal celebration at the Queen's Palace on planet Azur. We had made history by succeeding with intergalactic space travel and by managing to effectively redirect the eruption of a major volcano, Mount Pelorius on the Republic of Azur, averting certain disaster for millions of people and saving the Republic.

We had returned from Azur with the cancer-saving medicine for Hannah Lieb only to find our own Bad Love Gang and neighborhood under a coordinated KGB assault, which we effectively repelled. Borya and his wife Catherine had wreaked havoc across town in Knoxville, killing several of Ding's FBI team members and escaping with their two children, Bobbie and Natalie. Ding had intervened during that attack and prevented more loss of life. The Bad Love Gang had quickly regrouped and planned a time-travel mission back to Europe in April 1945 to get the life-saving medicine to Hannah.

Blue Nova One had recommended that we learn how to fly de Havilland Mosquitoes and meet in person with Prime Minister Winston Churchill. Half our group was sent by Churchill to destroy Hitler's Black Hole Project time-travel machine, while the other half searched to find Hannah. The Bad Love Gang, with some help from the British SOE and the Royal Air Force, learned some secrets from and then destroyed the Black Hole Project, along with Adolf Hitler's hope of escaping to the future. We found Hannah Lieb in Liverpool, England and gave her what Meatball called Bad Love Medicine.

We all returned to the White Hole Project and Oak Ridge, Tennessee on Saturday, January 10, 1976. The brief delay in returning gave Meatball and Hannah a well-deserved two nights together at the Adelphi Hotel, while the rest of us enjoyed our time together in Liverpool. Waldo, Bucky, Bowmar, and I had contacted President Ford on Sunday the 11th to give him a long-overdue update. Ford invited our entire Bad Love Gang to the White House for a very private, off-the-record celebration with the Bad Love Gang in the State Dining Room of the Executive Residence. The only one not present at our White House gathering was Meatball. He left Oak Ridge, Tennessee on Thursday, January 15, 1976, for Jerusalem, Israel to reunite with Hannah Lieb and his thirty-year-old son, Elijah. President Ford pledged to arrange for a conference call with Meatball and Hannah while we were all together. He also kept his promise to make new entries into the Book of Presidents about the exploits of the Bad Love Gang.

It was a wonderful, private celebration, with President Gerald Ford and First Lady Betty Ford attending. The Bad Love Gang provided some music, entertainment, and stories about our intergalactic trip to Azur and recent time-travel mission back to April 1945. At 9:30 PM, the first lady bid us farewell and President Ford put Meatball and Hannah on a conference call with all of us. The call, made through the White House switchboard, was crystal clear; it was 4:30 AM in Jerusalem on Sunday morning for Meatball and Hannah. Meatball and Hannah, honored to speak with President Ford, both sounded great and were already discussing wedding plans with Hannah's family.

However, there was a problem. Their son Elijah, who had distinguished himself with valor in the October 1973 Yom Kippur War, had become a member of Special Forces for the Israeli Defense Force (IDF) in late 1974. He had embarked on a top-secret military mission in November 1975 and was now officially listed as missing in action. Hannah had been pleading for more information, but other than the fact that he was missing, the military was mum.

I said, "That doesn't totally make sense to me, Hannah; when Meatball returned from seeing you and your family in November 1975, to tell us that you had terminal breast cancer, that was when he was introduced to Elijah for the first time."

"That is correct, BB. But I don't have breast cancer; I am in perfect health," Hannah pointed out. "The last time Meatball was here our son was taking a leave from the military to help take care of his sick mother. The future changed; I did not get breast cancer, and so Elijah was still on active duty in November."

President Ford interjected, "I will give Prime Minister Yitzhak Rabin a call. He cut his chops with the IDF. If anyone knows Elijah's status or whereabouts, he should be able to find out. But we have another problem to discuss before this party ends..."

ABOUT THE AUTHOR

Kevin L. Schewe, MD, FACRO, is the proud father of two daughters (Ashley and Christie) and two granddaughters (Gracie and Olivia). He is a native of St. Louis, Missouri and now makes his home in Denver, Colorado. He graduated from the University of Missouri–Columbia with a bachelor's degree in Biology and from the University Missouri Columbia School of Medicine as an M.D. He trained at the Medical College of Wisconsin to become a board-certified Radiation Oncologist. He is a Fellow of the American College of Radiation Oncology (FACRO). He has been in the private practice of radiation oncology for 34 years. He is an entrepreneur, having founded a skin care company called Elite Therapeutics (elitetherapeutics.com) and Bad Love Cosmetics Company. He serves as Chairman of the Board of a micro-cap renewable, green energy and animal feed company called VIASPACE, Inc. (viaspace.com).

Bad Love Medicine is Dr. Schewe's fourth novel in the *Bad Love Book Series*. His award-winning and highly-rated first three novels *Bad Love Strikes, Bad Love Tigers, and Bad Love Beyond* were released in September 2019, June 2020, and November 2020 respectively, and have all been Amazon bestsellers. Follow Dr. Schewe on Instagram @realkevinschewe and at his author's website at kevinschewe.com.

COMING SOON

BAD LOVE RISING
The Bad Love Series Continues...

Meatball and Hannah Lieb have been reunited in Jerusalem, Israel in early 1976. The Bad Love Gang succeeded in rescuing Hannah from her fate of terminal breast cancer. However, in doing so history changed and their son, Elijah, an Israeli Special Forces operative, is missing in action on a top-secret mission. President Gerald Ford intervenes to try and help find Elijah but also has more in store for the Bad Love Gang. Bubble Butt and Bowmar recall WWII physicist, Petra Vogel, from the past, and they use secrets that they gleaned from Hitler's Black Hole Project to expand the capabilities of the White Hole Project in order to meet the new challenges the Bad Love Gang is now facing. Time and space travel are inexorably intertwined as the intergalactic future, the mid-1970's, the WWII-1940's and the best recorded music in the history of the universe continue to collide with each other in dramatic fashion!

ALSO COMING SOON

BAD LOVE BEGINS

The prequel to the *Bad Love Book Series* follows the exploits of the Bad Love Gang as they are growing up together in Oak Ridge, Tennessee in the 1960s and before discovering the White Hole Project in June 1974. Getting to know each other and recognizing their various skill sets, they take crazy adventures. Sometimes they risk life and limb and other times they just have fun. One thing is certain, they are growing up fast and boredom is never an issue!

CPSIA information can be obtained
at www.ICGtesting.com
Printed in the USA
BVHW082126300721
613251BV00001B/105